ACQUIRED TASTE

Also by Clay McLeod Chapman
and available from Titan Books

WHAT KIND OF MOTHER
WAKE UP AND OPEN YOUR EYES
BODIES OF WORK
DEVIL INSIDE

Praise for

CLAY McLEOD CHAPMAN

"Clay McLeod Chapman has taken all that's troubling our nation in the current day and, somehow, makes it all more frightening."

Victor LaValle, author of *Lone Women*

"Few writers are as dependably, delightfully depraved… With stories like these, it'd be impossible to say no!"

Nat Cassidy, author of *When the Wolf Comes Home* and *Mary*

"Clay McLeod Chapman is one of my favorite horror storytellers working today."

Jordan Peele

"Daring and dread-inducing, creepy and clever, Clay McLeod Chapman defines contemporary horror."

Rachel Harrison, *USA Today* bestselling author of *So Thirsty* and *Black Sheep*

"A master storyteller."

Eric LaRocca, author of *Things Have Gotten Worse Since We Last Spoke*

"Chapman has an absolute gift for the unforgettably, mind-saturatingly horrific."

Ally Wilkes, Bram Stoker award®-nominated author of *All the White Spaces* and *Where the Dead Wait*

"Clay McLeod Chapman is a true master of horror."

CJ Leede, author of *Maeve Fly* and *American Rapture*

"An absolute blast of a collection, full of unforgettable imagery packed into tightly crafted, page-turning gems of short fiction."

Paste Magazine

"My favorite quasi-Kingian book is *Acquired Taste*…
whose excellent shorts recall the winking audacity of King's stories."

Chicago Tribune

"If you're already a fan of Chapman's writing, *Acquired Taste* is a must-own. If you're new to his work, it's the perfect jumping-off point."

Macabre Daily

"A modern horror maestro."

Dread Central

"*Acquired Taste*… will gross you out, make you laugh and get under your skin in the best kind of way."

Page Six

"Chapman excels in taking something familiar and twisting it to show that there are horrors beyond belief in ordinary places."

Library Journal, starred review

"A literary punch to the heart."

New York Times on 'Stay on the Line'

"Twisted, tender, deranged, Chapman has a singular voice that is strange and weird and beautiful, and does not falter throughout."

FanFiAddict

ACQUIRED TASTE

CLAY McLEOD CHAPMAN

TITAN BOOKS

Acquired Taste
Paperback ISBN: 9781835410790
E-book edition ISBN: 9781835410806

Published by Titan Books
A division of Titan Publishing Group Ltd
144 Southwark Street, London SE1 0UP
www.titanbooks.com

This paperback edition: June 2026
10 9 8 7 6 5 4 3 2 1

A CIP catalogue record for this title is available from the British Library.

EU RP (for authorities only)
eucomply OÜ, Pärnu mnt. 139b-14, 11317 Tallinn, Estonia
hello@eucompliancepartner.com, +3375690241

Set in Adobe Caslon Pro by Richard Mason.

Printed and bound by CPI Group (UK) Ltd, Croydon, CR0 4YY.

to R. Brooke Priddy
AHL forever

contents

the fireplace

The thought of tossing our baby in the fireplace first popped into my head a month or so ago. Around September, I'd say. Autumn was on its way, so—one lazy weekend, I figured I'd go ahead and get a leg up on winter and finally clean out that chimney. Get the flue all prepped for our first fire in our new house.

We were still only five months deep into our domestic bliss back then—no crisp nights curled up around the fire just yet. But before we even bought this place, all the way back when Chrissy and me first took a tour of the house—before it was ours, or anyone's really, lingering within that liminal space between seller and buyer, with all those hopeful families wandering about its rooms like ghosts; inspecting every nook and cranny in some spectral attempt to decide whether or not this is the house we would want to haunt—I remember waltzing into the living room for the very first time and locking eyes onto that inglenook. Its thick brick. The oak beam reaching across the top. Its swan-necked ironworks looked like the blackened ribcage of some prehistoric beast burned to its bones, the charred chest cavity the only remnant of its primitive existence left behind. Whatever it had been.

Check out the fireplace, I said. *Bet we'll save a fortune on our heating bill with that thing.*

Was that an offer I just heard? Chrissy whispered, hoping not to alert any of the other prospective homeowners that we were interested. *'Cause if it was, I can go find the realtor...*

Down, Simba... Take it easy.

I hadn't banked on the owners accepting our bid, to be honest. We were well beneath the listed asking price. I did it for Chrissy—but I knew there was no way in hell we'd ever get a house like this. Not on our annual income.

I mean—*come on*. An 1855 Victorian? With five bedrooms? Hardwood floors? There's no way we could call this place home. Not with that fireplace beckoning. We're talking the original chimney here. Nearly two hundred years old. The oldest part of the house at this point, I bet. The rest may have been remodeled over the years, but its brick bones remained, a spinal column of red clay holding this home upright.

We were crazy to've come to the open house in the first place. But Chrissy had begged to check it out. Outright *begged*. She's always had real estate lust, spending her Sundays sifting through every last email alert agents send her way.

It felt wrong, being here. Playing house like this. Getting her hopes up. Watching her eyes widen the deeper into the house we went, deciding which room would be whose—*this one's ours, this one will be the baby's*—I knew, I just knew we were cruising toward heartbreak. She kept rubbing her belly like there was a genie in there, ready to grant her wish.

Don't do this to yourself, hon, I warned her. *Don't get yourself all worked up.*

But the owners saw something in us, I guess. Our family-to-be.

Me, Chrissy.

And Colin. Nothing but a bump in his mama's tummy back then. He still had a few months in the oven to go before—*Ding! Baby's served...*

~

I'd never cleaned a fireplace before.

Never had an actual fireplace to clean—so there you go. First time for everything, I guess... *I am a man who now owns a fireplace, therefore I have become a man who must scrub it.*

Chrissy had been feeding Colin in bed, so I had the inglenook all to myself. Gave us a chance to get to know each other a little bit better.

It had a molded shelf embedded into the rear wall with a hinged spit-rack. A grand ol' rack. Had to date back to when this house was originally built, all those years ago. Turn of the turn of whatever century. They must've roasted enormous joints of meat back then. Could've fed a whole coven with what they cooked on there, I bet.

Kneeling before the hearth, I pulled the fire dogs out to scrub the floor. The grate weighed a ton. Took both hands just to tug that iron giant's ribcage out. Broke a sweat before I'd even started scrubbing, taking this metal-bristled brush and scraping at the interior walls. Swiping the soot away.

I was inside the fireplace now, on my hands and knees. Working on the rear wall. Tight, circular motions. *Wax on, wax off...* The grime never seemed to go away, though. Ten minutes of brandishing that brush over brick and it looked like I was just sweeping circles in the soot. This nibbling-on-tin sensation settled into my teeth. I could feel the steel bristles all the way up in my jaw, like chewing aluminum foil. *Skrchskrchskrch.* Throbbing right through me. My bones.

An exhale spread over my spine. I swear I felt somebody's breath drop down my neck.

I turned around.

No one was behind me. The living room was completely empty.

Then I felt again. This time on my temples.

Glancing up, I felt a stray draft creep across my cheeks.

The chimney flue had been left open, that's all. *Just the wind*, as they say.

Then something shifted.

Up there.

I couldn't see very far up, couldn't see much of anything—but my eyes tightened in on a pale shape centered within the brick funnel. A gray nimbus hovering in the darkness.

A baby.

I saw a baby. Trapped in the shadows. Its fetal form was curled into itself, crammed in the sooty womb of the flue. Its pale skin was covered in a layer of ash.

I reached up to touch it.

That's what people do in these situations, yes? If you see something that shouldn't be there—you poke it. Who cares about common sense? I'm staring at a baby stuck in my chimney, for Christ's sake. Of course I'm going to touch it.

The pressure from my pointer was enough to dislodge the infant from its floating position and fall onto my face with a hefty exhale of soot. I turned away from the plummeting bundle just as it dropped, so impact was actually on the back of my neck. I felt the softest thud, punctuated with a puff of ash, before it tumbled onto the bricks below.

I was breathing in way too much soot, coughing uncontrollably now. There was a solid three seconds of blurred vision. That cloud of ash slowly dissipated, clearing away to reveal—

A possum.

It must have been trapped in the chimney. Must've crawled down months ago and got itself stuck, starving itself to death up there. Its body was petrified, all its fur having fallen away, leaving behind its withered skin, covered in soot. Nothing but a mummified thing now.

Just a possum.

I figured it was best to get our little squatter out of the house before Chrissy saw it. She was not a fan of our furry four-legged neighbors, so I escorted the crispy critter by its shoestring tail, giving him a proper burial in our trash can among all the dirty diapers and coffee filters.

When I came back in, I could smell dinner cooking.

Buttery pork belly.

The halls were filled with it. My mouth was watering by the time I found Chrissy in the living room, bouncing Colin on her knee like a bucking baby bronco.

What's cooking, good-looking?

Nothing as far as I know... Had my hands a little full here.

What's up with the smell? I'm starving.

Chrissy gave me a look that would be put into constant rotation soon enough, hereunto categorized as—*What the fuck are you talking about?*

Sure enough, the oven wasn't on. Our kitchen was still a work in progress. Most of our appliances hadn't found a cupboard yet, still living within their moving boxes. A dozen cardboard nested dolls claimed any and every inch of free space. All our cutlery and dishes remained stacked in quick-pickable piles along the countertop for easy take-out meals.

Not that the smell was coming from the kitchen, anyhow.

It was in the living room. From the fireplace.

Bacon fat frying in the pan.

You practicing for Santa or something? Chrissy asked. *You're all covered in soot.*

I was cleaning the fireplace, I said. More to myself, but Chrissy answered anyway—*Hate to break to it you, hon, but... I think the chimney won.*

~

The house feels cold now.

Has for months. I've futzed with the thermostat and nothing seems to lift the chill. Every room I walk into, it feels as if I'm plunging into the tundra. My breath spreads out above me when I'm lying in bed. I've had to bundle up like it's the middle of winter, two or three layers thick, pulling out the parkas from their moving box, just to keep from freezing. *In August.* It's actually warmer outside than in. Chrissy looks at me like I'm nuts, which is the new norm now.

I could really use your help here, she muttered. *Can you take Colin? Just for a minute?*

What do we know about the house?

It's old. She shrugged, irked at me for not spotting the immediate problem at hand. *I know that much... Could you just take him? Please? I've got to start thinking about dinner. What're you hungry for?*

Colin was nothing but baby fat. Gripping him, I felt my hands sink into his sides. That plump swell of his pudgy tummy filling in around my fingers, like cement sealing us together.

Squishy brick and mortar.

When Colin was first cleared to come home from the hospital, I had given him the grand tour. *This is your room,* I whispered. Most were still overwhelmed with moving boxes back then, the walls eclipsed in cardboard. Our plans for unpacking before Colin was born were quickly hijacked the moment Chrissy's water broke. Not that we minded. We had our nest now. We had all the time in the world to settle in. Make this place feel like home. *This is where your mommy and daddy sleep... or where we're gonna try to sleep, as long as you let us. And this...*

This was the living room.

Her hearth had a thick cast-iron plate, surrounded by a brick enclosure. The entire house would embrace a fire, the heat circulating through the halls and swelling up within each room like the chambers of a heart filling up with blood. And on the spit-rack, roasting on the iron, a sizzling victual. Its delectable aroma filled the house. Grease dripping off the shank. Hits the hearth in this thin dribble. Each drip sizzles against the iron plate, bubbling over—*hsss.*

Hsssss...

Hsssss...

Chrissy's noticed I've been avoiding the living room. I turn in early now. Wrap myself up in a duvet and call it a night.

What gives? She asked. *You avoiding us?*

She asked if I wanted to light a fire. As if that would solve all our problems. Just tossed it out there last night, completely casual, like it'd popped into her mind—*Hey. How about a fire?*

The fuck did you just say?

Jesus... Don't snap at me.

What did you say?

A fire, she fumed. *All I asked was if you wanted to light a fire.*

Chrissy's breath smelled like peat. Decayed plant matter in her mouth. I could even see bits of turf in between her teeth. Tongue covered in earth. People used to harvest the peat from the bogs, carving out thick, sodden bricks, leaving them out to dry under the sun before bringing them inside and stacking them up in the inglenook. Those bricks burned slowly. The softest kind of kindling. Smokeless. Endless. It would warm the house for days and never die out. Warm its halls with dead vegetables and decrepit sedges, the pocosins and moss, compressed within the muck and mire of a thousand years, the bones of beasts long forgotten, lost to the bogs, the boreal peatlands slowing down their decomposition beneath our feet, now a fire, methane flames blooming in a beautiful blue, dancing about the hearth like will-o'-wisps. The aurora borealis in our living room.

Forget it, she muttered. *You're the one who's always complaining about how cold it is.*

I went to bed instead. Curled up into a cocoon of my duvet and tried to hide.

~

The house is only growing colder. Colder. Winter is nearly here. We're going to have to light a fire before long.

But I'm afraid what'll happen when we do.

What kind of kindling she'll need.

Colin woke us up last night, crying. It was late. Had to be three or four in the morning. I could hear him wailing, his voice drifting down the hall. Chrissy rolled over and mumbled for me to check on him. I pretended to be asleep, but that didn't fly.

Your turn, she mumbled, nudging me with her elbow. *It's your turn...*

A jolt of cold shot right up my legs the second my bare feet touched the hardwood floor. My ribs seized, locking on to my lungs, like an iron grate gripping at the air in my chest.

Colin wasn't in his room. Nothing but moving boxes everywhere. I could hear the soft pads of his fingertips grazing against the cardboard of one—so I opened it. Only I found a shriveled possum curled inside. Its withered pink tail looked more like an umbilical cord to me. The crying's coming from elsewhere. A different room in the house.

The living room.

I feel warmer the further down the hall I wander. A gentle breath brushes against my skin, drawing me in.

Warmer...

Warmer...

The fire's blazing. Our first fire in the house.

It's so warm in here.

There's a woman standing by the hearth. Her back is to me. For a moment, I think it's Chrissy—but no. This woman is much older. I see leaves tangled up in her gray hair. She turns just enough for her chin to reach over her shoulder. Her face is a dried riverbed of wrinkles. The one eye I see is fogged over. It's all milky to me.

She's smiling as she stirs.

There's a pot on the fireplace's hook. It's simmering. I can't see what she's cooking, but the pot boils over. Each drip sizzles against the iron plate along her hearth.

Hsss...

Hsss...

Hsss...

The woman holds out a wooden spoon to me, offering me a sip.

The broth is salty. And sweet. Like nothing I've ever tasted before. Butter on my tongue.

So I ask for more.

cyan, magenta, yellow, and key

The brave boys from Bear Scout Troop 237 were Pastor Nat's crusaders against corruption. His defenders of decency. His righteous knights of the highest order. These scrupulous scouts had exceeded the highest of the pastor's expectations, gathering around a thousand comic books, all told, for their purification drive. Each uniformed boy shuffled up with a Radio Flyer filled to its hilt with comics confiscated from around town, dumping the smut into a heaping pile for all to see.

These boys had purged the pharmacies of their indecencies.

They had eradicated the newsstands of their filth.

Here was the cancer that had crept into their small town, insinuating its sinfulness within the minds of the youngest, most innocent citizens, stacked six feet high and rising.

Mount Pornography.

Their flimsy pages flittered in the wind as the heap kept growing. *Swelling*. Toppling over in an avalanche of sex and violence. Wanton lust. Repugnant busts. Nothing but pages upon pages of illustrated licentiousness.

Keep 'em coming, boys, Pastor Nat called out. *Toss 'em all in! Every last comic... I want our pyre to reach as high as the heavens!*

L'il Lonnie Wilder couldn't even reach the peak anymore. When it was his turn to contribute his comics to the pile, that poor pudgy boy had to drag his feet up to the fire and lift himself up onto his tippy-toes, holding his shoe box over his head and shake them all out, each filthy issue showering down.

Tales of Terror.

Killer Comics.

Crime Pays and You're Buying.

L'il Lonnie didn't realize that Nat was well aware of the fact that this was his own *personal* stash. The pastor knew he was a peruser of these prurient pamphlets. All through Sunday school, he'd find L'il Lonnie flipping through the pages of one of his so-called horror comics. He'd confiscate it faster than you can say *sodomite*—but just like the head on a hydra, the very next Sunday, out sprouted another copy. The pastor had a whole file cabinet crammed full of comics commandeered from none other than L'il Lonnie. His poor saint of a mother had high hopes that the Bear Scouts would pull him out of his lecherous shell. Build up some character in him. Add a dash of moral fiber to flush out his objectionable habits once and for all.

Well, you better believe the pastor put in a personal call to Mrs. Wilder first thing after kick-starting his comic campaign, suggesting she *might* look under L'il Lonnie's bed mattress to see if he *might* be squandering a copy or two that she *might* wish to contribute to their crusade.

And me oh my, what a treasure trove of atrocities did Mrs. Wilder find waiting for her...

Bare-Knuckle Bulletin.

Fearsome Funnies.

Sci-Fi Sarcophagus.

Poor L'il Lonnie had tears in his eyes. He'd been at the back of the line for quite some time, letting every other troop member step ahead of him. Seemed to Nat that the kid was stalling, as if he thought Nat would decide at the last minute they had enough kindling and L'il Lonnie could keep his comics.

What've we got here, scout? The pastor pinched Lonnie's copy of *Petrified Pages* from the back of his belt loop, as if he couldn't see it poking out from the boy's pants. As if he'd actually spare it. *Were you hiding this from me, Lonnie?*

No, sir...

Don't mumble now. Speak up.

Yes, Pastor Nat, sir.

Pastor Nat flipped through, glancing over all the decapitations and half-dressed harlots running from lumbering corpses. An endless parade of four-color fornication.

His eyes halted upon a particular story—if you could call it a story—some pornographic paean to a cloven-hoofed demon of some sort. Lord only knows what kind of debauchee comes up with this stuff. He was only half-reading it, to be honest, impatiently perusing the pictures as if to prove a point to our L'il Lonnie here that he would not tolerate harboring smut such as this.

Frankly, Nat wasn't sure what exactly he was looking at. Some necrotic abomination. It had the blackest skin. Red eyes sunk deep into its sockets. And if he wasn't mistaken, there, between its legs, dangled what he could only presume was a grinning python. His fingers *just so happened* to rub over the image. Its black-as-pitch visage smudged, cheap ink smearing across his skin. It burned.

Do you find these types of stories entertaining, young man? Pastor Nat held the foulness up to L'il Lonnie's face, practically pressing the page against the boy's perspiring cheek. *Do you enjoy the objectification of the female form? The reverie of rape and murder? Do you, Lonnie?*

No, Pastor Nat, sir...

Look at me when I'm speaking to you. Do you know what you're doing to your poor mother, reading this rubbish? Do you know what you're doing to yourself? To your own mind? I imagine it must look like Swiss cheese by now. Cramming it full of stories of this... deca—

Decarabrian. He hissed its name with such venom. Lonnie snapped his head up at Nat, pinching his eyes into the thinnest slits, each crab-apple cheek turning a deep purple.

There was defiance in those beady eyes.

Pastor Nat saw rage.

It's indecent is what it is, young man, and it has no place in our homes. He rolled up the copy of *Petrified Pages* into a tight tube, as tight as he could, a four-colored fagot for their comic-book conflagration. *Which is why I want you to have the honor of lighting the fire, Lonnie...*

Click! The flash of a camera briefly blinded Pastor Nat, flaring up before him. It took a few blinks to bat the spots away. He had put in a call to the local newspaper to cover today's event. He'd given them the exact time and place—noon on Saturday in our church's parking lot. He even waited an additional twenty minutes after their designated start time just to be sure the photographer had arrived.

Showtime, folks...

We have gathered here today to take a stand against the insidious rise of comic books within our community, Pastor Nat announced to his prepubescent audience. There had to be over three dozen boys circled around the mound by now. Their doe-eyed future. *It is our firm belief that this type of literature poses a morally objectionable threat to the mental and physical well-being of our children—which is why, today, before the watchful eyes of our lord and savior, and our parents, we pledge to commit these desecrations on the page to whence they came.*

It was utterly unnecessary, Pastor Nat knew, but he went ahead and soused the pile with a hefty dose of lighter fluid, like dousing a dollop of holy water on the damned. They'd have themselves one heck of a finale here. He wanted the fire to be seen as far as two counties over. Let everyone know their town would not stand for this type of pictorial pederasty.

Gather round, children, he called out. *Don't be afraid. Circle in, nice and tight...*

Pastor Nat lit L'il Lonnie's comic with a match, letting the flames chew through that dirty devil *Decarabrian* and his dark ding-a-ling before handing it back to him.

Do you, boys and girls, consider comic books to be the ruin of many a youthful mind?

We do, the cheerful crowd chanted back.

Do you pledge to take a stand against this type of corruption from this day forward?

We do!

Then let us purify our minds and bodies once and for all.

Pastor Nat nodded to Lonnie. The boy only stared back with his bovine eyes.

Nat gave a gentle cough. *Lonnie.*

They all watched him toss his comic. Watched its flames coil in a comet's tail.

Watched it land on top of the pile.

An incendiary hiss filled the air. Smoke rose up from the smoldering heap, roasting for just a moment before combusting altogether. It all went up. And what a glorious fireball it was! Such diminutive kindling. The pages hastened a retreat, wilting within the intense heat before the inevitable singe swept over, *the Power and the Glory,* punctuated in a sizzle and pop.

The flames towered over their heads.

Such wondrous colors.

Cyan. Magenta. Yellow. And key—black, black key. The four inks used in the color printing process were pirouetting throughout the blaze.

Dots. Nat realized the flames were made of... *dots.* Hundreds upon thousands upon millions of tiny half-toned spots clustered together to compose a single continuous image.

Of fire.

He had to look away. His eyes were watering. Too much smoke. Nat rubbed them with his knuckles, then glanced back to see Troop 237 capering around the flames. They clutched each other's hands and spun about the fire, lascivious hips, gyrating in obscene circles. Voices lifting. Singing something. They had talked about belting out "The Star-Spangled Banner" once the fire was up and burning, but this—this didn't sound patriotic to him. Or English, for that matter.

Pastor Nat couldn't make out the words. Couldn't understand what they were singing. They all buzzed in some larval harmony, prancing and chanting as the flames reached higher.

Higher.

One boy began ripping the merit badges from his uniform. Just tore them off, one after the other, eating them. Why was he eating them? When that hadn't sated him, he kept clawing. Tearing through his uniform. His undershirt. His skin. He dug as deep as his fingernails would allow, clawing up chunks of his own flesh. Eating his skin by the handful.

Pastor Nat watched on as another boy plucked his eyes out from his own sockets. He perched them in the palm of his hand so the pastor could see. The reflection of the conflagration lit up in his eyes, burning with an intensity that dared not subside. He popped one in his mouth. Swallowed it with a smile. Then gulped the other.

Another boy forced his hand into the mouth of his friend, snapping back a few baby teeth in the process. His fingers disappeared. His whole fist. Lips wrapped around his wrist. When he yanked that glistening fist back out, painted red, he brought his fellow scout's uprooted tongue with him—and ate it.

They were eating each other. The whole troop. Pastor Nat's Bear Scouts had their own intestines dangling in their hands, garlands weaving about the fire, as they continued to dance and sing.

An eternal ring. A snake devouring its own tail. Infinite. Boundless.

You unleashed him, Pastor Nat... The voice had piped up from behind him. Nat wasn't sure if he'd even heard it at first, or if he'd just imagined it—but when he spun around, he found Lonnie, L'il Lonnie Wilder, staring back with empty eyes, blood dribbling out from his hollow sockets and running down his pudgy cheeks.

Decarabrian, he said, rather matter-of-factly. *The sixty-ninth spirit. The darkest star on the pentacle. He's been imprisoned for years. Now he's free. You set him free, Pastor Nat.*

Lonnie kept talking, but truth told, the rest of what he said was a bit garbled to Nat's ear, considering he was now chewing on his tongue. He couldn't help *tsk-tsk*ing the boy for talking with his mouth full, but this wasn't the time nor the place for a lesson in politeness.

A breeze blew through, whisking off with a few comic panels. The embers were so thin—the cinders instantly disintegrated as soon as they cooled, dissolving altogether in the afternoon air.

Sulfur lingered in the church parking lot, scorched and organic. An unavoidable smell which crept into Nat's nostrils. The odor of calcinated tissue wafting along.

Flesh. Pastor Nat smelled flesh on fire.

Their fire. His victory against idolatry.

Nat glanced at his arms and discovered they were covered in colors. Colors that shouldn't be. Cyan, magenta, yellow, and key—the four inks of the apocalypse.

A countless amount of the tiniest dots came together along his flesh to form images.

Panels. Actual panels scabbing his skin.

So he flipped through his leprous flesh. Each page revealing another image. Another layer on this endless comic. Down, down, all the way down to the bone.

One more sermon from me, Pastor Nat thought, *and then I'm done: As a boy, I had always been obsessed with the saints. During church services, I would stare up at the stained-glass window of St. Giles. I would lose myself counting the scabs scaling his face. The sun would seep through his cheeks, lighting up his leprosy, the colors casting themselves across the aisle—and I would place my hand underneath the beam. The redness of his sores soaked into my skin. I'd make believe I had been afflicted with whatever sickness this saint had. And at my most prideful, I would imagine what it would be like to have my own stained-glass window. What it would take to have my own image soldered along with all the other apostles. Boys and girls for years to come would look upon my window and pray unto me.*

St. Nathaniel—Patron Saint of the Pure. The Innocent. Protector against pornography. Crusader against comics...

Saints make sacrifices of themselves.

So Pastor Nat stepped across the scorched asphalt, through the ash pockmarking the pavement, over the burned Bear Scouts, the heap of their blackened bodies, into the purifying fire.

who brings a baby?

What kind of pissant for a parent brings their baby to a horror movie? A nine o'clock screening on a Monday night, no less... If you can't afford a sitter, then sorry, you shouldn't shell out fifteen bucks for a flick. Put that money aside for this kid's therapy bills, which will no doubt be coming, thanks to mom and dad dragging their child's diapered ass to some slasher rehash and ruining the movie for the rest of us.

Remember when theaters used to be a sacred space? Holy temples for celluloid? The point is to immerse yourself in the filmgoing experience. The world outside the cineplex simply melts away as soon as the lights go down and you can get lost in that tenebrous cosmos. Your very soul elevating itself out of your body, drifting along with everyone else in the audience and entering that vast expanse of the silver screen, as if the pearly gates just opened up to us all.

We go for that cinematic rapture.

But now we have cell phones to contend with. Texting and blooping and bleeping all through the movie, for Christ's sake. Once I was forced to listen to some preteen drama queen prattle on with her acne-saddled gal pal from the seat behind me, gossiping over the phone rather than watch the movie we all paid to see—that *I* paid to see. *Why piss over the film for the rest of us*? I shouted over my shoulder so that everyone in the theater could hear. *Why not just stay at home, young lady? Netflix and chill out somewhere else?* Do something—*anything*—other than step into my temple and blather on about whose boyfriend is cuter than whose during my cinematic sermon.

Guess who received their own round of applause from the audience after sending *that* wailing banshee out of the auditorium? That girl probably cried all the way home to her mommy.

Good riddance.

Someone needs to protect this hallowed space from unruly customers. *Someone* needs to hold the line. The very integrity of the filmgoing experience is at stake and if you won't risk your life to defend it, then what in God's name is the point of going to the movies anymore?

But nothing—I mean nothing—desecrates a film quite like listening to the four-alarm fire of some wailing baby overtake an entire auditorium. Sound carries differently in a theater. It doesn't matter where you sit: if your kid is bawling in the back row, we're all going to hear it.

Case in point: tonight, less than ten minutes into the film, I sense this sniveling infant from somewhere deep in the darkness. I can't pinpoint the exact location. The whimpering is coming from somewhere in the rear of the theater. It begins with a chainsaw sputter, just a few tugs from this kid's lungs, like yanking back on the pull-cord of a power tool. But once that wet engine gets revving, I know in my bones this little bastard is going to roar all through the movie.

Where is the little shit? I peer over my shoulder to try and pinpoint this family. All I see are the silhouettes of heads. The theater is practically empty, save for a few scattered shadows. No bouncing baby bopping along in the darkness, even if I can hear it. Am I the only one bothered by its staccato sobbing? It's only growing in volume now, gaining momentum with every clenched breath. At a certain point, just as a courtesy, you'd think mom or dad might heft their newborn foghorn into the lobby. Just don't, you know, *stay*. Don't sit in your seat and act like nothing's happening, *nothing wrong here at all*, as your kid shrieks and shrieks and shrieks.

Who's even following the storyline anymore? I certainly can't. Is anyone paying attention to the movie? I could alert the manager and complain, but that pimple-faced excuse for a spine won't do more than stutter through some scripted excuse for a scolding. They never do a thing.

No, I'll take matters into my own hands. I'll answer that baby with my own battle cry:

Sssh! I hiss over my shoulder. *That* should do it. Loud and clear. I'm completely anonymous here. Mom and dad will never know it was me, sitting in the third row, second from the aisle, but they'll know that we the people of this movie theater have collectively spoken.

But this baby...

It won't stop bawling. Jesus, how big are this kid's lungs? The sound of its crying expands and contracts, eclipsing everything onscreen. What the fuck is wrong with this child? Is it malnourished? Did it just take a cataclysmic shit in its diapers? We've now entered a new phase of wailing—short, glottal retorts that pepper the theater with auditory depth charges. If this were a war movie, I'd imagine the crying was just another sound effect. But no—these sonic hand grenades are coming from behind me, blasting at my ears. Total surround sound.

So, I do what any rational-minded moviegoer would do. I simply turn to the back of the theater and shout: *Some of us are trying to watch the movie!* That'll shut it up. Take that, tyke!

But this baby...

Now the crying is closer. Where the hell are they? It's as if the family has moved forward a few rows, just to mess with me. Toy with me. The blackened space compresses itself, so it now sounds like that caterwauling kid is sitting in the row right behind me, bawling just at my back.

Over my shoulder.

At my neck.

Something nicks my left ear. Just the slightest slice over the lobe. It stings, my shoulder springing up in a defensive reflex. There's a warm trickle dribbling down the length of my neck.

I'm bleeding. How am I bleeding?

This baby...

Now the crying creeps into my right ear. There's a thin wriggle against the lobe and I can't help but imagine a worm burrowing its way through the canal. I turn in time to catch a passing glance at a pale, pudgy pinkie finger reeling back into the blackness behind me.

Now the crying comes from up front. In the aisle. The baby just won't stay still. I can't nail down the sound anymore. It's everywhere and nowhere all at once, circling around me.

Closing in.

Something brushes against my right ankle, slicing through my sock. Both my legs pitch upwards as I scream, sending popcorn into the air.

Sssh! Other audience members hiss back, as if I'm the problem. But there's something strange about the timbre to it. It doesn't sound like a pissed-off patron. They're mocking me.

Somebody help, I shout. But no one answers. Searching the theater, I notice none of the silhouettes I'd spotted before are there anymore. Where did everyone go?

A very cold thought enters my mind: What if those shadows weren't actually people? What if I've got the whole theater to myself?

I plunge into the row of folding seats. Old soda seeps through my pants. Or maybe it's blood. I've got a good view of the floor now, among the candy wrappers and shriveled popcorn.

I'm going to wait for that baby. This time, I'll see it coming. This time, I'll be ready.

Where is it where is it where is it where... I hear the soft pads of its paws peeling off the sticky floor, all covered in coagulated cola, but I can't see it. *Where is it where is it where...*

The vaguest shape slips past me. An albino flash. Was that a rat? Are there mice in the movie theater? It's not too late to escape. I can just crawl into the aisle and run for the exit.

Where is it where...

There! A pair of eyes glint in the dark, as gleaming as the silver screen. It's a baby alright, crawling on its hands and knees, but not like any newborn I've ever laid eyes on before. I don't think this child has ever seen the sun in its entire life. Its skin is practically translucent, mottled in multicolored tumors. The cysts shimmer in the dim glow cast from the movie projector.

Wait—those aren't tumors. Those are Jujubes. That gelatinous candy that always gets caught in your molars. Teens toss them at the screen to see if they'll stick, but this pustulating infant is covered in them. A rainbow-hued leper. There's a speckling of stale popcorn flecking its limbs, nodules of kernels clustered across its shoulders, like lopsided vertebrae all over its back.

The baby's blistered lips—*Do I still think this is a baby?*—are dusted in white nonpareils—those are Sno-Caps—and I can't help but think its erupting in abscesses.

Something slashes the back side of my hand. I cry out in pain and the crowd hisses, *Sssh!* But it's not coming from the audience. There is no audience. This is an imitation of a shush, a cruel mimicry of my own hiss getting echoed back at me... and it's coming from all around. *Sssh!*

There's another baby in the aisle now.

And another.

Their eyes are silver, as blinding as the screen itself. I count three of them—no, make that four—five—each scabbed in candy from the concession stand, Swedish Fish and Mike & Ikes and Junior Mints and Raisinets and Goobers and Skittles and Gobstoppers and M&M's...

There was never just one.

They're closing in on me now, slowly crawling across the floor on their hands and knees, each inch forward punctuated with the tacky peeling of their skin.

They're not crying anymore.

Oh God, they're giggling.

Sssh... Sssh... Sssh...

This theater was never my temple... It's their hunting ground.

the spew of news

Fax News took my mom and dad away from me.

You know their stupid slogan: *Just the Fax*—cheekily misspelled in some outdated Reagan-era wisecrack. But it was true: some right-wing propaganda machine masquerading as a twenty-four-hour news network reprogrammed my parents.

I hadn't spoken to either of them in weeks. Maybe a month by then. Our phone calls had faded due to my "hectic schedule". Which was a lie. I swore up and down that I wasn't purposefully giving them the silent treatment, and my wife and I certainly weren't holding their grandkids hostage, denying them their weekly FaceTime chat with Thomas and Benjie, even though I'm pretty positive that's precisely what Mom and Dad were thinking. Too late—the delusion had taken root in their heads and now there was no yanking it out. We were being blamed for brainwashing our boys with our own liberal agenda, turning our sons against them.

This was more than some silly ideological divide between generations. This wasn't just about the election. Who's voting for who. As much as Candice and I tried to convince them of picking the better candidate—Christ, *any* other candidate than *that* one—we'd accepted the fact that their minds were made up and now there was no changing them. We moved on.

No—this had everything to do with the news. *Who* they were getting their facts—sorry, *fax*—from. How their very channel of choice was changing my mother and father from the inside out. *Altering* them, somehow. I barely recognized them anymore.

What they were becoming.

I know how easy it is to slip into hyperbole when you start talking about politics, but whenever I spoke to Mom on the phone, the things she said—about the president, climate change, our healthcare system—none of it sounded like her. It was her voice, *sure*, but the words weren't hers. They sounded like somebody else's. *She* sounded like someone else.

Everybody knows the virus isn't as bad as the media is making it out to be...

Everybody knows all that climate stuff is just a hoax...

Everybody knows the kids in cages is just more fake news...

Who the hell was this person and what had she done with my mother? Where had that sharpened edge in her voice come from? The spite? Why was my mom so *angry* all the time?

You have to understand, my mother wasn't one of *those people*. She never had a political bone in her body. Our family always had the uncanny knack of repressing their politics. Growing up, I never even knew what my parents' political affiliations were because we never talked about them. Who you voted for was something you kept private. It wasn't for polite conversation. No ruffling feathers at our dinner table during the holidays and that was that.

Then something changed.

The *channel* changed *them*.

~

It started with Dad. He was such an easy target once he retired. Most days he simply sprawled himself out in front of the television for hours on end, barely getting up from his cozy recliner. Cable news was his default, imbibing a steady stream of world events filtered through Fax. I was already out from under my parents' roof by then, living in an elite east coast city with my own family. Our time together tended to follow the familiar pattern of holiday visits, which is just to say I wasn't around anymore. I wasn't there to witness the gradual decline of my father's political prehension in real time. I wasn't there to try and stop it before it was too late.

The shift started subtly enough. At first, he'd lob these odd, offhand comments into conversation. Casual remarks just left of the Kaiser, such as—*Well, has anyone actually seen his birth certificate?*

That quickly escalated to—*A vote for her is just another step closer toward socialism.*

Only to finally land at—*Who's to say Sandy Hook actually happened, anyhow?*

Our conversations became untenable, to be honest. I didn't want to talk to him anymore—my own father—because the dialogue always sounded the same. Poorly written conspiracy theory fanfic. Just hearing Dad spout out these outright lies was like listening to him read lines off Hitler's teleprompter. I could even hear the echo-effect of his opinions, regurgitating the viewpoints of someone else rather than doing the actual thinking behind them.

It was simple to discredit Dad's crackpot talk. He was just getting older. Crankier. Candice and I poked fun at him, opining the fate of every white man entering the twilight of his years.

That'll be you one day, she teased. *Just wait.*

Shoot me now, I begged. *If I ever become some raving lunatic, please, you have my full permission to put me out of my misery...*

Then Mom started to sound just like Dad.

Mom, who gave birth to me.

Mom, who raised me to be a *thinking man*, as she always put it.

Who cut the crusts off my peanut butter sandwiches.

Who always teared up during commercials about auto insurance.

That mom.

On our last phone conversation together, she said—actually said—*Everybody knows there's a secret Democrat pedophile ring in DC.*

I couldn't breathe. I felt as if my ribs had just gripped my lungs and kept on squeezing. I had to take a moment to simply process the words that had just oozed out from the receiver.

Jesus, Mom—do you even hear what you're saying?

It's true. Look it up. There was something different about her voice. She sounded congested. There was a gravelly drag to her breath, every word raked over wet rocks. It could've been a cold, but this sounded thicker. Phlegmier. Even over the phone, I heard the fluid filling up within her lungs, sloshing around as she talked. *They're hiding it from us.*

You honestly don't believe that—do you, Mom?

That's what they said on the news...

News. You mean Fax?

Just the Fax, she echoed.

That's not news, Mom. That's right-wing BS getting pumped straight into your head...

You just don't understand, son. There was the slightest edge of belittlement in her voice, which frustrated me to no end. I'm forty-three. I'm married and have two children of my own. And here's my mother—some faded facsimile of her, at least—treating me like I was a child. *You don't see it yet, like we do. But you will. One day, when you're older, you'll understand...*

I know it's absurd to blame the news. But it's true. I genuinely believe my parents had been brainwashed by Fax News. The empty rhetoric had infected my father first and now somehow the sickness had spread to my mother, contaminating her with the same vitriol.

I couldn't listen to it anymore. Couldn't talk to them. It just wasn't worth wasting oxygen over, I thought. The older they got, the more entrenched in these opinions they'd become. But these weren't even their opinions! That's what was killing me! They were being spoon-fed this poisonous punditry, night after night with these rancorous newscasts, listening to Stepford hosts spout out their harmful bombast and then rehashing it as if it were their own.

Fax News was taking my parents away from me. Fax News was driving this wedge between my mom and dad and the rest of the family—from reality—sealing the two of them in this suffocating bubble of bile and racism and I just couldn't put up with it anymore.

So I refused to listen.

I refused to engage.

I refused to let our children anywhere near them as soon as they hopped on to their acrimonious discourse high horse.

Our visits over the summer were compressed. We were in and out over the holidays. It was obvious what was happening, even if nobody said anything about it. Not out loud. Certainly not to each other. I mouthed off about it to my wife any chance I got, when it was just the two of us, safely out of everyone else's earshot. Now even she was getting sick of me complaining.

How long are you gonna do this? Candice asked. *Why not just say something?*

Don't you think I've tried? There's no reaching them anymore...

I don't know, hon... Your family has always been pretty conflict-averse.

So you're saying this is my fault?

What I'm saying is you're choosing to look the other way...

So, what should I do, huh? Stage an intervention? Try deprogramming them?

Talk to them, she offered. *Tell them you love them. You still love them, don't you?*

Yeah, but... Not the way they are now. Not what they've become.

Maybe it's not too late.

They're not changing their minds... That much is obvious.

Then just listen to them. Hear what they have to say. Try to understand where they're coming from... Who knows? Maybe they're still in there, somewhere. You just have to find them.

~

Then they stopped answering their phone. Mom's cell went straight to voicemail whenever I called. No ring or anything, simply sending me straight to her mailbox. Dad had a cell phone, but he never used it. Calling him was pointless. But they should've at least picked up the landline. I called when I knew they'd be at home—should've been at home—but it simply rang and rang.

I thought about asking the neighbors to check in, but then I realized I didn't even know who their neighbors were. I thought about calling the police but that seemed to be taking this to an awkward extreme that I'd never be forgiven for if it all turned out to be one big misunderstanding. That was still a possibility, wasn't it? That they were OK? That I was simply overreacting? Who's to say they just didn't want to talk to me? Maybe this was their silent treatment. Maybe they were giving me a little bit of my own self-righteous medicine here. *Two can play at that game*, they were thinking. Giggling to themselves every time my name popped up on the caller ID.

I had to go down there. I had to hop in the car and drive the two hours—three, if there's traffic on I-95—all the way to their house and see them for myself.

Jesus, I had to confront my parents.

On any other trip, the whole family would've piled in and headed down with me—but something about this visit made me feel like it was better if I went solo. I still couldn't shake the feeling that something was wrong, even if I didn't know what. I had the whole ride to imagine all the worst-case scenarios. There was a gas leak and both of them had asphyxiated in bed. I'd step into the house and find their bodies still tucked in next to each other, as if they were just sleeping, their skin gone gray with the waning days that I hadn't done anything sooner.

What if it was something worse? What if there had been a break-in and the two of them had been held hostage in their own home?

Trapped by addicts looking to lay low for a while? Would I find their bodies in the basement? Hands bound behind their backs? Mouths sealed shut with duct tape? Their muffled voices calling out for me, their only son, to save them?

They should've picked up the phone, for Christ's sake. They should've answered.

Unless something was wrong.

Something very, *very* wrong.

Nothing seemed off when I pulled into their driveway. The house looked fine. The grass was a little taller than normal, but that was no reason to panic. Dad always liked to keep his lawn perfectly level, but I was choosing not to sound any alarms over the ragged grass. Not yet.

I had my own key, so I let myself in. *Hello?* I called out. *Anyone home?*

No answer.

The smell found me first: a sourness in the air, old fruit gone bad. But wet. Can a smell even be wet? I felt like I'd just entered a damp cave. There was a certain humidity sweltering throughout the house. Nobody had opened a window in here for a while, and they had no air-conditioning.

I heard voices coming from the living room.

It wasn't Mom or Dad.

Someone was talking. Reporting. The television was still on. The volume was cranked up pretty loud, as loud as it could go, the authoritative voice of some bombastic newscaster kept pumping throughout the halls of the house, filling up every room with his discordant words.

Mom? Dad? I had to speak louder. *Everybody OK? It's me...*

The voice only grew louder the closer I got to the living room. But I couldn't focus on the words for some reason. Whatever he was saying, they didn't sound familiar to me.

It was the news. Had to be the Fax.

The smell intensified. It was coming from the living room, too.

The air dampened, clinging to my skin. Like sweat, but not mine. This perspiration had an oiliness to it. A viscosity.

I stepped on something squishy. The floor simply went soft, the very floorboards seemed to sag under the weight of my body. The heel of my shoe slipped out from under me and I almost fell over backward. I reached out for the wall to hold me up, pressing my palm against something like algae. Whatever it was, it was on walls. Covering the picture frames of our family. It spread across the floorboards, thin filaments branching out from the living room.

I found my father first, or what was left of him. His corpse remained in the recliner, the footrest outstretched so that his body was leaning back in a resting pose, facing the television.

His skin was now covered in wet tendrils that seemed to reach out from the screen. They ran down the wall and tangled across the floor, as if it were some blackened pumpkin patch, connecting to the swivel base of his chair and worming its way over his limbs. His lower jaw hung open, slackly dangling all the way to his chest. His cheek muscles had given out, stretched like taffy. What was left of his tongue had gone green, coiling together with several tendrils in a braid of ivy and desiccated muscle. It was all connected. Every tendril.

The television was a wet, black web. The screen rested at its center. Every filament, every oily thread seemed to vibrate with the newscaster's voice. Humming, almost.

What was he saying? What were the words coming out from his mouth? I felt like I was just at the precipice of hearing them, of understanding.

I turned to face the TV. I couldn't help but wince at the fluctuating colors, swirling in oily distortions. Something was off about the balance. The settings kept recalibrating themselves, the contrast rising and lowering, up and down, until the image began flashing in some hypnotic pulse. It left me with a queasy feeling in my stomach. Inside my head. But I couldn't look away.

Now the newscaster somehow drifted a few inches off the screen, peeling away from the plasma, hovering outside the television. Reaching for me. Broadcasting to me as if I were the only person listening. Witnessing this telecast. His voice reached in and found me. *What were the words what were the words what were the words what were the words what were the—*

The remote was still clasped in what was left of Dad's hand. *Don't touch it,* I thought. I had to pry the remote out from his hand, snapping off a few of his fingers in the process. My fingertips burned with the slightest singe in my skin.

Dad suddenly blinked—I believe he blinked—at me. Just the slightest dip in his eyelids, nothing but green veils over his oil-slicked sockets.

I pressed the off button and was suddenly met with silence.

The moan came from behind me. She may have been groaning all this time and I just hadn't heard her yet, but now that the television was finally off, I heard her—*Mom*—mewling from the far corner of the living room. I found her body tucked behind the couch. She had been trying to crawl underneath it, from the looks of it, as if to hide. She was on her back, partially hidden beneath the couch's underbelly. It was a weird image to imagine, but from where I was standing, it looked like Mom was servicing her car in the auto shop, sliding beneath the chassis to change the oil, only to get a face full of black gunk for her troubles. It had pooled in her mouth. Her eyes. I tried to pull the couch away to get a good look at her, but it wouldn't give. The couch was stuck on to her. They were adhered to each other. The latticework of tendrils that had once been Mom's arm now branched over the floor, gluing her to the couch's inner framework. Peeling it away would've been painful, I surmised from the sounds Mom was making, so I simply gave up on separating her from the furniture and let her rest on the floor.

Mom was still able to turn her head. She looked up at me with eyes that didn't look like eyes anymore, but pools of oil. Her mouth opened and out bubbled more of that black bile, the same fluid that seemed to be dribbling out from the television screen, covering just about every inch of the living room. She opened her mouth to say something, the shriveled root that had been her tongue slowly emerging from the tidal pool of her lips. I couldn't understand her.

Jss...tth...fffxx...

Dad still had his rifle locked up in their bedroom closet. He blinked again when I brought the barrel to his forehead, or the fungus that covered his skin approximated some flex that could've been misconstrued as blinking. I wanted to be quick about it. *Put the ol' man out of his misery.* But I kept hesitating. The rifle was too heavy. The trigger slippery with sweat. I couldn't do this. I couldn't. But Dad wouldn't stop staring. Blinking. Begging with his milked-over eyes.

I apologized as I pulled the trigger. I don't know if he heard me or not.

Whatever was left of his brain splattered out from the rupture in his skull, oozing down the back of his recliner. Green fluid seeped into the fabric.

I couldn't look at Mom. I had to turn away. I heard her moan once more just before I squeezed the trigger—and in that moment, I wished, almost wished, I'd left the television on.

Just to drown her out.

The walls shuddered. The tendrils retracted, the latticework reeling back into the television set. Not completely, but just enough for me to understand that I had hurt whatever this was.

The black screen looked oiler than before, now that it was turned off. I thought I had severed the connection. That Fax News was cut off from pumping this house full of hate.

The television turned back on.

By itself.

No newscaster this time. Only variations of light. An oil spill swirling about the screen. A spiral of brilliant, beautiful colors. I took a step closer to the television. There was a warmth spreading across my cheeks. The patterns expanding across the screen wouldn't keep still, spiraling outward, almost spreading beyond the screen itself. I swear I saw something slithering within the pigments. Something behind those bands of light. Something staring back at me.

I'd never seen such wondrous colors before.

Such truth.

And somewhere deep within my mind, some very far echo of an image came to me: a pelican. Its wings sheathed in oil. White feathers tethered in black. Struggling to free itself from the muck.

All I wanted to do was sit and watch.

To bear witness.

I could've sat there for hours if the police hadn't arrived. The neighbors had heard the shots and called it in. When the pair of officers walked into the living room, apparently they found me, rifle still in hand, sitting Indian-style—sorry, crisscross-applesauce—between the bodies of my mom and dad. Just watching the news.

I know how the mainstream media is reporting this. I know what's being said about what I've done. But let me ask: *Who are you getting your information from? Your Fax?*

My mom and dad were dragged into an alternate reality. I know that now. Or, more to the point, an alternate reality was getting dragged into them. *Replacing* their reality. Their minds, the soft tissue of their bodies, were contaminated, rotting them from the inside out.

Their TV was changing them, quite literally, into something else. Something not of this world.

I'm speaking directly to you, whoever you are. If you're listening to me, then I have to assume a few things about you. Your political affiliations probably lean a little to the left. It's not a given, but still. Odds are I'm right. And what's right of left? Left of right? Who knows anymore? I don't. But I know what I saw. I know what I heard. You have to believe me.

Chances are you have parents of your own. Who live alone. Such easy targets. They're probably in their homes right now, as we speak. Probably watching the news. But it's who they're getting their news from that's important here. Who's feeding them their *fax*. Their truth.

This isn't just my parents. This is your mom and dad, too. This is happening everywhere. So, before you head home for the holidays to break bread with your family, I want you—need you—to find out where they're getting their fax from. What channel. Have you noticed something different about them? Their voices? The words crawling out across their lips?

It's not too late for you. There still might be time to save them. All you have to do is...

Change the goddamn channel.

It's too late for me. I can feel it—the need to tune in—even now. The news is out there. Twenty-four hours a day, seven days a week. Someone needs to be watching it. Absorbing it.

Taking it in.

Sometimes a remote control isn't strong enough to sever the signal. Sometimes it takes a pistol. For the truth's sake. For the fax.

Sorry. Facts. For the facts.

Fax.

Facts.

Fax.

Just the Fax. Just the Fax. Just the—

stowaway

Mom got so mad at my *itsy bitsy teenie weenie fluorescent pink hey-boys-come-fuck-me* bikini. Guess her stupid rule came back to haunt her, didn't it? *If you want this junk so badly*, she totally droned, *buy it with your own money*. But that was gift shops ago. She was referring to some dumb bottle opener keychain with my name engraved on it. SARA. No "H." Most mementos always put the stupid "H" at the end, so when I saw this keychain emblazoned with my name, I was all like—*Oh, finally, someone actually spelled it right*. That's when Mom's Sunday school upbringing decided to suddenly kick in for once in her life. She put her foot down, saying—*I can't justify buying a bottle opener for a fourteen-year-old*. It's not like having some dumb keychain would send me downward-spiraling into alcoholism or whatever, but she wouldn't budge.

Like $1.99 would break our vacation's budget, anyway. She bought Peter that stupid hat that said **BEACH BUM**, a pair of pale butt cheeks under it, but Mom apparently didn't have any moral quandary over that particular purchase. She can be such a fucking hypocrite sometimes.

I spotted the shoestrings dangling on the rack back at the last hotel, along with all the Budweiser beach blankets and god-awful T-shirts.

CHECK OUT MY LADY NUTS.

I NEED AN ALCOHOLIDAY.

SHELL YEAH, BEACHES.

That's what I totally thought they were, at first. Neon lime shoestrings. Cotton candy laces. Just a few loose threads suspended from a coat hanger... but no, those were totally meant to cover your boobs. As in, that's it. Nothing else. Just some fluorescent floss and a pair of triangles. Nipple pyramids. I knew it would piss Mom off, but what was she going to do? Stop me? It was *my money*. If I wanted any of *this junk so badly*, I could *just buy it myself*. Her words.

Now I never take it off. It's my highlighter-pink protest for the duration of our family vacation. If I'm going to be stuck in the car for two weeks, suffering next to my dipshit baby brother and his incessant nose-picking, then I'm wearing my brand-new bikini through our whole road trip, rain or fucking shine, and nobody can stop me.

At least put a shirt on while we're in the car, Mom grumbled from the front seat. She wouldn't look at me, couldn't deign me with eye contact, speaking out the windshield instead.

What's the big deal? It's not like anyone's watching.

Truckers are watching. Biker gangs are watching. Anyone who drives by is watching...

She's wrong. Nobody's noticed me. Yet. No sixteen wheelers honking their horns or bearded, beer-bellied Hell's Angels revving their engines as they pass our car on the highway.

The bikini definitely has taken some getting used to. At first, I kept covering myself with my arms. Too many exposed moles. The seat belt saws at my chest, chafing against my skin.

Dad hasn't waded into the bikini discourse aside from suggesting I should put on suntan lotion, even in the car. *You're destined for skin cancer without it.* He's more focused on the road, to be honest. Reaching the next destination. No HoJo's for our fam, no sir. It's been backroads and roach motels for the Pendletons all the way. Dad's so hell-bent on his Americana Tour, steering clear of the interstates as much as possible for what he says is *a real good look at what's left of the country.* The forgotten America, he calls it. Let's see it before it all fades away.

Whatever that means.

I've sulked next to just about every pool within a three-thousand-mile radius of our house. At least now I can do it in style. See how Mom feels about all the creeps checking me out. I don't care who's looking. Let the dads all stare for all I care. I definitely don't. Care, that is. The acne-riddled hotel clerk with the protruding Adam's apple can stare, too, if he wants to. Or the dudes who seem to be living out of the back of their trucks or the traveling Bible salesman or any of them. I just don't care. *Hey, everybody, let's all have ourselves a poolside peepshow!*

This was supposed to be my spring break. We could've gone anywhere, but no, we all had to pile into the car and make every single pit stop Mom and Dad wanted, just to see the world's biggest ball of twine or some prehistoric tar pit in the middle of nowhere.

I was missing my friends for *this*?

~

The war started between me and Mom after she took my phone away. Dad made some grand sweeping statement at the beginning of the trip that he didn't want to see our faces buried in our screens while there was a whole world just waiting outside our windows for us to witness, but he didn't enforce it or anything. That was up to Mom. Dad focused on driving while she always got to be bad cop. We battled over who got to charge their phone and I lost out because she said she needed hers to navigate, but Dad won't let her even turn on the map app. He says *that defeats the whole purpose*, which I completely agreed with, taking his side much to Mom's annoyance. She still wouldn't let me use the charger. She took my phone away after three warnings, which I didn't really think she'd do because who even does something like that? But here we are. I told her I was taking pictures of our trip to share with my friends—*You know, all my friends, who are all having the time of their lives in Daytona with their families right now*? Not like there's any reception out here on the highway, anyway. It's been zero bars all week.

Hand it over, Mom had said. *Now.*

What the hell am I supposed to do?

I don't know, hon, she said. *Read a book.*

I picked up some dumb paperback left behind at the last hotel. Someone must've read it, then abandoned it. There was a whole shelf of forgotten novels. Beach reads. Boddice rippers. That sort of thing. I found a copy of *A Million Little Pieces* and figured I'd give it a spin. The cover was curling over, the spine cracked so much you could barely read the title anymore. But it was about drugs, and I could tell Mom didn't want me reading it, so I had that going for me. She asked to read the book description on the back, so I gave it to her and watched her face pucker as she took it all in. *I remember this,* she said, tossing it back. *Turns out it wasn't true.*

So? I asked. *Still pretty stimulating.* To prove my point, I read a particularly heinous passage from the back seat for all to enjoy. The one about the teeth. The root canal stuff. Peter started crying so Mom made me stop. *What's everyone's problem?* I asked. *This is literature.*

No, Mom retorted, *that's just you, pushing your brother's buttons.*

You could just give me my phone back...

Not happening.

~

Every motel has the same setup: some concrete pool just off to the side of the parking lot, wrapped in a rusted chain-link fence. No umbrellas, so the sun soaks into the asphalt. Plastic lawn chairs. Not beach chairs. *Lawn* chairs. There is no ocean out here. No sand. All we have are these roadside oases. Concrete beaches just next to the highway. The water usually has a slight greenish tint to it. Who knows the last time anyone dumped any chlorine in. I can always feel the algae clinging to my skin whenever I climb out, totally coated in this sticky thin film of slime that dries into a coagulated crust, like soda. There's always a bevy of dead bugs drifting along the water's surface. Fist-sized mosquitos. Beetles paddling on their backs.

These pools are supposed to be the main draw for most traveling families. Some motels have a putt-putt, or free HBO, never any Wi-Fi, but the pools are the real lure. Always with a sign NO LIFEGUARD ON DUTY posted on the fence. There are always a couple kids splashing around, floating on some inflatable unicorn. It's a miracle there aren't any drowned babies bobbing along with the bugs. Mom makes Peter put on these inflatable arm bands that make him look like a total 'tard. As soon as we pull into the hotel, or motel, or no-tell, l'il Petey leaps out of the car and races to the pool faster than Mom can blow up his rubber biceps.

Take a wild guess who's always on babysitting detail?

Keep an eye on your brother, Mom said.

Why.

You want to unload the car instead?

Fiiine.

I could tell Mom was hating our vacation just as much as I was. Maybe even more. The only people who seemed to be enjoying themselves, or pretending to enjoy themselves, were Dad and Peter. Mom seethed through each state. I almost felt bad for her. Almost.

I plopped down in a lawn chair next to the pool while Pete had the water all to himself. Nobody else was out here, thank God. I had a pair of sunglasses that kept the rest of the world at bay, just in case. I had dragged my paperback halfway across the country at this point, but I'd barely made a dent into it. I didn't even open it. I was just carrying it around as an excuse not to engage with anyone, anyways, so I simply flipped to a rando page and stared off somewhere, anywhere else other than the words, hiding behind my sunglasses and just tuning the fuck out.

Good book?

Where the hell had he come from? The skin on my arms prickled from his proximity. One second, I was all alone—the next, there was a stranger, invading my space. Probably somebody's dad, bored with his own family, singling me out and hoping to flirt. Ick.

I side-eyed the guy but pretended not to've heard him. He wasn't in my field of vision, even if I could feel him close by. I didn't want to turn my head and acknowledge that I'd heard him, not yet, but I still couldn't quite clock his location. Which was weird. Where was he?

I felt his eyes.

On me.

I suddenly found myself wishing I was wearing a T-shirt. Too much of my skin was exposed to this creep. The laces of my bikini slowly constricted around my torso, the strings tightening like a garrote at my chest, squeezing against my ribs until I couldn't breathe.

Never read it. This guy clearly wasn't taking the hint, so I closed the book and turned.

That's when I actually saw him.

He was sitting two lawn chairs down from me, an empty seat between us. Which was weird. I could've sworn he was sitting right next to me. Leaning over. Sharing the air between us.

How was he so far away?

I had to bring my hand up to shield my eyes from the sun to see him, almost as if he was hiding behind the light, his silhouette keeping his features in the shadows.

What I could make out was cute enough, so he at least had that going for him. He looked like he was in his thirties, I think. I don't know, it was hard to tell. Older guys just look old to me. I have this affliction called *adult blindness.* He could've been thirty or fifty or whatever and I really wouldn't even know the difference.

He was alone. That much I could tell. No beach towels or inflatable pool toys. No bottle of sunscreen or six-pack of Bud. He wasn't even wearing a bathing suit. Just dull adult clothes.

...Well?

Well, what? Ugh. That was the best I could do? Echo his question like some dumb parrot.

Do you like the book?

It's OK, I guess. My shoulders sprung up in an involuntary shrug.

Just OK? I'll pass. Life's too short for "just OK." I want something that'll change my life.

That could've easily been the end of the conversation. I was already feeling the urge to pick the book up and hide behind its pages, but he kept looking at me. Staring. Not at my bikini or anything. At me. Like, my eyes or something. There's a difference. He seemed genuinely curious. It felt weird. I didn't really know what to say, so I said nothing.

This guy seemed totally OK to just sit and stew in that awkward quiet for as long as he wanted. He smiled even. Just basking in it all. He knew he was in control of the silence and it was going to be his decision to break it, like popping a tiny bubble of saliva clinging to my lip with just the tip of his finger—*plip*.

So, where you heading?

West, I said, even if I had no idea if we were coming or going. One of those noncommittal answers that doesn't give away too much information. I wasn't an idiot. I wasn't about to give him our home address or anything. But it was enough of a breadcrumb to keep the conversation going. He could come back for more if he wanted. Follow me, if he wanted.

You with your family?

Yeah. I turned to look over my shoulder, just to see if I could pinpoint my parents. They must've still been checking in to our room. Unloading the car. They certainly weren't here, protecting their kids against the poolside advances of some potential serial killer. Thanks, guys.

Must be a drag.

You said it. He didn't say anything in response to that, so instead of stewing in even more awkward silence, I managed to ask, *How about you? Are you with your family?*

Ugh. Even I could hear the yearning in my voice. It was too much. I'd given him too much. I could feel the blood rush straight to my solar plexus, this rash spreading across my chest and here I am, wearing a shoestring for the love of God and I can't hide it. I sounded like such a cooze and I was full-on blushing with nothing to cover myself up and I was so—

No family, he said with the slightest exhale of a laugh. Maybe it was a laugh. *Just me.*

That must be fun.

Sometimes. Feel like I've been stuck here for ages, though...

OK. This was interesting. Here's this guy, this stranger, offering up a little something of himself. To me. This was the first honest conversation I'd had with anyone in like, days. Weeks.

Does it get lonely? I had to ask. *Traveling all by yourself?*

Depends. Every so often I meet somebody nice. We get to talking and it doesn't feel so—

Sara! Mom's voice cut through the air, snapping me out of our conversation. I spun around in my chair to find her standing in the parking lot, arms planted on both hips. Even from across the lot, I could sense the exasperation seeping out of her pores. She waved me over, beckoning me back to the car with a single sweep of her arm, as if that's all it took to get me to come trotting. Couldn't she see I was in the middle of something here? Couldn't she just, you know, give me a minute to finish my conversation? *And pull Peter out of the water!*

Fuck. Peter. I'd totally forgotten him. Luckily, he was still alive, bobbing about the water with his floaties. Not floating face-down or anything. Thank God for small miracles.

Sorry. I felt all of me blush. My whole body this time, not just my chest. *I gotta go...*

No worries, Sara, he said—and I could tell, I could just tell, he knew my name didn't have an "H" at the end of it, saying it so succinctly, so sharp. *You know where to find me.*

It wasn't until after I left that I realized I didn't even know his name. I hadn't asked.

Totally slipped my mind.

He was still there after dinner. Just sitting by the pool by himself. Nobody else was around. The sun had sunk down, so the lights kicked on under the water, casting this cerulean sheen across his face. The water was still. Nothing broke the surface except for the dead bugs.

Hey, I said. *This pool taken?*

You came back... I don't think I went back for him. Not exactly. But I was curious. Just to see if he was a man of his word. From the way he was sitting, I would've believed he'd been there this whole time, except he wasn't sunburned or anything like that. The pool was pretty close to the highway, so everything had a burned asphalt aroma to it. You could almost taste the tar. The thickness of it clung to my tongue, and in a way I imagined that's what he tasted like. If we were to kiss, which is totally not what I was expecting to do, but still, if—*if*—we did, I imagined he'd taste something like the road. Like concrete and exhaust. Like heat waves oscillating off asphalt. Even his skin probably felt rough as pavement. Gravel and broken glass.

I was hoping you'd find me, he said.

Yeah, well, not like there's much else to do here...

There's plenty. He didn't offer up any suggestions and it felt weird to ask.

I dipped my legs in the pool this time. The water felt warm. I gently kicked my legs, sending these ripples radiating across the surface. The light now warped and danced, casting these baby blue shadows over his face. Why were his features always hiding from me?

So, have you been, like, staying here a long time? I asked.

Something like that.

Where are you heading?

Don't know just yet... Who knows? Maybe I'll follow you.

He was flirting. Obviously. But it was the way that he was doing it that felt so—I don't know—uncharted. Most guys just go in for the kill, *God you're so hot*, but he was talking in this way that felt both extremely direct and frustratingly indirect at the exact same time. Like, if I called him on it or something, he could easily say I had just misunderstood him and then I'd feel like a total idiot. He was subtle. Casting out these lines like I was a fish he was hoping to lure in.

Finally, I said, *You wouldn't want to be trapped with my family, trust me.*

Says who?

What? I suddenly felt bold. *You wanna come with me?*

Maybe I do.

Liar.

Who says I'm lying?

But it's... My voice faded. I couldn't find the right word. Boring. Stupid. Soul-crushing. None of them felt right to say right then. They all sounded like something a kid would say.

But... what? What is it, Sara? He said my name like he'd known it for years, like we'd been sitting by this pool, stranded at this hotel together forever. Like I was his and he was mine.

Endless, I said.

~

He wasn't at the pool when we checked out the next morning. I never got to say goodbye. Never got his name. It's strange, but the further away from the hotel we got, the further his features faded away from my memory. I couldn't remember what he looked like.

If I ever knew at all.

The rest of the day was spent pretty much in the car. Dad found the world's biggest ketchup bottle in Collinsville, so we just had to stop there and snap off a few pictures.

I held my paperback in my hands during the ride but never really opened it. I just pressed my temple against the window and stared out at the world slipping by. I rolled down my window at one point to take in a deep breath, just inhale the aroma of the road through my nose, take the highway into my lungs, but Mom scolded me for letting all the A/C out.

The next hotel wasn't any different than the last hotel. Same setup. Same pool.

Same man.

When I first spotted him sitting in the lawn chair, I accidentally dropped my suitcase. Mom told me to pick it up, but I wasn't really listening.

He was *here*. Sitting by the pool, like always. Like nothing had changed.

Staring at me.

Smiling.

I didn't go to the pool right away. I waited until after we'd checked in, and even then I wasn't in a rush. Peter kept begging to go to the pool, whining like a tea kettle on the stove.

Sara, Mom pleaded, her face buried in our bed for the night, her muffled voice seeping out from under the pillow, *take your brother to the pool, pleeease?*

Had he gotten in his car and driven ahead of us? Had he somehow checked in before we did? How did he know this was where we'd stop for the night? It couldn't just be a coincidence.

Was he following us? Following me?

Hotel to hotel?

Pool by pool?

I almost said something to Dad, but I knew I'd be blamed for ruining our trip by seducing some total stranger with my choice in poolside apparel. Somehow this would all be my fault.

Other people were at the pool, thank God. Kids splashed in the water. There wasn't anything he could do to me. Not in broad daylight. Not with so many other families around.

How did you find me? I asked.

Who says I ever left you?

I'm going to tell the manager you're following my family. They'll call the cops.

Sure. You could do that.

OK, that wasn't the reaction I expected. He didn't seem worried at all. Just happy to see me again.

Who are you?

Someone stuck on the road. Just like you.

What do you want?

What you want, he said. *Someone to talk to.*

If I see you at the next hotel, I'm telling my Dad and he'll—

Who are you talking to?

It was Peter. In his pajamas. Picking his nose. The sun had gone down. The pool was empty. It looked just like the last pool, which looked like the pool just before it, and on and on.

Wasn't I supposed to look after Peter while he went swimming? Or was that yesterday?

Which hotel was this? How many pools had there been?

Mom says it's time to come inside, Peter prodded.

Go away.

But Mom said to—

I said GO!

I stopped wearing my bikini. Not that Mom noticed. She hasn't said much of anything to me for the last few days—I think it's been days—on the road. She just stares out her window. We've all been. Everyone's been so quiet in the car lately, like we know something's changed.

Mom knows. She senses it. Smells it, maybe. I'm not a little girl anymore. I don't need a stupid bathing suit to prove it. Whatever's been unlocked within me happened at one of these rundown hotels and I think that scares her. When she turns around in her seat to look at me now, I just stare back. No pithy comeback. She doesn't recognize me anymore.

Where did her little girl go? *Oops, sorry, she must've gotten left behind at the last hotel...* Should Dad pull over? Turn around and go back? *Nah, it's been miles now...*

We've all come so far.

Seen so much.

I'm not a girl anymore. I'm a woman now.

He told me so.

He was waiting for me at the next hotel. And the next. Wherever we pull in, it's like he's been sitting next to the pool all along. Just waiting. Smiling as soon as he lays his eyes on me.

We talk about all kinds of things. *I'd been stuck at that hotel,* he said—the one where I first found him, I guess—*for years. Maybe even longer. Time sure loses shape out here.*

But... how's that even possible?

Your guess is as good as mine.

I was the first person to see him, he said. Actually *see* him. Which is weird 'cause I still couldn't tell you what he looks like. Couldn't describe his features. I don't know if that's true, but I want to believe him. That means I'm special, then. Different than all the rest.

I was the first to see him. And he sees me. For who I am.

A woman.

Some of the things he says don't really make much sense, but none of this makes any sense. None of this feels *real.* But here we are, sharing the road together. The endless road.

He tells me about the rooms. Every hotel room we stay in together. Everything that's ever happened inside them. Things that, if you knew, really *knew*, you'd never check into a hotel again. He points out bloodstains under the beds. Brown spots speckling the mattresses. Moles of mildew. The solar flares of urine stains radiating out beneath the bed sheets. The sun-dried patches of old blood. The rusted crust just under the bathroom sinks, still clinging to the faucet. All the nooks and crannies where the bleach couldn't reach. The hidden crevices the cleaning ladies never found.

These rooms are bad places. This is where he's lived. Where he always lived. He calls these hotels home.

But now he wants to come home with me.

Whenever I try to change the subject and ask him why he was stuck at that first hotel, he closes up. It's weird because he's so open about everything else—*An open book*, he said—just not about that.

It doesn't matter anymore, he said, *because we found each other.*

I imagine he must've been left behind, like a brush or book you forget in your room, abandoned beneath the bed until the cleaning lady picks it up and tosses it in the lost and found. I imagine him as some forgotten item accidentally stranded at the hotel until someone—me—came along and claimed him. Books get left behind at hotels all the time. When somebody finishes their paperback, rather than throw it out in the trash, they just leave it for someone else to pick up and flip through. They pass it along. You never know where it might end up.

Who it ends up with.

Where are you? He asks me. *You seem distant...*

Miles away.

Tomorrow we'll finally make our way home.

Dad mapped out the rest of our trip and he says we'll reach our house in less than eight hours, as long as we wake up early enough and don't make any more pit stops.

We'll all be sleeping in our own bed tomorrow night, he said. *Doesn't that sound nice?*

Hallelujah, was all Mom said.

I don't have the heart to tell *him*. I know I need to. Say goodbye. But I don't know how he'll take it. If it'll hurt his feelings or something worse. I don't know.

But he can't come home with me. He can't.

So I end up saying nothing.

I say nothing for the rest of the ride home. All eight hours.

All the way home.

Dad had been hell-bent on finding the Forgotten America. Maybe he found it, I don't know. All I saw were so many forgotten spaces. Forgotten rooms. Full of forgotten people.

Maybe we forgot ourselves out there, somewhere, leaving something of us behind.

My forgotten family.

At least I made a friend.

Mom's breath catches as soon as Dad pulls into our driveway. She sees it first. I lean forward in my seat and glance out the windshield, even though I don't need to see.

What's wrong? Dad asks. He doesn't know yet. Doesn't see.

The front door's open, Mom says.

baby carrots

Emma brought home a bad batch of baby carrots. You could tell just by looking in the bag. Gnarled things, really. Like fat fingers, their pudgy knuckles pressing against the clear plastic.

I had volunteered to help unpack the groceries, as a peace offering, finding the ugly nubbins nestled in between the OJ and the eggs. I grabbed the bag and tossed it in the air a couple times, feeling those baby carrots slap and settle into my palm.

Think these might've gone beyond their sell-by date, hon...

Look fine to me, Emma replied without *actually* looking at me, or the baby carrots, leaning her head into the fridge instead.

Most times these babies were moist. Plump and crisp. But I don't know... this bunch looked downright desiccated to me. They're supposed to be smooth, sanded down to a perfect rotund tube. These ugly little buggers certainly must've slipped right past the carrot-inspector while they rumbled along the assembly line. They were segmented. *Crooked*. A few were even tumorous, bubbling over with cysts. Warts on a witch's finger. I couldn't shake the feeling that they were pointing at me—*This is all your fault! You're the one who's leaving the family!*

I brought the bag up closer. They looked like grubs to me. Orange larvae. Gravity dragged the carrots down my wrist, still in the bag, slithering against the clear plastic along my skin.

I could've sworn I felt them wriggle.

Sean absolutely *loved* baby carrots. It was just about the only vegetable Emma could ever get him to eat. Our crisper was always stocked with a bag or two. They never lasted long. The turnover for taproots was pretty swift in this house. For lunch, Emma packed him a ziplock full of them, a whole handful, to crunch on at school. It was the only snack he ever asked for—*Mommy, I want baby carrots, Mommy, Mommy, I want baby carrots, pleeeeeease...* I'm surprised his skin hadn't turned orange yet, to be honest. Wasn't that a thing? Too much unsaturated hydrocarbons flushed your flesh into this gingery hue, as if you'd spent a few too many hours in the tanning bed? All that excess beta-carotene entered your bloodstream, stored in your skin, giving your fingers a yellowish tint?

I had nothing against baby carrots. But people needed to realize they were not really babies—right? It was all a lie. One big capitalist fib. All about the rebranding, you know?

Baby carrots were actually just the ugly-nubs of adult carrots, sliced and sanded down to yummier-looking stubs. They had been bathed in chlorine, bleaching out the foodborne bacteria, rinsing away any E. coli still clinging to your carrot. My son's favorite snack was soaked in the same solution that obliterated poo in the community pool. Pretty appetizing, right?

Emma would suggest that I get over myself. *They're just baby carrots*, she'd probably say. I could even hear that familiar shard in her voice. *Does everything have to be a consumerist conspiracy with you?*

I was not, nor had I ever been, a card-carrying member of the anti-baby carrot lobby here, I swear! I just found it a little off-putting that *certain people* in our household preferred to eat some *selectively* bred, *fabricated* brand of trademarked "*baby*" carrots instead of the real organic deal just because they were cute.

Just because they were *babies*.

~

Emma and I weren't sleeping in separate beds. *Yet.* We probably should have been, but... we wanted to be adults about this. There was still some love between us. Somewhere. We just had to find it. Even though I was the one who floated the notion of a trial separation, Emma and I could still curl up under the covers next to each other. We still took turns spooning. Our bodies shifted beneath the bedsheets until settling into that perfect fit.

Tonight, Emma had already assumed a facing-out position.

Facing away from me.

I didn't know if this was a statement in and of itself, that I shouldn't swoop in for a spoon... so I simply slipped under the sheets and faced the opposite direction. The two of us were back-to-back, the chasm between us only expanding the bed. A gulf.

Romance was never *really* technically out of the question in these final breaths before falling asleep, was it? We just had to act fast, dragging our partner out from the quicksand of their drowsiness with a little romantic overture, such as a gentle kiss that extends beyond the pleasant goodnight peck. Or a nuzzle in the neck. A wandering hand. That sort of thing.

I felt Emma's finger. More like her thumb?

Well, this is a pleasant surprise, I thought. Emma was probing. Exploring. Her skin felt cool against my lower back as she wormed her way toward the base of my spine.

This was totally unlike her. Emma never went back there.

Whoa, hey now, I said. *Where are you heading there, tiger?*

Emma's breath purled in her throat. Her body had slackened against the mattress, still facing away from me. How could her arms bend backward like that? Wouldn't her elbow pop?

That's when I felt her thumb take the plunge.

No—not her thumb.

Not Emma at all.

Even when I knew it *couldn't possibly* be her, seeing her fast asleep, I kept thinking my wife's disembodied thumb was the culprit. I reached back to swat her hand away—*See?*—but no one was there. No wrist or arm or *anything*. But that finger kept at it. Squirming forward.

Tunneling.

So I clenched. I rolled over on my back, taking most of the sheets with me, elevating my pelvis into the air like I was in some sort of frenzied yoga-pose. *The Timid Oyster* or *The Puckering Tortoise*. Nothing was getting in back there. I put whatever muscle mass I had in my ass, batting down the hatches long enough for me to take my fingers and pluck out this marauding member.

It *wriggled*. My grip kept slipping. Greasy little bugger.

I had to dig in. Literally dig my nails in just to pinch it. Flecks of its brittle flesh clumped under my fingernails as I finally extracted this phantom finger from my ass.

But of course, it wasn't a finger. *Of course.*

It was... It was a carrot.

A *baby* carrot.

It squirmed in my grip, writhing between my fingers like a panicking maggot. If I let go, I was pretty sure it would roll right off the bed and crawl away and I'd never see it again.

What're you doing? Emma mumbled from behind me, oblivious to all this. Even when she was half asleep, I could still hear the icepick in her voice.

I'd already leaped out of bed, rushing for the kitchen. *Just getting some water,* I said.

Tossing the baby carrot into the sink, I watched it loll about the basin. *I'm losing my mind*, I thought. The stress of the separation was getting to me. *I'm seeing things.* If I closed my eyes, took a deep breath, the carrot would go away. I needed to take a beat, calm down, and—

Still there. Still wriggling.

I don't know how long I stared at it, watching it worm over the dirty dishes, attempting to scale the marble and escape.

So, I turned the faucet on. The rush of water sent the baby carrot tumbling down the drain, into the garbage disposal.

I flicked the switch and the garburator chewed through it with a gargled drone. I left the disposal on for longer than I needed to, just in case, the high-pitched whine and whir of the blades humming up from the drain. Just to be sure. Just to know nothing came crawling out.

Oh Jesus, I suddenly thought. *What about the others...?*

I turned to the fridge to find out.

The bag had been torn open. Ripped from the inside out.

Totally empty. What remained of the plastic was still resting at the crisper's bottom, *flaccid*, as if somebody had eaten all the baby carrots and forgotten to throw the bag away.

Where did all those baby carrots go?

~

This wasn't something I could share with Emma. Or Sean. Obviously. Emma and I had already discussed me breaking it to our boy that I'd be moving out. I was supposed to have The Talk with him today, after school—but my mind was elsewhere. On other things.

Such as: Did you know that most bags hold up to forty-eight baby carrots? Give or take?

Forty-eight.

All morning, if I saw a flash of orange from the corner of my eye, I would stop and turn. Wait and see if anything wriggled.

But nothing was there. Nothing was ever there.

Of course.

I called in sick as soon as Emma left. I had the run of the house all to myself, so I spent the day peeling back the carpet. Pushing back the couch. Flipping the cushions over. Rummaging through the pantry. Digging into the freezer. Pulling out the canned vegetables in the cupboard. Sifting through the sock drawer. The closets. The bathroom cabinet. Under the bed.

I couldn't find them.

Any of them.

I found a few AA batteries. Plenty of pocket change. A picture Sean had drawn of the fam. Just the three of us, holding hands. Smiling with our crooked Crayola lips. No peach crayons for Sean. No, he had decided to color our skin all orange.

Emma's desktop woke up from behind me, the screen reviving itself.

There. Crawling across the mouse pad.

A baby carrot. I fucking knew it. They're here. Hiding. Messing with me.

Get it, get it, get—

Too late. By the time I reached her desk, the carrot had wriggled away. *Fuckity fuck.* It wasn't in her chair or burrowed in the drawer, hidden amid her office supplies. I swore I saw it. All I was left with was Emma's revived workstation, her browser still open with a million tabs.

Her email.

I don't know why I clicked through her account. I can't quite say I even knew what I was looking for. Did I think I was going to find something? An infidelious email? Adulterous correspondence? I couldn't help myself. I just wanted to look. See for myself.

One tab caught my eye.

RECIPES.

Honey-glazed carrots. Roasted carrots. Carrot fries. Carrot patties. Carrot—

The hell was this? What was I even reading here? Why did Emma want recipes for...

She'd say it was for Sean. Get him to eat his veggies.

These weren't recipes.

They were a curse.

~

It was my turn to pick Sean up from school. Time for The Talk. But from the moment—and I mean the absolute second—he hopped in the car, all he wanted to talk about was food.

He kept saying he was hungry. That he wanted, *needed*, a snack.

In a little while, sport. Promise. But first, I was hoping you and I could have a little chat.

My tummy's grumbling...

I hear you, pal, but—please. There's something I wanna talk to you about.

Can I please have some baby carrots, pleeeeease?

No, I snapped. *We're all out of baby carrots! I'll get you some goddamn Doritos, OK?*

I'm not saying I was the best father or the best husband or even the best *human being*. All I'm saying is: People grow apart. That's nobody's fault. It happens. The most we can hope for if it happens—*when* it happens—is to understand no one's to blame. Not Sean. Not Emma.

Not me. I didn't mean for any of this to happen. It just did.

I swear I felt something wriggling between the bottom of my legs and my car seat, but when I slid my hand along the leatherette, I couldn't find anything. The car didn't feel clean. Infested, somehow. I could've sworn I heard something rummaging around the glove compartment, but the second I popped it open, all I saw were road maps. Old napkins. Nothing.

Where in the hell were they?

I was the one growing in my own direction. I could help but wonder where. Into what.

What was I growing into?

~

Dinner was pretty stilted. Sean wouldn't look up from his plate. Emma kept grating her knife through her food, mangling her meal. *Dissecting* it rather than *eating* it.

Lord knows where my head was at. I couldn't even clock what was two inches in front of me, let alone what I was eating.

Until I noticed something orange under my nose.

There. On my plate. Nestled next to the spare ribs. A steaming heap of baby carrots. Soaked in olive oil, all soft and soggy. Flecks of diced parsley clung to their charred skin.

I pushed my chair back, wood grinding against wood as its legs scraped over the floor. *What the hell's that?*

Butter-roasted carrots, Emma spoke slowly. Very measured, I might add.

Those are baby carrots.

Yes, they are.

Where did you get them? I asked.

...From the fridge?

Where? Where in the fridge?

In the drawer. She sounded nervous now. *The recipe says you can use baby carrots.*

Sean speared one on his fork. He hesitated before biting, realizing I was staring at him.

At his fork.

He looked frightened. Yes, yes, he should be frightened. Look! Look at the carrot, look at the *baby* carrot! That squirming auburn worm, writhing about the tines!

I smacked the fork out of Sean's hand, sending it clattering to the floor.

Can't you see it, I shouted. *Can't you see?!*

I slept on the couch that night. Normally, I don't rest on my back—but tonight, I stared at the ceiling. Waiting for them.

I had asked—*begged*—Emma to forgive me. I'd gotten down on my knees. She only stared down at her hands in mine, tangled together, unable to take in the whole of me.

I fucked up. I did, I know it. But—please. Make it stop.

What're you talking about? She asked, confused. *You're the one who wanted this...*

I was wrong. I'm sorry. Just—please. Just take them back.

Take what back?

The carrots, I pleaded. *Take back the baby carrots.*

What is wrong with you? I hadn't realized she was trying to pull her hands away.

I didn't realize I hadn't let go. *You sent them, didn't you?*

Let go of me.

You cursed me. Cursed me with carrots.

We agreed that I'd check into a hotel in the morning as long as I could stay the night.

The living room was still. Nothing was moving at this hour. I couldn't hear anything.

Not a carrot was stirring...

I eventually drifted off into a dream. A dream about carrots.

The first carrot.

Daucus carota.

Its roots stemmed from Persia. Cultivated for its aromatic leaves and seeds. It would take centuries before its woody core would become the focal point of its majesty. The original taproot was bitter. Arboreal. It had medicinal properties. It possessed aspects of magic. Used for fertility rites.

For babies.

Its fleshy cortex reached deep into the earth.

The ideal soil was soft.

Warm.

Moist.

It needed space to grow...

To flourish...

For its roots to reach...

down...

...deep.

I woke up choking. Oh God, I was drowning on my couch. I couldn't breathe. It felt like someone had poured cement over my face, sealing off my nostrils. My mouth. I could even feel it working its way into my ears.

I sat up, gagging. So I hocked and hocked and—*hyyyuuulp!*—I finally dislodged the obstruction in my throat.

The baby carrot landed at my feet. It glistened with saliva as it wrapped around my toe. I kicked, flinging it through the air. It landed on the living room wall and rolled over the floor.

Oh, I could feel them. All of them. The baby carrots. Worming their way in through every orifice. Massaging and flexing and tensing with their desiccated skin.

They wanted to come in.

Take root.

I stumbled into the bathroom, shaking as many of them off as I could. The pitter-pat of baby carrots thumped along the floor.

When I flicked on the bathroom light and found my reflection in the mirror, I still gasped, even though it shouldn't have come as such a surprise.

My left nostril was distended. It looked as if I'd been punched right in the face, the flesh bruised and bloated to abnormal proportions, wadded up with something or other.

Another carrot wriggled in my ear. Its stubby tail coiled about the air while the rest of its orange body burrowed into my ear canal. Already, I could feel the nub nuzzling at my ear drum.

So I swatted at the side of my head until I dislodged it.

Victory!

Short-lived. What was going on in my nostril?

The baby carrot in my nose had forced its way up my septum. Even then, I had to take a moment to look, to marvel at my reflection as the baby carrot continued to crawl up. Up. *Up*.

Then it was gone.

There was nothing for me to grab hold of. Nothing to stop it from creeping into my nasal cavity and into my cranium. All I could do was pinch the bridge of my nose in hopes of halting it.

Tweezers!

I took Emma's tweezers from the cabinet and dug in but I ended up accidentally pushing the baby carrot in deeper, sending a crunching surge in my skull. My eyes were stinging. I couldn't see. I felt it wriggle, forcing its way up, *up, up*, each fleshy segment undulating like an inchworm. I could feel its pulse pounding against my nasal cavity, a low-wattage throb.

It had a heartbeat.

It had a *heart!?*

My best option, my only option now, was to stab the baby carrot. The tweezers' fangs sank into its cortex. It was just a matter of me easing the taproot out from my nasal cavity at an angle. I couldn't just yank it. I needed to keep pressing down, pinning it against the inner canal of my nostril and sliding the baby carrot out. Slowly. Slowly. If I lost my grip, that baby carrot would simply worm its way back in, aiming for the soft tissues on the other side of my septum.

I blew my nose. And blew. Blew all the air I had pent up in my lungs, flushing the tanks.

It finally popped out.

I was free.

Free!

Fuck you, baby carrot, I shouted. *Fuck yooooooou!*

There was blood. A sheen of mucous slickened up the baby carrot, like flecks of placenta and afterbirth still coating a newborn baby. My blood had seeped into its furrowed skin, filling in its wrinkles so that it looked like a latticework of red veins tethered against its orange body.

I sank my teeth in.

It was still crisp.

I felt that satisfying *crunch* that you get at the very back of your molars, my teeth singing in its mastication.

My tongue worked over its crinkles. It had a bitter taste, rusty, unwashed. This was a woody-textured taproot. An ancient thing. Uprooted right from the very earth.

I chewed and chewed. God help me, I swallowed.

I let them take root.

Emma found me on the bathroom floor, clutching my stomach.

My distended belly looked like a bag full of baby carrots. I'd eaten them all in one sitting. *What have you done?*

One of them just kicked, I said.

I'll call 911—

No, please, stay with me! Stay!

What's happening? What—

Here they come! Here they come!

Emma kneeled next to me and took my hand. She told me to breathe. *Breathe...*

Please don't leave me, I shouted. *Please.*

Just keep breathing. Emma squeezed my hand. *That's it. Just one more push. One more. You can do it...*

I wailed. The distended patch of flesh along my belly ruptured with orange buds. Green sprouts of hair. Glistening and slippery and blind and beautiful.

Look. Just look at my babies.

My baby carrots.

fairy ring

It's not Mom anymore. The doctor warned me that, once the dementia took root, I'd lose a little bit more of her every day. *They call it the long goodbye for a reason*, he said. *The woman you've known will slowly begin to fade away.* But the body in the bed isn't her. Her jaw has locked to allow the fibrous stalk that had once been her tongue to branch out and blossom. The fleshy veil ruptured just above her nose, its cap a warm pink. A blushing umbrella. I spot another button already peering out from her left nostril. More morels are about to sprout. It won't be long before Mom's face is gone altogether, replaced by a fresh bed of fruiting bodies.

Hey, Mom, I say. *It's just me today. Sarah's at home with the kids.*

She blinks, taking me in. Her eyes remain cognizant while the rest of her ruptures. The doctors aren't certain if she can still hear. Her ear canals keep clotting with these yeasty cysts. The nurses rinse out the fungal infection with a saline solution, but the thrush always comes back. Now the whole lobe looks more like a honeycombed Morchella, all spongy and yellow.

I take her hand. Squeeze. Even through the latex, I can feel the warmth of her skin.

There you are, I say, managing to smile.

Her room was supposed to be sterile, but nursing homes are so understaffed and overworked, they're the perfect breeding ground for a drug-resistant fungus. *Colonizations*, they're called. The germs hop from room to room, clinging to the nurse on call as she makes her rounds, infecting the resident in the neighboring room. The growth rate is so rapid that, seemingly overnight, the morning nurse at any one of these retirement homes will walk in and discover a colony of fruiting bodies where the resident went to bed just the night before.

It's happening everywhere now. We've all seen the images of hospital beds that look more like community gardens. CNN broadcast a time-lapse of a senior citizen succumbing to the fungus, recorded over the span of eight hours, then sped up to look as if their body erupted in a matter of seconds. First, their skin rippled with pinheads. White buttons branched out from their fingertips. Patches of puffballs cropped up from the cervices in their flesh, around the armpits and groin. Jelly ears fanned out from their temples.

Gone, just like that.

That can't be a person, I remember thinking. But it was. That mass of branching hyphae had been somebody's parent.

Their mother.

~

You thirsty, Mom? Want some water? I'm failing at this one-sided conversation, simply filling up the silence with nonsense. *How about some sunlight? Should I open the window?*

Every visitor puts on a mask and gown over their clothes before entering. Even if Mom could remember, how would she recognize me, her own son, under all the protective gear? I must look like any one of the faceless physicians who have paraded through her room over the last couple days, trying to figure out how to halt the infection before it spreads any further.

They warned me about what she would look like. It wouldn't be her anymore, they said, not in the strictest sense of the word *her.* It was all conjecture at this point, but there was a working theory that human contact slowed the process down. There was no proof, but any interaction with loved ones hypothetically decelerated the transfiguration, as if to remind the body who it belonged to. I was being asked to make my mother remember who she was.

I thought maybe today we'd do a little reading. How's that sound? I brought one of your favorite books... I hope my voice is enough to trigger some memory for her. That it is enough.

Mom makes a sound. It seems like she wants to say something, but it's no longer her voice. No longer her mouth. Her lips have fissured into vermillion gills. The doctors put her on a feeding tube the day before. The fungus keeps forcing it out, rejecting every blended meal they've fed her. The nurses would reinsert the tube until finally they just gave up. Now there's a patch of small nodules around the incision in her neck, a dozen toadstools surrounding the slit.

It reminds me of a fairy ring.

Remember them?

I found one in our backyard when I was a boy. I dragged Mom out of the house to show her the circle of toadstools enshrining our lawn. She warned me never to set foot inside. *Anyone who breaks the ring will have bad luck,* she whispered. *That's where the devil dances.*

A ventilator breathes for her now. Her doctor insists the respirator is all that's keeping her alive. Her lungs are full of fungus, every exhale alive with spores. Even now, the yeasting particles persistently push the pipes out from their respected vents, rebuffing the IV drips inserted in her arm, over and over again, as if they were battling over her body. The doctors are losing their ground. They're retreating already, stepping back as the front line spreads. Before long, there won't be anything left. My mother will be an empty field. No one will know what happened here, who died on this patch of land. Life will move on without her.

No one will remember her or what happened here.

It's still Mom, I remind myself. *She's still alive. In there—under there—somewhere.*

~

She was the eighth resident to be infected. The fungus swept through the memory ward in a matter of days. Sitting ducks, the whole floor. There was barely any time to warn families. None of the prescribed antibiotics stopped it. Antifungal drugs have proven useless. Isolating the residents in their bedrooms was the best they could do, but too many people were coming and going. There was nothing anyone could do, the admin said, as if this was all inevitable.

Now I have to let her go. Let nature take its course.

It had been my call to move Mom into Greenfield. Her memory was only getting worse. She still had control over her faculties when we first took the tour, but it was only a matter of time. The doctors agreed. In less than a year, she would need full-time care, someone who could look after her twenty-four seven, which was more than my wife and I could provide.

Memories were already slipping away. Little things. People's names. But I could tell she was beginning to forget. She confused me for my father once, embarrassing us both.

Greenfield was the solution. My solution. The best possible option for us all. Mom would have a room all to herself. Daily care. She'd be surrounded by other residents. She could make friends. This is where she'd live out the rest of her days.

We'll come see you every chance we get, I swore to her. *Nothing's going to change.*

Our visits were at an even clip at first. I'd bring the kids and we'd stay for an hour or so. Maybe get lunch in the dining hall. But sometimes life got in the way. Work. School. Plus, coming here was always a little uncomfortable for the kids. The residents in the memory ward would wander over and ask if they were here to visit them. *Whose grandchildren are these? Mine?*

Even before the quarantine, I was losing her. Answering the same questions. Trying to explain who I was. Where Dad was. Why he wasn't here.

I'd visit when I could. I'd see Mom's eyes light up whenever I entered her room. How relieved she was to see me. See anyone. I realize now it wasn't so much that she knew who I was, that she was happy to see her own son, but that someone, *anyone*, was here to see her.

That same look is still in her eyes now. Her cheeks have mottled into a yellow morel complexion. The tip of her nose has cauliflowered, the skin slowly boiling over. Her wrinkles ripple with mycelium. Threads of flesh lift into the air, a bacterial colony of tawny-capped toadstools rising up from her body.

Mom—can you hear me? Mom?

The stems along her throat oscillate with every exhale, bending with her breath. Her body no longer wants the respirator or needs a feeding tube. She's pushing every piece of plastic out from her cavities. All she wants is to flourish. Take root.

I was told I'd have an hour. There are tests the doctors need to run and it's better that I'm not here to see it. No one says it outright, not any of the nurses or the administrators, but I know I need to say goodbye. Whenever I ask what's done with them—their bodies—I'm always sidestepped. Nobody tells me. Do they bury them? Cremate them? Where will my mother go? Will there be a place I can visit her? Some patch of land in the woods where she'll be planted?

Where will her fairy ring be?

I adjust her bed so that it's level. Mom doesn't need to sit up anymore. It's better on her back. *How's that?* I ask. *Comfy?* I comb what's left of her hair with my fingers. If a nurse was here, I'd be reprimanded. Possibly quarantined. But they've left me alone with her, so I pull down my mask and kiss her forehead. The skin is soft, too soft, the underlying bone spongier than before. My lips leave the slightest dimple in her temple, her skull sinking for a few seconds before swelling back up again.

I tell her I love her. That I'm sorry for bringing her here, that I hadn't done more for her when I had the chance.

The fairy ring around her throat swims. Each toadstool fans in tandem to one another, back and forth, swaying in some imperceptible breeze. Perhaps it's her pulse. It's mesmerizing, watching the mushrooms dance like that.

I break off a cap from her neck. It pulls away without any resistance. I bring it to my nose. There's a meaty aroma to it. Raw chanterelle. Even after I put the mushroom in my pocket and leave, I can still smell the earthiness steeped into my skin. It's in my fingers.

At the first stoplight, I pull the cap from my pocket and roll it around in my palm. It has an ovate shape. A tiny egg. Pale ivory. We've been warned that the fungus can spread. Children seem to be asymptomatic carriers. It's only the elderly and those with autoimmune deficiencies that need to worry—while adults my age, the children of the victims, the ones who abandoned their parents in these nursing homes, leaving them to rot, we seem to be out of harm's way.

We've been spared.

I shouldn't have taken the mushroom. I should throw it away. Just roll down my window and toss the cap out. But it's my mother. A part of her, at least.

It's all I have left.

I pop the cap into my mouth. It has a delicate, lacelike texture. My tongue feels fuzzy, almost numb, after I swallow. I wish I had a bottle of water to wash it down, stuck with this peppery aftertaste.

The stoplight warps over the windshield, breaking down into bands of color, as though the lights are refracting through a prism. I tighten my grip around the steering wheel. I don't know what's happening. The temperature in the car climbs. I'm starting to sweat. I reach for the A/C when my vision splits. Rifts right in half. I'm still in the car but outside of it at the same time. A memory resurfaces and I know it's not mine. It's someone else's. Whose is it? It's from my mother. Not *of* her, but *from* her. I'm looking through her eyes.

I shouldn't be driving. I need to turn off the car. Need to pull over to the side of the road. Get out. Run. I'm seeing myself as a boy, no older than three. She's chasing me through our backyard. Her hands are out, ready to catch me. *I'm gonna get you*, she sings, *I'm gonna get you!* I keep running, squealing with laughter every time I glance over my shoulder to see if she's getting any closer. We run ourselves in circles, until Mom finally grabs me and we both fall across the lawn. We lay there, catching our breath, giggling, as the blades of grass prickle against the back of our necks.

Don't break the ring. Keep running in circles.

Don't break the ring.

Keep running.

room with a boo

I never believed in ghosts. *Never.*

Not until self-isolation.

Not until Charlie.

He'd say he was here first—and technically speaking, that's true. Realtors swear up and down that they aren't technically *legally* bound to let prospective tenants know who's been murdered in an apartment if nobody asks. But in New York you've got a fifty-fifty chance that somebody's died in your place. Simply accept the fact that most apartments here are probably haunted. You can live in a five-floor walk-up and never even know you've got a ghost living in the building with you. Or sharing the same one-bedroom apartment.

Here, let me introduce you.

Charlie? You there, hon? There's someone here who I want you to meet...

He'll show up, I swear. Sooner or later. Sorry about the mess. Charlie hardly picks up after himself. It's his turn to clean up the apartment.

...Charlie?

He's a bit shy at first. Always disappears whenever we have guests over. I feel like I need to perform a séance just to drag him out from hiding. Just give him a sec. He'll pop up before long. To be completely honest, we didn't start talking, *truly* communicating with one another, until maybe a month into quarantine. I'd been sheltering in place for weeks before he even spoke a single word to me. Can you believe that? Talk about the silent treatment! But I knew he was in my apartment—*our* apartment—long before then. The slamming doors. The flickering lights.

I knew I wasn't alone.

This isn't an old pre-war building settling or wood expanding or the radiator rattling. I know what those all sound like. Trust me, I went through the Skeptic's Checklist first thing: *Is it the plumbing? A rat? Noise from the neighbors seeping through the Sheetrock?*

I am an extremely rational person.

Logical to a fault, my friends always say. But they're not stranded by themselves. They all got to shack up with their significant others, spending their quarantine spooning.

While I got this bachelorette pad. A one-bedroom, half-bath studio in Bushwick. Never mind that the floors sag in the center. Please don't pay attention to the crack in the ceiling just above your bed. Don't bother with the black mold in the bathroom. I've never met my neighbors, but I sure can hear them arguing through the walls, working through their marital strife nearly every night.

You get what you get and you don't get upset.

Anyhoo, I was blissfully ignorant I even had a roommate at first. We simply settled into our separate routines. Never crossed paths. Our flight patterns around the apartment were on completely different schedules. I'd wake up early, head off to Condé Nast, work late hours, come home and crash, then repeat the whole thing the very next morning, while he—he just drifted through the apartment all on his own, lounging around all day. Probably didn't even put on his pants. But then came coronavirus and I was furloughed from work and... well, our domestic balance got totally thrown out of whack.

That's how we found each other.

I had just broken up with my boyfriend back in January. Hence the move into a new apartment. Talk about shitty timing. There had been this teeny-tiny part of me that wondered if I could *just* take it back, *just* endure my ex's bad habits for a little while longer, *just* a few months more, *just* until this whole coronavirus thing blew over, *just* to have someone to shelter in place with like everybody else.

Just so I wasn't alone.

I wanted the warmth of someone. I wanted to cohabitate. I wanted to wear pajamas all day with somebody else and make breakfast for dinner and binge on Netflix and *just not care.*

But all I could do was look out my window at the other buildings on the block. Spy into the lives of everyone else. The family dinners. The Zoom chats. The flicker of other people's TV screens. That phosphorescent glow of someone's iPhone floating through the dark of their bedroom.

We were all ghosts haunting our own homes now.

One day I got so bored, I eavesdropped on my neighbors. Just pressed my ear against the wall and listened in. I could almost make out their muted conversation. Something about scallops, I think. Maybe scabies. I couldn't quite make the words out. But I closed my eyes as their voices seeped through the Sheetrock, until it almost felt like they were whispering to me.

(*whisper whisper whisper*)

Someone touched me. I swear I felt something—like fingers—graze past my arm. You know when two people accidentally brush up against one another? That's what it felt like.

I spun around. Nobody was there. The hairs on my arm stood straight up, galvanized by somebody else's presence. Electrified. Someone was here. Someone was in the room. With me.

My friends tried to make it feel less lonely. We had our regularly scheduled Zoom cocktail parties every Friday. I'd look at my laptop and see them all cramming together in their digital windows, these little blurry boxes made for two, the cute couples squeezing onto the screen. The laptop's battery overheated on my legs. The heat seeped into my skin, burning me.

Who's that? I remember one friend asking.

Who's what?

Nothing, she said. *I thought I just saw something move behind you.*

Charlie's not a rebound ghost.

He's not. We found each other at exactly the right time in our lives. Or afterlives. When we needed each other the most. He was knifed in the heart by his last girlfriend, bled out on the kitchen floor. No wonder they laid down that awful-looking linoleum. His spirit is bound to this building while I'm stuck inside until Cuomo says it's safe to come out again. It's perfect.

He was pretty passive-aggressive at first. Believe me, opening up is not one of his strong suits. I'd wake up freezing in the middle of the night and wonder where the bedspread had gone, only to find it flung halfway across the room. Doors would open and close all on their own. He'd turn on the kitchen faucet while I was reading on the couch. He'd knock over my laptop. Spill wine on the carpet. A chair might move by itself, skidding across the floor. He'd unplug my charger at night so my phone would die on me.

Ever spoon with someone who isn't there? It's the strangest feeling. At first, I thought I was imagining it. Feeling this presence press up against my back, only to peer over my shoulder and find... nothing. Sensing invisible arms slowly slide over my stomach and hold me.

Ever cook with someone else in a kitchen that's meant for just one? The brushing limbs? The accidental collisions with each other? That friction in your skin? It leads to a caress. A sharing of space. We syncopated our movements before long, cutting together, hand over hand, holding the same knife and slicing. We would make a meal together, even if I was only eating for one.

Ever share a cramped bathroom with a phantom? You're in the shower and they race in to use the toilet? Ever mistake your toothbrush with a ghost because they don't have their own? Who drank all the orange juice?

The problem is, we've just been seeing way too much of one another. Our shared space feels more cramped now. We're intensely aware of one another's bad habits. His inability to pick up after himself. Always leaving behind a mess for me to clean. Playing tug-of-war over what little space we have. It's always been a small apartment, but these last couple of months have made it feel oppressively petite. Suffocating. I only signed a year lease, so I can understand his propriety over the apartment, but we need to figure out how we're going to go about cohabitating together. He needs to learn how to share.

The fridge is littered with alphabet magnets. Charlie's begun leaving me messages.

GET OUT. GO. RUN.

Very subtle. But it did give me an idea. A Ouija board might help us. I couldn't go out and buy one, so I whipped one up with whatever items I found around the apartment.

It could be fun, I thought. *An arts and crafts project. We could do it together.*

I thought it might help us. We've had problems communicating with one another, so I saw this as a step toward discussing our relationship in a way that he wouldn't find overbearing. I wanted to establish a foundation for ourselves, a safe space, where we could talk about these things and not feel like we were accusing one another. Blaming each other.

Charlie wouldn't even push the planchette. He wouldn't engage. I feel like I'm single-handedly trying to save our relationship while he prefers to simply drift through the apartment and pretend like nothing's wrong.

I feel like he's giving up. Giving up on us.

On me.

Last stop—the bedroom. You're going to love it. It gets great light in the morning, thanks to the fact that it's facing the—

Did you hear that? Sorry, I thought that was him. My mistake.

Charlie won't even speak anymore. He's been giving me the cold shoulder for days. So I started whispering in the walls. Banging on the pipes. Tugging the plumbing. Leaving magnet messages on the fridge just for him. Shouting from across the void. Even throwing books at him from across the room. Just to get him to notice me. Pay attention to me again.

The whole apartment—it feels cold now. Empty. Like he left. Like I'm all alone again.

Who's the ghost here? Who's haunting who?

pump and dump

I found it at the back of the yard sale, practically abandoned, tangled in a wired knot of its own translucent tubing.

I had no clue what I was even looking at, to be honest. Not at first. It wasn't in its original packaging, whatever it was, tossed into an unmarked cardboard box with a bunch of old DVD player remotes. This thing looked more like some long-forgotten video game console, a Nintendo system with its controllers garroting itself. But the deck was a different hue than the Nintendos I remember as a kid. The buttons weren't the same candy apple red. Maybe it was some off-brand Atari? Had Sega come out with an early system that I just couldn't recall now?

What the hell is this thing?

Turns out the plastic appendages weren't joysticks at all, but a pair of semitransparent satellite dishes with hollow reservoirs. Bottles—*milk* bottles—hooked to their own rubber hose.

A breast pump.

I tugged the bellows up from the box. Exhumed it. Certainly had some heft. Ten pounds, easy. It was a bit on the clunkier side as far as these lactation-contraptions go. Not the most portable pump you'd find on the market nowadays. Probably an earlier model. One of the first pumps to come home with new parents, I bet. Jesus, I'd need a dolly just to lug this thing home.

It still had all the parts and pieces, from what I could tell. The tiny instruction pamphlet was folded, rolled and rubber-banded inside one of the empty plastic carafes.

A message inside a milk bottle.

I'd already moved on, plopping the pump back in its box and making my way to the next card table full of castoff toddler items—partially gnawed teething rings, a diaper genie with a busted hinge, a baby monitor missing one of its cables—when I hesitated. Turned back around.

What does the message say?

I couldn't help myself. I was curious. I ambled back to the breast pump. Popped the bottle's top and peeked, eager to read its secret missive, as if it had been written just for me.

Well, who do we have here?

I very rarely read instruction manuals, but this one had pictures. On the cover was a pencil-sketched illustration of a woman—a mother, presumably—strapped to this tendriled apparatus. *Smiling.* Her graphite eyes were fixed on some nebulous point beyond the pamphlet, not the pump itself, as she expressed her milk. The suction pumps looked like a mollusk's eyestalks, the kind of eyes you'd find extending from the head of a snail. Or perhaps a crab? Hard to say what it was. It could've been a squid for all I knew, its clubbed feeder-tentacles twining around this woman's body and latching their suction pads at her nipples, the two wrestling against one another in a bloody battle over breast milk. Kraken versus leviathan.

The Pure Essence Platinum Breast Pump is the perfect blend of advanced technology and time-proven assistance, the manual read, *offering one-of-a-kind care to clinicians and mothers around the world.*

It was the 1994 model. Over thirty years old by now. Who keeps a breast pump for nearly three decades? Had it simply been collecting dust in their attic all that time?

Just how many breasts has this thing pumped from?

It seemed strange to me to think about buying the machine that performed such an intimate function as this—drawing the milk from another mother's breasts.

A stranger.

But our family's been on a budget ever since we brought Lonnie home. *Moderately preterm* was what the doctors called him. His body was so small and yet his head looked so big when he was born more than a month premature. He barely weighed five pounds. His features were sharper, less rounded than a full-term's, due to the dearth of fat stores. Lonnie lacked the muscle reflexes for sucking and swallowing. He simply couldn't latch on. He would always pull away from Mimi's breast every time she brought it up to his lips, turning his head, as if her nipple was some affront to his newborn disposition and he simply refused to even look at it.

I feel like it's my fault, Mimi confessed to me once we were finally able to bring our son home. *I feel like he doesn't want me or he's rejecting me or—or—*

You know that's not true, I cut in, gently dragging her back from her downward spiral.

I'm just saying that's how it feels.

I understand that, hon. All I'm trying to say is—

No. You don't *understand. You* can't *understand how this feels. It's not your* milk.

Mimi was right. Of course she was right. I wasn't Lonnie's primary food source. I wasn't the one Lonnie was pushing away. I was simply some glorified escort, ferrying the two of them to their lactating workshops every Saturday morning. I had nothing to offer but a ride to and from home.

Here I am, killing time at this goddamn yard sale while Mimi and Lonnie work on their latching tactics. And look at what I found. Stumbled upon, really. Like fate.

Perhaps this pump would be the answer to all our prayers.

The newer models I'd seen online were well over a hundred

dollars—and that was just on the lower end. Some pumps run as high as three hundred bucks. We couldn't afford that. We were scrounging just to meet our premiums every month. These baby monopolies always offer some brand-new hopped-up model of the same overpriced device you're only going to use for a few months of your life and then never need again.

But who buys somebody else's breast pump? Who purchases a maternal mechanism that's been attached to some other woman's body? It doesn't matter how many times you wash it, sanitize it, irradiating every last bit of bacteria that could be clinging to its console...

It still carries the essence of another mother.

Doesn't it?

The Pure Essence Platinum Breast Pump model #3926 offers moms enhanced flexibility, comfortable interplay, and multiple suckling options. It is the ideal pump for those women returning to the office who need a discreet means to express themselves... and their milk!

I found myself flipping through the instruction manual, transfixed by its pictures. This hand-drawn woman wore the same docile expression in nearly every illustration throughout the pamphlet, each diagram showing the user—*showing me*—how to strap the harness on, attach the suction shields to my nipples, how to flip the switch and let the machine begin to extricate the milk from my body. There was no eye contact, no breaking the fourth wall between us. She simply stared off into the distance while that mollusk latched itself directly on to her breasts, a parasite siphoning the lifegiving elixir from her body, taking what it wanted.

Our piston-pump generates a simulated stimulation that feels both natural and comfy. It offers numerous suckling variations to mimic a newborn's suckling movements, easily adjustable to match the feeding habits of a maturing child. As your baby grows, so does our pump!

Five bucks for this clunker. Talk about a song. They were practically giving it away. Mimi could express all her pent-up milk and Lonnie would get all the nutrients he needed to grow into a healthy, happy boy. Who cared if this pump wasn't the latest model? As long as it worked...

It still worked, right?

Cheaper than a cappuccino. Six bucks just for some foamed milk. Worth a shot.

~

It dawned on me that I'd bought it and brought it home without even flipping the pump on. This wasn't a battery-powered model. It needed to be plugged in. I got tangled in the tubes, wrestling against the kraken in our kitchen, just looking for the right cord. *Let's give this pump a test run. Make sure everything's in working condition.* That meant cranking this crustacean up.

Just like the mother in the manual. Look how sublime she seemed, tethered to it. Connected.

Look at her smile.

The Pure Essence Platinum Breast Pump features six unique suction settings and four adjustable speed cycles to simulate your baby's own nursing patterns. Our patented Platinum technology helps our product achieve comfortable, smooth expressions.

I don't know why I put it on. I'm not entirely sure I can answer that question. Something about the illustrations, I guess. The pencil-sketched mother seemed to be having—I don't know—a *pleasurable* experience with the pump. Always smiling. Not a posed grin. She wore the same beatific expression in every last drawing, no matter what position she was in.

Ever seen *The Ecstasy of Saint Teresa*? She looked like that. Only she's breastfeeding this mechanized mollusk in every image. I'm not sure if it was lazy rendering on the illustrator's part, or if the expression signified something consistent. *Eternal.* She was enjoying herself. Losing herself in the gentle rhythms of the pistons as they pumped. Her body may have been here, harnessed to this machine, but her mind was drifting. Soaring. Christ—her soul itself looked as if it was off and rocketing beyond the parameters of her earthbound form.

I wanted to feel that, too. Experience whatever she was experiencing.

Could I?

(*Not your milk.*)

Nobody else was around. Mimi must've fallen asleep with Lonnie upstairs. It was just me and our new (*used*) breast pump, its translucent tentacles reaching out for me. For my body.

Who would ever know?

There was a Velcro corset. A girdle, I guess. I wrapped the elastic band around my chest, strapping myself in and making sure the eyelets were positioned directly across my nipples. Both nips slipped through the stitched slits, so my torso now looked like Zorro with pink eye.

Why do men even have nipples? What purpose do they serve?

(*Not your milk.*)

Our pumps use an internal rotating piston that creates a waveform akin to an infant's suction. It follows the exact patterns of a baby's feeding habits: builds, peaks, and releases...

I felt silly. The Velcro cut off my circulation. I couldn't breathe in this thing. But I'd come this far. Might as well keep going, right? Just to know what it felt like? See for myself?

The mother in the manual. Just look at her. *Just look.* Her half-closed eyes. Her smile.

A lactating Mona Lisa.

(Not your milk.)

I pressed the button on the control console. A slow-churning purr suddenly whirred up from within. Lord knows how long it had been since this machine had last been used, but here it was, lurching back to life. Invisible pistons emitted their thin but persistent hum, high in pitch.

I felt the first tug.

Whatever air was caught between the suction shield and my skin was vacuumed into the cup. It started pulling at my nipples. Suckling. It tickled a bit. I couldn't help but imagine the suction shields were two tiny mouths—doll mouths—working their rubberized lips over my chest. A *menage a trois* with Barbie and one of her pals. It was funny at first, but a queasy unease suddenly settled into my stomach. This felt wrong. All wrong. *I shouldn't be doing this...*

I should turn the pump off before Mimi walked in and caught me. I should get rid of it. Toss the thing into the trash. It was a stupid idea. Picking up a used pump. What was I thinking?

Stay, the mother in the manual seemed to say. *Stay with me...*

Those suction shields opened and closed over my chest, opened and closed, opened and closed, a pair of arid gasps alternating between each nipple, left then right, left then right.

Stay...

I flipped to the next page in the pamphlet, hoping to occupy my mind while the pump nuzzled at my nipples, left then right, left then right.

Babies change their sucking speed to achieve multiple milk ejections during a breastfeeding session. Mothers can adjust the Pure Essence Platinum Breast Pump to increase their speed to trigger multiple milk expressions or lower the speed to drain the breast.

Oh, so there were speed ranges. Between 30–80 cycles per minute. That's interesting. I could make it go faster, if I wanted. Did I? The pump even had fluctuating suction levels. 30–250 mmHg. I could make the machine suck harder or softer with just a simple flick of a switch.

The choice was all mine. How far did I want to go? How deep?

Stay with me... Stay...

The pistons lifted in pitch as I adjusted the controls. The pump worked harder now. Hummed under its own mechanical strain. The tiniest of vibrations tittered out from the console. I gasped at the sting as the pump reached deeper. Going further than my skin. I swear it felt like the pistons were suddenly siphoning something elemental out from within me, an oil derrick for breast milk. What was it going to find inside my body? What did I have to offer?

(*Not your milk.*)

Stay, the mother in the manual cooed in the other.

I cranked the controls even further now. Up to their hilt. The engine strained, lifting in pitch. Its pistons puckered, suckling nothing but pockets of air, greedy for something wet. Something slippery.

Stay with me...

My skin was really chafing now. But the tugging intensified. It felt like my nipples were slipping into the suction shields, abruptly pulling away from the rest of me.

Ow, ow, oooow...

Reality bent a bit. There was a certain elasticity in my physical form now, like my flesh was no longer bound to my body. It was pulling away. Tearing like taffy tugged to its hilt and now snapping in half. All my soft tissue was suddenly funneled into the pump. The skin. The blood. There wouldn't be anything left of me but the bones, nothing but a skeleton strapped to this apparatus, while the rest of myself was vacuumed into the tubes and filling its milk bottles.

I let out a cry. *Christ*, I needed to turn this thing off. *Turn it off, turn it off, turn it—*

Stay, the mother in the manual whispered. *Don't let go. We're close.*

So close.

Stay...

This goddamn machine could care less if I was a mother or not. It only knew how to do one thing and that was to extract the very essence from its host. The life-giving fluid. The milk.

Turn it off, turn it off, turn it ooooooffff—

I yanked the cord out from the wall socket. The pinched purr of its pistons faded. I was out of breath. Nipples aching in a full-on throb. I finally, slowly opened my eyes and realized...

The bottles were sodden.

Ink? A viscous liquid sloshed around the bottom of both reservoirs. Less than an ounce in each. *What in the goddamn fuck...?* I brought one bottle up for a closer look. Bands of swirling purple and green spun across its surface, a lactated oil spill, whirling in pearlescent hues. Something you might find puddled along the pavement of a grocery store parking lot. But these colors kept fluctuating, vibrantly spiraling: red, now blue, now pink. These colors were *alive.*

Where the hell did that come from?

There had to be an explanation for this. Perhaps some engine grease had leaked out from a gasket, trickling into the milk reservoirs or something. This moo-juice jalopy was so old, practically an antique, it wouldn't have been so surprising if it was oozing motor oil everywhere.

I disconnected the suction shields from my nipples. I wanted it off. *Now.* Just feeling the pump still tethered to my body, its rubber tubing cold and inflexible against my skin, turned my stomach. I felt impure; violated somehow.

Each satellite dish peeled away from my sore skin with a gummy smack. I pushed the pump's console as far away as I could, the inert machine dragging its tentacles across the kitchen counter, taking its milk bottles with it.

I was dribbling.

My nipples were beading. Pebbles of pitch. But how was that even possible? I lightly tapped at my chest. Hissed at the sudden sting. This sticky black resin clung to my fingertips.

That's not blood, is it? Where is this stuff coming from? What is it?

So, I did a sniff test.

A pungent aroma wafted up from my finger. Hints of Limburger. It wasn't bad, exactly. Just strong. Earthy, almost. Like loam. I didn't mind it as much on the second whiff. Or the third.

This came from me, I couldn't help but think. *I made this. Me.*

So I licked.

Salty. Sweet. Sour. Bitter. Umami.

What if there was a sixth flavor profile? Something new? An uncharted taste we have yet to experience? To indulge?

It burned. A steady heat spread across my tongue, enveloping my taste buds.

I gagged at first. Not because I was nauseous, but because I was there and not there at the same time, my consciousness schisming from my body for the slightest second. I couldn't focus for a moment, feeling outside of myself. I juddered. Like a film strip skipping in the projector. I just barely caught a glimpse of something else—*somewhere* else—outside my body.

I had to settle back into my skin. Sync up again. Get my breath to settle.

One taste had done all that. Just a simple lick.

What would a whole gulp do?

So I took a sip.

(*My milk.*)

Then the other.

(*My milk.*)

I polished them both off. Swallowed it all down.

(*Mine.*)

Even if I tried to explain what it tasted like... even if I wanted to share this feeling with Mimi or anyone else... express the sensation of taking my milk into my body for the very first time and entering a realm outside of our digestive systems... outside of our nourishment...

There was no taste like this. Our tongues are not equipped to handle this milk.

My milk.

I swallowed a black hole.

~

You've barely touched your dinner, Mimi said.

It took me a moment to realize she meant the meal on my plate. *That's not food*, I thought. I don't know how long I'd been sitting at the dinner table. My stomach still hadn't quite settled. I felt in between digestive realms. Mimi made some pasta dish. Too much garlic.

You feeling OK?

Fine, I said, belching a bit. I could still taste the loam at the back of my throat.

You want me to make you something else?

No, no, I'm good. I couldn't look at my plate. The noodles seemed to slither. Constrict. I forced myself to take a bite, for Mimi's sake, but the spaghetti just ended coming back up.

What's wrong?

Just a little indigestion... More like a cesspool in my intestines. I clutched my stomach.

Can I get you—

I'm fine, I'm fine, excuse me— I rushed to the bathroom before I threw up in front of her, feeling those few pasta noodles rise up my throat like earthworms during a heavy rain.

I needed something to ease my tummy. Maalox or Pepto-Bismol or—

my milk

Research has shown that pumping at your highest comfort level yields more milk. Our Pure Essence Platinum Breast Pump allows mothers to adjust their speed higher or lower to meet their own comfort level while maximizing their output.

The mother in the manual understood. She knew how to soothe me.

I needed to express myself. Needed to pump again.

Needed to drink.

~

I've kept the breast pump for myself. It was a doorway. Mimi and I would figure something else out for Lonnie. I'm not as worried about his feeding habits as I was before. Not anymore. He'll get his sustenance somehow. He'll feed. There's plenty of milk to go around now.

I don't eat much anymore, and Mimi's definitely noticed my meals go uneaten these days. I've tried telling her I'm fine. Better than fine. I'm getting all the nutrients I need. It's hard to explain, but I'm not quite ready to share my milk with her just yet. One day. Maybe. We'll see.

The pump unlocked something within me. Found something. Brought it out.

If you could just taste it, I wanted to tell my wife, *you would understand... Understand how it feels. You would see for yourself.*

See everything. There's so much to witness. To taste. It burns at first; hollows you out, but when the indigestion eventually settles and there's little left of your intestines to scorch, you'll come to understand that there's nutritional value in the blackness.

There's such wondrous sustenance to be had.

It doesn't matter if my teeth are falling out. I don't need them anymore. All I need is the milk.

My black milk.

I find time to pump. Whenever I can grab a few minutes by myself, I'll take them. It doesn't matter where I am or the time of day. I'll hook myself up and express myself.

I have so much to give. To offer. The mother in the manual showed me.

I'll slip off to the bathroom and connect, attaching its tendrils to my nipples. I'll rest the console in my lap, cradling it, while the pumpjack unearths the milk from within. It's so hard not to guzzle it all myself. After those first few pumps, I ended up drinking everything. Made myself sick. I felt like I woke up halfway across the galaxy, wrapped in a ghastly plasma of starlight.

I had to learn the hard way you can't gorge yourself on this stuff. It has to last. *Savor it.*

Besides, there's Lonnie to think about. His frail body. He needs me. His father.

My milk.

~

I keep finding myself wanting to leave this life behind.

I'm desperate to drink my way back to that blackness.

I'll take travel nips. Just little swigs when I can. Simple quick trips across the cosmos.

I carry a flask full of milk with me wherever I go, in case I need a quick pick-me-up. Not that I go anywhere lately. My physical body at least. I'm limiting my errands to absolute essentials. Leaving the house—in this form—takes too much out of me. I'm all tuckered by lunchtime.

I know Mimi's noticed, but if only she knew where I've been. Where I'm going.

You mind picking up some diapers? We're all out.

Do I have to?

There are none in this house. At all. So, unless you want to wrap him in your favorite Dave Matthews T-shirt, I'd suggest you get in the fucking car and get some goddamn diapers.

A quick trip to the grocery store usually takes less than ten minutes, but fuck if I haven't been stuck in the parking lot for I don't know how many hours, wrist trembling, straining to keep my hand steady long enough to unscrew the cap and bring that flask up to my lips and feel the curdled cosmos creep down my throat, that warm buttery swell spreading through me, thick and viscous, slowly enveloping my insides with a gelatinous layer, and oh God, I feel everything roil, it's turning me inside out, a galaxy expanding in my stomach, a supernova in my bowels, so massive this car cannot contain me, this parking lot cannot contain me, this world cannot contain me, our universe cannot contain me. I am limitless, traveling unfathomable distances.

I am a lactating astronaut. Bands of curdled light warp around me. A black Milky Way.

Look at what I'm leaking, bleeding out into outer space. What dribbling constellations I produce. What wonders I have to share.

What a gift my milk is. I want, *need*, to share it.

Let me feed you, son...

~

I'm stockpiling.

I'll freeze the extra helpings in a plastic baggie with the date written in Sharpie, *best served by,* tucking them in the rear of our freezer where Mimi can't find them. She hasn't asked me why my nipples are so swollen. Why they bleed through my tees, a pair of bloodshot eyes blossoming from the cotton. I've been Band-Aiding my nipples. I change before bed, where Mimi can't see the suction marks along my chest. It looks like I've been attacked by a squid. She just wouldn't understand. *Not her milk.* She hasn't seen what's on the other side of that first sip. What vitamins are swirling within the pitch, pink, now purple, now green.

It's all we drink now, Lonnie and I. All I feed him on. My milk.

My rapturously black milk.

We're doubling up on breastfeeding duty whether my wife knows it or not. I'm sneaking my feedings in between Mimi's. Lonnie's getting twice the milk. First hers, then mine. I might be a bit biased, but I think our boy likes my milk better. He drinks it all. Down to the last drop.

Mimi's? He spits hers out. He wails and wails whenever she comes closer with her breasts, practically pushing her away with his reedy arms.

It just takes time, I offered. *You two will connect eventually. I'm sure of it. Until then, I'll just keep bottle-feeding him.*

Lonnie needs milk.

His father's milk.

Look at him. *Just look.* He's finally gaining weight now. At long last. All wrapped in fat. Pleasantly plump. He wears a docile smile that I swear I've seen before, somewhere, on someone. The woman from the instruction manual. Of course. His eyes cast off into the cosmos.

Stay with me, she said, her voice crawling across countless stars. *Stay...*

I notice how the color of Lonnie's eyes are changing. When I gaze into them after I feed him, I swear I see the blackest tidepools swirling about his sockets. My son has oil spill eyes.

His father's eyes.

That's it, I say. *Drink it all up.*

keep it civil

Some time ago The Journal advocated in its columns the erection of a monument to the living and dead soldiers of this county who responded to the call of Virginia and the South and followed the fortunes of the Confederacy from Manassas to Appomattox. Each one of these heroes, many of whom sleep in unknown and unmarked graves, is entitled to a high place in the affections of the people of Mathews and their heroic deeds should be commemorated by the erection of a fitting monument to their memory...

Confederate soldiers of Mathews, awake and respond to the sacred duty resting upon you to pay the deserved tribute of a shaft of marble to the memory of the comrade who slept by your side in winter's cold and summer's heat, and who fell under the rain of the enemy's bullet with his face to the foe, whose life blood baptized the soil of our mother State and who died in defense of his country's honor, with face as calm and smile as sweet as patriot ever wore.

Sons and daughters of the Confederacy, arise in the strength and beauty of your youth and proclaim to the world your pride in the splendor of courage and wealth of self-sacrifice shown by your fathers upon the battlefields of Virginia, and honor their deathless valor and their unexampled patriotism by lending your youth and your strength to the erection of this monument.

—*The Mathews Journal*, March 8, 1906

They're toppling our monuments. Ripping our history right on down. Look at what those rioters are doing in Richmond. They've laid siege to that city—the goddamn heart of the Confederacy—singing and dancing in the streets as they tear down every last statue.

First, it was General Williams Carter Wickham in Monroe Park.

Then it was Jefferson Davis on Monument Avenue.

Now the city itself removed ol' Stonewall. Got one of those telescoping boom cranes to roll on in, cinching its winch around the general's bronze horse and hefting them both off their pedestal while all those protestors cheered, snapping off selfies with their goddamn phones.

Those statues have stood for well over a hundred years and their mayor's got the gall to pull them all down? Whose statue are they coming for next?

Not our monument, no sir.

We only got one stop light, but Mathews County sure as hell ain't sitting back and watching our one and only statue get torn down like they've done in Richmond. We're not turning our backs on our heritage. You damn well better believe we're protecting our legacy.

A group of us boys have taken it upon ourselves to stand watch, keeping vigil over our Confederate memorial, just in case any looters decide to take a little road trip here to Mathews.

Go ahead. Try knocking our monument down, I dare you. Let's see how close you get before you're whistling Dixie through your freshly ventilated chest. Open-carry is legal here in Virginia, last time I checked, so you better think twice before coming after our statue.

Our militia is strictly volunteer. Ain't nobody getting paid to stand watch. We consider it our civic duty to protect our monument. And you better believe there's more than enough folks around here willing to enlist in order to protect it. Let's see, there's myself, Walt Tompkins, Hank Reynolds, Jimmy Litch. Ben Pendleton bailed on us after the first few nights, so he's out.

We're taking six-hour shifts. Day and night. Seven days a week. We gotta dance around each other's work schedules, which ain't that hard for me, considering I'm in between jobs at the moment. Walt's the only one with a nine-to-five, while the rest of us gentlemen tend to take work wherever we might find it. Makes it easier for us to commit to our call of duty.

Our memorial might not look like much compared to the big boys on Monument Avenue, but it's all we've got. We give our statue the respect he deserves. Back in 1906, the Daughters of the Confederacy put out the call for *a monument that commemorated the men of Mathews*, those boys who responded to the battle cry of the South and *followed the fortunes of the Confederacy from Manassas to Appomattox*. Each one of them boys were heroes—*our heroes*—many of whom *still sleep in unmarked graves* to this very day. Damn straight they're entitled to *a high place*. They deserve to be on a pedestal overlooking the courthouse square.

It's a fitting tribute, if you ask me. A shaft of marble reaching twenty feet straight up in the air. Nobody knows who that reb standing on top is. He's no general. There's no name on the inscription. He's just some unknown soldier boy who once called Mathews home, a brother in arms *who slept in winter's cold and summer's heat, who fell under the rain of the enemy's bullet with his face to the foe, whose life blood baptized the soil of our mother state and who died in defense of his country's honor*. Us boys all call him Mathew 'cause—well, because this here is Mathews County. For as long as I can remember, ever since I was a kid, that's just what everyone around here called him—as in, *Hey, meet me under Mathew*, or, *Turn left at Mathew and just keep on driving till you hit Route 611*. It's a nickname that sticks. Our very own mascot.

I looked up to him. Literally.

As a kid, no older than eight or nine, I'd stand under the statue of Mathew and stare up at those bronze eyes of his, cast out 'cross the horizon. I always wanted to see what he'd seen on the battlefield. He's looking at it right now, always staring at the aftermath along the front, the outright carnage of it all. I remember wanting to be like him, growing up and serving my country—most of it, at least—just like he had. How old was he when he went to war?

I'd talk to him. If nobody else was around, I'd end up asking: *What was it like? Believing in something so much?*

But Mathew never answered. Sometimes I imagined him talking back to me. Still do. Ain't like I'm the only one, either. Hank was convinced he'd conversed with Matthew one night a few years back, but that was after a twelve-pack of Pabst, so nobody's buying his ghost story.

What I wouldn't give to see the things he'd seen.

I've lived here my whole life. Mathews is my home. Mathews is my people. I've been taught to respect where I come from, even if it's fallen out of fashion. To hell with what the history books say. Teachers are whitewashing whole battles out from their lesson plan. Kids these days don't even know what war's been fought right under their feet. Who died on this very ground that we're standing on now.

This statue is all the history I need. The erection of this here monument is a fitting tribute to the *courage* and *self-sacrifice our forebearers showed on the battlefield*, *honoring their deathless valor and patriotism.* It stands as a testament to the Confederate sons of Mathews County who gave their lives to the cause. If that ain't worth protecting, then what the hell is?

~

I pull the midnight shift.

Walt is asleep in his Chevy when I come up on him, so I give that boy the scare of his life by pounding on the hood, thunder rumbling all around as I shout—*Antifa are attacking!*

You should see the look on his face as he springs up in his seat, eyes wider than a pair of hubcaps. Probably pissed in his Pampers. I nearly keel over, busting my gut.

The hell, man... I coulda shot you!

You'll have to wipe your ass first, after the crap you just shat in your pants...

Mattie's all yours, asshole, he mutters before turning over the ignition and driving off.

See you tomorrow... Bring a fresh pair of underwear!

There's a picnic table in the courthouse square, situated next to the monument, just under Mathew and his musket. Gives me a clear sight line between Church and Fisher Street.

I prefer keeping my vigil outdoors. Boredom settles in pretty quick behind the wheel. Ain't no surprise Walt dozed off. Luckily, it's not raining tonight. I got myself a front-row seat to a jam session between the crickets and cicadas, sawing their asses off in the dark.

Nobody is awake at this hour. Just me and Mathew, standing our watch. He's leaning against his musket made of marble, its buttstock between his feet as he stares blankly out at the horizon—while I got my 9mm on the table, simply listening to the spring peepers. There's a slight breeze coming in from the Chesapeake, so I get a good whiff of salt water in the air. It's pushing 1 a.m. and it's still more humid than Hades right now. I can feel the mugginess cling to the back of my neck, summoning the sweat all across my skin, rising right out of me.

Whaddya think, Mattie? I ask the statue. *See anybody up there?*

Nobody's come for my main man so far. That don't mean either of us ever let our guard down. This vigil here is to hold the front line. We're letting the folks in Richmond know we won't sit idly by while these looters take to the streets and bowl over our legacy. There may be over a hundred miles between the state capital and our town, but we all know how these things go. I've heard all about their night raids, spray-painting statues across the state. Last I heard, defacing public property was a crime—and around these parts, the law still stands for something. It don't matter if it's a can of spray paint or a Molotov cocktail; they're carrying a weapon and nothing would make me happier than to show them the business end of my pistol.

Ain't that right, Mattie?

He don't answer.

Never answers.

We're taking a stand. The culture wars end here, my friends. If those protestors come marching our way, you better believe we'll be ready for them. I'm holding the line just like my great-great-great-grandfather held the line over two hundred years ago. I even got myself a great-aunt who disguised herself as a man and fought on the ground. That's how deep our roots go. So, you damn well better believe I'm here for the cause. Ain't nobody taking Mathew down.

But Christ, does it ever get boring. I've glanced at my watch five times in the last twenty minutes alone. Mosquitoes are downright murdering my ass, making a meal out of me.

It's the last hour of my shift. The sun will be softening the horizon before long. Once I see that egg-yolk yellow seep through the trees, my vigil will be done.

I can't remember who's picking up the morning shift. Either Hank or Jimmy. They better not sleep through their alarm and leave me hanging like last time. To hell if I'm abandoning my station, though. Until one of them shows and relieves me of my duties, I'm sitting right here.

You hear that, Mattie? I ask. *Just you and me...*

Nothing, someone whispers.

I leap up from the picnic table. I grab my 9mm and circle the perimeter once, then twice.

Ain't nobody around. The streetlamps are getting battered by moths, but that's just about as much as I can see moving in either direction.

Who's there? I weigh the words down with enough concrete for this son of a bitch to know I mean business. *You got three seconds to show yourself. One...*

The streets are clear. Ain't no one hiding behind the pillar.

Two...

The safety's off. Finger on the trigger. I'm listening to the cannon blasts of my own heartbeat battering against my chest as I try balancing my breathing through my nose.

Three...

Silence.

There's nothing. The voice sounds closer now. I can't put a bead on where. It's faint, more air than utterance, as if the word itself was exhaled from the mouth of whoever said it.

Sounds like they're right on top of me. Whispering from above. So, I tilt my head back.

The monument is empty.

Mathew is gone. As in, he's no longer there. The pedestal is empty.

I stumble back, away from the monument. I'm not looking where I'm going, so when I collide with whatever's behind me it feels like hitting a brick wall. But this wall's got arms.

I spin around and find myself face-to-face with him.

Mathew's staring back at me with his chiseled eyes. Nothing but gray marble sanded down by a century's worth of bad weather, a pair of rotten robin's eggs settled in each socket.

Do you want to see? I swear I hear him say it, that sandpaper rasp summoning the words up from his marble throat. He's shaking his head as he steps closer to me. *See for yourself?*

Before common sense seeps in and I second-guess myself, I hear myself answer...

Yes. I want to know. I need to see.

See the war with my own eyes.

Mathew—this statue, this man made of stone—takes hold of his own face, simply gripping his eyes with both of his weatherworn hands and digging those brittle fingers into the sockets. The rock crumbles under his clutch as he pulls in opposite directions. Pulls at his face.

Wait, I say. *Don't—*

The stone gives, brick flesh separating along the bridge of his nose. His fingers have plunged so far into his sockets he's able to break open his own skull, splitting it vertically in half like an arid coconut and now I see what's been hidden within the tomb of our nameless soldier's face. Look at that chasm. That abyss. It's endless. I can't see the bottom.

Nothing, Mathew whispers to me as the halves of his head envelop my own. *There's nothing to see.*

Now I see it, too. See that vast grayness for myself. At first, it feels like smoke, a vague haze suspended over the terrain, but there's a brittle chill coming off it, a cloud cover of cataracts eclipsing my vision—and in the very moment his head seals up again, closing over my skull and trapping me inside, I hear them, their voices rising up from the mist, so many soldiers pleading for their mothers, their wives, wailing like lost children. I can just barely make out their writhing silhouettes, bodies roiling over one another, rooting about the mud. Their stumps pierce the fog before getting swallowed up by it all over again. So many missing limbs.

I try blinking them away, but I can't close my eyes anymore. They're held open. I don't know what's happening to them but the lids won't shift. If I strain to close them, I can feel this brittle crackle, like dry clay, along the surface.

My eyes. My eyes are hardening. I feel their weight growing heavier by the breath, a pair of rocks settling into their sockets. Every time I blink, my eyelids scrape over coarse stone.

Nothing's there anymore. Nothing to see. It's all gone gray for me.

The battlefield, at last.

battlefield séances

I am looking for Seaton. Seaton B. James. C Company, 39th Massachusetts Infantry. Seaton—can you hear me?

Such a deafening field. Practically impossible to sift through the din of soldiers. Me and my sisters could hear them clamoring from miles away, all that hollering overwhelming my ears. The seeds of a migraine had already taken root right between my pigtails, well before we even reached that pasture—the sound of these soldier-boys shouting out for me, for anyone really, cultivating my headache until it was in full bloom. Couldn't concentrate with all that racket. Couldn't hear clearly. Kept begging Daddy to turn our carriage around. Take us all home before it got any louder. But Mrs. James had paid top dollar for this session—and she was expecting results. She'd dragged the whole family down from Rochester, spending two days straight traveling by train. Plus the countless hours crammed into that carriage with Lela and Kate. Ever since word had spread that the three of us had established contact with little Willie Lincoln right there in the White House—we were always traveling nonstop.

One barren battlefield after the next.

Shiloh. Bull Run.

If it was good enough for the First Lady, well then—you better believe it was going to be good enough for mothers like Mrs. James. Poor woman. I recognized the expression on her face from the first time I laid eyes on her, seeing it everywhere I went nowadays. This eclipse of exhaustion and despondency overshadowed every glance, every desperate interaction between herself and me and my sisters. She would stop at nothing, and I mean nothing, running herself absolutely ragged until she finally found her son.

Seaton—I have your mother here. She misses you very much. Would you like to speak to her? Is there anything you'd like to say?

Help me...

The first skull I found was half-buried between my feet, the surface of the earth leveling along the bridge of its nose. Its yellowed dome looked more like an unripe pumpkin—not the crown of some cranium. When this field had been nothing but ruddy mud, taking on a red tint from soaking up all that blood—the soil must've seeped inside the eye sockets, eventually hardening over as cement solidifies itself, gripping on to the bone and just refusing to let that soldier go. What was left of him at least.

Seaton? Is that you?

Take me home...

Spring was bringing plowing season back to the southern states once and for all, returning farmers to their own fields for the first time since the war had ended. The number of unknown bones still littering these fields reached right on into the thousands, even a year later, all those soldiers decaying away in their hasty graves. Federal or Confederate—they were still here, all fallen and forgotten. The mutilation of human remains by farmhands tilling the soil had become something of a common offense down here, pushing their ploughshares over all the unprotected corpses before they could be properly interred. The desecration of Union graves was absolutely forbidden, no matter where those bones were buried. Not that that had stopped any of these farmers. There's this one story getting whispered around New

York about a plantation owner wanting to expand his cotton fields an extra acre or two, plowing up more than thirty Federal skeletons in the process. He had his men deliver those bones *in bulk* to the nearest cemetery, a heap of femurs and ribs all anonymously jumbled together. Now there was just no telling whose bones were whose anymore. Left it up to heaven to sift through and sort them out, they did.

Wilderness. Cold Harbor. It was happening everywhere nowadays. Acres of farmland were now housing the aftermaths of battle. Nothing but a harvest of death. No matter where you stepped in this country, there seemed to be a body buried beneath your feet that just didn't belong there. If there was any hope of these families ever finding their relatives before the horses plowed through—parents were going to have to act fast, seeking an *alternative means* of reuniting with their loved ones.

Hence the sessions with me and my sisters.

Can you hear them? I asked, pressing my ear to the earth.

Hear whom? Mrs. James asked.

All the soldiers.

There are no soldiers here, she said, shaking her head. *Not anymore.*

But there were. At our feet. Behind our backs. They were everywhere, surrounding us, the sound of their voices seeping up from the mud. Thick and peaty. All of them begging, repeating the same supplication—*Take me home, take me home, take me home...*

Some would even say they were Seaton—but I knew that just wasn't true. These boys would say just about anything to leave this field behind, lying right through their loose teeth. The shrill whistle of their breath flitted along with the wind, the breeze blowing through their bullet wounds. The fractures in their skulls where the shot had shattered through were now like finger-holes on a flute, all of them playing along in some tuneless song, echoing the same refrain over and over again.

Take me home, take me home, take me home...

There were just too many dead nowadays. Couldn't bury them

fast enough. Not with the war wiping through. Half of the country's boys had suddenly gone missing, all because their bodies had been left behind. It wasn't clear to the folks back at home if their relatives were dead or if they'd just up and disappeared. Mothers didn't know if they should start mourning or not, if they could still cling on to what little hope they had left. Nobody knew what to do. Not until the war was all over. Everybody started heading down after the South had surrendered, hoping to haul off our dead. Even then, though, the chances at distinguishing one skeleton from the next were nil to none. By the time these burial parties combed through, looking to dig up all the unmarked graves and ship their remains back up North where there was a headstone waiting a couple summers had already passed by, the intense heat wiping the identities of these soldiers right away. The weather and decay. The insects and wild animals whittling them down to the bone.

Wasn't anything to put in the ground for most families now. Not anymore. They'd lost their loved ones without even having a chance to say goodbye.

So call upon the Fox sisters.

There was sweet little Lela. No older than eight. Couple years back, she'd come down with a case of rheumatic fever—only to lift herself back out of the illness relatively unscathed, healthier than ever. She claimed her recovery came by an "intercession with angels." Ever since, she's become inseparable from this ratty blanket that she swears was the winding sheet of some ghost. She yanked the blanket free from the spirit, leaving him naked now. Half the time she uses it as a handkerchief, carrying the rag with her wherever she goes—sniffling all the time, always wiping away the ectoplasm running down her upper lip.

Elder Kate had just turned sixteen, her body suddenly undergoing its own series of paranormal activities. Changing in ways Lela and me just couldn't comprehend yet.

While for myself, the middle child—my talent was clairsentience.

Clear feeling as my daddy called it. I take on the ailments of those non-corporeal entities that establish contact with me, experiencing the very same maladies they had right before dying. Whether it's bleeding out from a buckshot wound or withering away with typhoid fever, I'll feel it. Know that sensation in my very bones. That way, when these mothers ask just how it was that their sons died I'll be able to show them. Families can watch those last few moments of their boy's life as I slip off into a trance, my body overtaken by his wandering spirit, watching me approximate his death throes exactly the way they happened on the battlefield. If these parents are willing to pay the price Daddy's calculated to cover the physical toll of me undertaking such a traumatic form of trance-mediumship, they can watch it all for themselves now. Down to the very last detail.

Entry wounds. Last rites. Coughing fits. Final prayers.

Everything. Right before their very own eyes.

The spirit world is no longer inaccessible to the living. Immortality is here! We three are the key, the bridge between the living and the dead. The very voices from the hereafter are whispered right into man's ear, using our mouths as their own. The nimble lips of my little eight-year-old sister can now channel the final transmissions of private Wilber Hunt of the 23rd regiment, Pennsylvania, asking as a favor to inform his father of his death not two days prior to contacting us. We let his daddy know he died a valiant death on the battlefield, serving his country up to the very end. Now spirited away by the graceful hands of God.

We've been blessed. Me and my sisters have been given a gift. We're serving our country the only way we know how. It is our patriotic duty to deliver communications from those fallen soldiers back to their families, reporting to relatives that their loved ones had died well. Given the Good Death.

We are here to bring you home, Seaton, I said. *To give you a proper burial.*

Bet you I find him first, Kate said.

Wish you would. Then we could all go home.

Searching for just one boy out here, buried among all the others? I swear. Needle in a haystack.

Just keep looking. He's out here somewhere.

The rate we're going, she muttered. *I'll be turning seventeen before we ever see home again.*

Kate had been acting surly all morning. The bags under her eyes were surefire proof that she'd spent all of last night with Lieutenant William Bradshaw from the 34th Division again. He'd been trailing after Kate ever since we found the remnants of his skeleton scattered halfway across Shiloh. Some farmer's hogs had been left free to forage through the battlefield, living off the dead for days on end without anyone shooing them away. Those pigs dragged poor William's body in every which direction. Took us all afternoon just to find the missing pieces, the distance between his limbs now reaching some twenty or thirty yards. All on account of the swine.

Kate had come across his mandible sticking up from the mud, assuming it was a horse shoe. She tugged his jaw up, shaking off the earth, suddenly catching sight of that boy's sly grin for the very first time, only to make the mistake of smiling right back at him, giving him those deadly doe eyes of hers. Now he'll never let her go. Always following a few steps behind, wherever she goes. Her own little lost puppy. He's been our family's spirit guide ever since, helping us locate lost soldiers—though, as of late, William's been more interested in spending his evenings with just Kate, *alone*, the two of them spiriting away from the rest of us every chance they get.

I caught them sitting under the shade of some tree just off to the side of the pasture, hearing her get all giggly.

What are you doing? I asked.

Mind your own damn business.

We're supposed to be looking for Seaton.

Well—better get to it, then, and leave us alone.

My sisters and I had decided to separate, agreeing we could cover more ground that way. We each took off in our own direction, waltzing along the empty field, reddening the hem of our dresses as we trudged through the mud, while Daddy pacified Mrs. James as best he could by detailing her in our rather *unconventional* methodologies. We needed quiet. Needed time to find her son. A séance of this sort could take hours, days even, combing over these grounds until we were able to establish contact with the other side—if not with Seaton himself, then possibly some other soldier he had served with. A fellow fallen member of his company might lead us in the right direction, tell us where he now lay.

Such communication had always been my sister's strong suit. Elder Kate could chat to these boys better than me and Lela, since she was the closest to these soldiers in age. They all thought she was cute. Telling her she was pretty. Ever since she started receiving compliments from the afterlife, Kate's been wearing her hair down. Letting those long curly locks just roll off her shoulders—as if none of us knew what she was up to. Batting her eyelashes at the air like that, as if no one were there watching. But Lela and I knew better.

I'm gonna tell Daddy you're down here with William again.

You do and I swear you're gonna regret it.

William was alright-looking, I reckon. I'd seen cuter boys out here. There was that one soldier who escorted me toward his corpse back in Antietam, taking me by the hand and showing me the way to his body. Eldridge—that was his name. Eldridge Darwimple from Tennessee. Daddy would've killed me if he'd found out I was walking with a Confederate soldier. But boy, was that man ever handsome. Carrot-red hair. Green eyes. It was hard to tell whether he actually had freckles or not, what with all the drops of dried blood peppering his cheeks. But I swear I'd never felt so weak in the knees for a soldier before. When I saw what was left of him, just laying out there in the field, the earth barely even blanketing his body, I felt my heart break into a million pieces for that poor boy. Absolutely shattered.

Is there anything you want me to tell your family? I had asked him. *I could find them for you, if you wanted me to. Let them know what happened.*

Nah, Eldridge said, shaking his head, a bit bashful about it all. *What I would say to my family the world has no right to hear...*

Kate had caught on that I was up to no good, seeing me blush the way I was. She asked William to have a word with Eldridge, the two of them taking to the battlefield all over again. Brother against brother one more time. I could've murdered her for it, sicking her pit bull on poor Eldridge like that. She knew Daddy would've had my hide if he knew who I'd been talking to, forcing me to bite my lip and keep quiet about it all. As if what she was doing was any better. Just 'cause William was a member of the Federal army didn't make him any more harmless than the rest of these men, wagging their maggoty-assed tongues at the three of us. Listening to them whistle from their shriveled lips the second we stepped onto these battlefields.

Hey there, young lady! they say. *You got yourself a boyfriend?*

You leave her alone!

Don't be shy now! I promise I won't bite...

You want to talk to her, Kate would say, *you're gonna have to go through me first.*

Sounds fine by me!

Spiritual phenomena had always followed us girls around. Ever since we were younger, it was clear that we'd been touched with clairvoyance. Moving furniture. Ghost lights. Materialized hands hovering through the air. Daddy first discovered our talents when the three of us had been playing in our basement. We had handcrafted our own planchette, taking a heart-shaped chunk of wood and cutting a hole right through the center of it. We used a newspaper as an impromptu talking board, laying the morning edition down flat across the floor so the planchette could glide from letter to letter. Before long, we had made a new friend, channeling the spirit of a child, a little girl who had been murdered by her father right here in our very own home. We would contact her every chance we had, eager to excuse ourselves from the dinner table so we could head downstairs and play.

We were receiving dispatches from the afterlife regularly once the Civil War had started. Once word got out about our talents, there was just no stopping it. Missing children could now find their families. Questions left unanswered for the living could now be remedied by the dead.

Parents weren't the worst of it, honestly. It was all these soldiers. Telegrams from the world beyond our own were sent with such alarming frequency, fueled with such urgency, there were times when there was just no way we could sort through them all. Sometimes these boys just wouldn't shut up. Hearing their voices all at once—we were losing sleep now. Daddy had to take us out of school, all because of the commotion we were causing in our classroom. Wasn't our fault these soldiers wouldn't leave us alone long enough to learn our arithmetic, asking us to contact their families all the time. Let them know where their bodies were buried. Which battlefield. While all we wanted was to practice our math equations, simply trying to act as if nothing was happening. Nothing at all.

Just act normal, Daddy had instructed us. *Don't pay any attention to them.*

But they keep begging us, Daddy, I said. *They won't go away!*

If their families really want to know where they are, they're the ones who will contact us. Not them, you understand?

Daddy managed our accounts now, receiving anywhere from three to five hundred dollars a session. We were in such demand with families the country over, we had to be tutored as we toured.

You girls sense anything? he asked from the battlefield. *Time to find Mrs. James once and for all.*

Please don't make us do this, Daddy, Lela said.

Come now, Lela—just do as we've practiced.

But I don't feel so good...

The sooner we make contact with this young man, the sooner we can all go home and get some rest. Now hurry, honey.

Poor Lela. Her health had been waning ever since we hit the road.

She had a knack for manifesting ectoplasm, usually in thin rivulets, seeping out from where these soldiers had been shot as proof palpable of a spiritual presence. She was a fountain for it ever since she was a little baby. Daddy always thought it was bad allergies, her runny nose refusing to let up whenever there was a ghost in the room, channeling itself through her body. Just bleeding for these boys. Lela rarely got the attention the rest of us received, all on account of her talents lacking certain *sanitary* aspects. She didn't have a chance of standing in the limelight with Kate around, anyhow. All eight years of her life had been spent in her older sister's shadow.

Let's circle up and get this over with, Kate said. *Come on—grab my hand.*

What about Lela?

We don't need her.

I don't think I can do it without her.

What? Poor little Margaret's not strong enough?

Shut up.

You need your little sister to help you?

Kate was just jealous, if you ask me. If it weren't for my skills, we'd still be playing with one of those Ouija boards in our basement up in Rochester. She never would've met William without me. He'd gotten her started on drinking whiskey behind Daddy's back. First William will get her all tipsy, then have her channel his ghost—just so he can intercept the intoxication all for himself. Saying it brings them together, uniting their souls or something like that. She's drunk half the time now. Can't even stand on her own two feet, let alone know where to look for any spirits beyond that bottle. Now Kate's got the gall to say she's pregnant with William's baby, just to raise Daddy's hackles. Can you imagine that child? Must be such an ugly little thing, tethered to a ghostly umbilical cord, connected to a placenta full of ectoplasm. Feeling it kick in her belly like a burst of bad gas.

Well, are we gonna do this or what?

Why don't you find him yourself?

Maybe I will!

Girls, Dad interrupted. *We're wasting daylight...*

I was a better medium than Kate. Always had been, with or without William guiding her along. Something about my youth made me a riper vessel for these spirits to enter. *But it hurt.* Couldn't stand on my own two feet after I was done. Daddy would have to drag me off the field, I'd get so exhausted.

I closed my eyes. Took in a deep breath.

We are speaking now to the spirits of those soldiers abandoned on this battlefield.

We sense that you are with us, Kate said. *Those who cannot rest.*

We sense your presence. Will you speak to us?

There was safety in a contained séance. A small group of people, no more than five or six participants at a time. All sitting around a table. Lights dimmed, save for a single candle. Speaking to spirits in someone's parlor was more manageable, much more controlled—while, out here, touring these battlefields, there was an overwhelming presence on the front line, dense with spectral phenomena. There's no protection against that energy, no shielding us from the sheer number of spirits stranded on these vast stretches of land. We had no choice but to let them enter our bodies once we started, leading them into battle all over again.

Will you communicate with us?

Will you come through to us?

Will you speak to us?

We are here to help you.

Will you speak to us?

Who are you?

Will you speak to us?

What is your name?

Where are you from?

Where is your home?

What is your name?

How did you die?

Is there someone here you wish to communicate with?

Will you speak to us?

Will you tell us why you are not at rest?

Why do you not feel at peace?

Why do you remain?

Will you speak to us?

Tell us—what happened here? What happened on this field?

Tell us, dear spirits. Tell us and you will be free...

Let us see and you will be released from this muddy plane.

Tell us...

Tell us...

Tell us...

The first cannon blast came from the northern corner of the field. The phantasmal sound of mortar shells ripped the air open like thunder, crackling just over our heads. Me and Kate dropped for cover, while Daddy and Mrs. James simply remained standing upright, hearing no sound whatsoever. Lela didn't duck in time, watching her eyes capture the cannonball coming right at her. Her head exploded in a flurry of ectoplasm, a ghostly green sheen showering down over the rest of the field. I could feel a wetness spread across my face, this boy's blood running down my cheeks. Nearly blinding me.

Rifle fire hissed through the atmosphere, mud sputtering up in clumps wherever the shot struck the ground. The soldier just next to me fell to his knees, looking down at his own chest to see himself bleeding. He fell over onto his face, dead before his body could even hit the ground.

I can hear screams. Screams coming from everywhere. This field's alive, boiling over with soldiers. Clutching their muskets, firing at each other.

They're dying. They're dying all around me now.

There—right over there. One boy just took a bayonet thrust into his throat. He's got his hands held up to his neck, palms open and facing upwards, as if he were trying to catch his blood. Save it or something. It's seeping through his fingers, between his knuckles, running down his wrist—but he keeps holding his hands out, cupping his own blood as it spurts up from the wound.

And there—just over there. A soldier has lost his leg. A cannonball just bowled right through a whole row of soldiers, taking out every limb that was in its way. Now the only soldier left standing is this one boy hopping up and down on one foot, the only foot he has left. His arms are held out at his sides to help him keep his balance. He's got his own leg in one hand, the boot still buckled up and everything. Using it as if it were a hammer, knocking another soldier over the head with his heel.

I turn just in time to see a swarm of Confederate soldiers rushing toward us, this blur of gray heading our way. Kate comes charging at me with her musket, driving the end of her bayonet right through the middle of my ribs. I can feel the blade enter my body, parting through my flesh with the ease of a warm knife cutting butter. But the blade gets caught, stuck between my ribs. Kate can't pull free from me. We're connected now, tethered together by her bayonet. There are only a few inches between me and my sister—so I grab her by the throat, choking her with my bare hands. I can see the soldier inside her, his Confederate resonance settled into her eyes, staring back at me, imagining the man who must be inside my body, this echo of a Federal soldier maneuvering through.

Gonna kill you, you Yankee son of a bitch, Kate muttered under her breath.

Seaton. I can feel him struggling from within me. These pinpricks scatter all over my skin. The lack of oxygen suddenly dulls my senses. These tiny black specks start bubbling up inside my eyes, until there's nothing else to see. The last thing I notice is Kate, the look of determination in her face as she drives her bayonet further and further through, pushing me over, the tip of the blade sticking me to the ground like a butterfly in a glass case, framed and dried—then it all goes dark. Absolutely black. I'm numb all over as the cannon-fire fades, the sound of screaming dissipating back into the air.

The battlefield goes quiet again. A silence like the living have never heard.

When I finally come to—I find myself on my back, blinking my eyes. Lela and Kate are off to my side, squatting on the ground. Kate has her face buried into her hands. I can just barely hear her sobbing through her palms, while Lela runs her fingers through her older sister's hair. Combing it back from her face.

Daddy and Mrs. James are hovering above me now. All the color has rushed right out from Mrs. James' face, the blood in her cheeks washing away.

What happened? she asks. *Did you—did you see him?*

Turning over, I manage to pick myself up onto my knees. I'm staring down at the grassless ground directly beneath me. I take a deep breath and begin digging with my bare hands. The earth's still soft here. Parts open so easily for me. I've only got a few inches to go before I reach the front slope of his skull, slipping my fingers around its domed surface until I can uproot it from the mud. I try wiping off the clumps of red clay still clinging to Seaton's face, cleaning him up as best I can for his mother.

Found him.

pick of the litter

Look at them go. Nothing but a knot of limbs, all tangled up into one another. You've got to hand it to the mommy who's generous enough to donate a whole box of sidewalk chalk to the rest of the playground—but there's blood in the water now. These kids are like kindergarten sharks gnashing over the last scraps of chum. Wouldn't want to reach my hand in there. Probably wouldn't get all my fingers back.

Careful, kids! Watch out for the little ones. No biting now. Elbows down.

Playgrounds can be pretty intense with the pecking order, can't they? The children are one thing, but I'm talking about the parents. All the adults just sit back on the park benches, ringside seats, letting their kids have at it. See who survives.

You've got the nannies, who could give a crap. They simply toss their kids into the mix and then chat on their phone for the next few hours. They barely glance up from their manicure while their ward is off getting garroted with the swing set.

You've got the daddies—but they're a rare bird around these parts. Might as well be looking for a unicorn out here. They never know what they're supposed to be doing with themselves.

And then you've got the mommies. All the mommies. They cluster together in their corner to compare juice box brands or whatever. They're more interested in chatting among themselves than whatever's happening out here. Don't get me wrong. They'll occasionally look over their shoulders, just to make sure it's somebody else's kid that's screaming their little head off—not theirs.

Is anybody even watching their kids out here? Did you just see what that boy did to that other boy? Did anyone see what just happened to that little girl?

It's like a free-for-all out here. The punching. The dry-humping. The kicking and clawing. The spitting. The hair-pulling. The gnashing and the gnawing.

Does anybody even care what happens to our kids?

I come here to relax. I actually find it peaceful here, believe it or not. With all the wrangling I do back at home, it's just nice to sit here. Take a breather.

I'm not going to lie—I steer clear of the other mothers here. Their club. I'd rather just watch the children. They're more interesting, anyways.

Ever try to guess whose kid is whose? All you've got to do is scan the crowd and see if you can pinpoint which kid belongs to which parent. It's fun.

Come on. Let's play.

That girl. In the sundress with the pink flowers? My guess is she belongs to that mom over there. They share that same air, that hoity-toity, *me-me-me* vibe.

That boy. The one with the skinned knee? Tough call. I'm going to go out on a limb here and say he belongs to—*wait*. I'm going nanny on this one. With the way he's acting out there, there's no way his mother's got eyes on him. Like a freaking Tasmanian devil. Get that kid on his Ritalin already. He's nanny material all the way.

How about her?

Over there. On the slide. With the pigtails. It's like the whole park belongs to her. She's not bossy, like the others. Everything else seems to... just seems to radiate around her. It's her playground. The rest of us are just playing on it, you know?

They're so perfect when they're that young. It's a shame to think she'll lose that cuteness in a few years. The older they grow, the more they lose that beauty.

Can't stay cuddly forever, I guess. Everybody's got to grow up sooner or later.

That's usually when I give them back. I'll just drop them off at the playground—any playground, they're all the same—and pick up a new one.

Which one's mine? Good question. I haven't quite decided yet. Usually, the right one just kind of comes to me. I'll know when I see her. Or him. I'm not picky. It's just a matter of knowing when to swoop in when their mother isn't looking.

Everything comes to those who wait.

There she is.

Excuse me.

sisterhood of the salamander

Sister Asís was the first to lick the salamander's back. All by accident, she confessed. Eventually. Such a flighty child. Always with her head in the clouds. Handling the *ajolote de fuego* is a sacred act. It must always be done with rubber gloves, to protect our skin against its neurotoxic exudations. *No part of your bare body shall ever come into contact with that of the salamander.* This has been the way of our sisterhood for generations now. But such precautions must have slipped Sister Asís' mind as she carelessly wiped the sweat from her brow while still gripping a mature axolotl in her hands. The mustard from its flaming mane rubbed across her lips, numbing themselves in seconds. As she inhaled its herbaceous fragrance, the ruddy musk settled into her lungs until it burned to breathe, every last branching bronchiole on fire in her chest.

Its mustard was so pungent. So piquant. Sister Asís found herself craving a taste. Who among us could resist a simple lick? Just the tiniest dash on the tip of her tongue. Surely no one here would fault her for such a minor trifle as this. Not even God would judge her for sampling one of His small wonders. But once she began lapping at the salamander's skin habitually—shall we say *ritualistically*—during her tenure tending to the axolotl, there's no denying Sister Asís experienced something the rest of the vestals never had before.

Something miraculous.

I saw her, Sister Asensio, she vowed to us on one of our daily visits, checking in on her as she convalesced in her quarters. *Such beauty. Such warmth...*

Sister Asís is one of our youngest nuns. Just a girl, really. Her calling remains in question among the rest of us. Always given to flights of fancy, even before her visions.

We went ahead and asked her who. *Who was it that you saw, child?*

The Virgin, she beamed, already drifting off to images only her eyes could witness. *I saw the Virgin Mary, wrapped in flames...*

The Basilica de Nuestra Señora de la Arpía sits atop one of the highest peaks in the region. The convent was built in the early 1500s from stones dredged from the local quarry. Those stones were dragged up the mountain. They became our home. Our cloister has stood overlooking Lake Pátzcuaro for centuries. Less than a dozen nuns live here now. Though our numbers have dwindled over the generations, each has answered a singular calling.

We are the Sisterhood of the Salamander.

~

The mural of the Virgin was painted well before our generation. See the lake. See the salamanders swimming within its blue waters. See the Virgin Mary walking along its surface, hands held out at her sides, her flaming blue fingers pointing to the heavens above, the water below. We do not know who painted this vision, but it is a vision—a dream—we sisters have all had at some point in our life. This vision, this dream, was our calling. Once we had this dream, we knew where our paths led. The dream brought us here. To this basilica. To the salamanders.

Our convent's primary congregant is the *ajolote de fuego*. You will not find pews here, but aquariums. Dozens of murky tanks line the crumbling plaster walls, stacked one on top of another, each filled with water taken from the lake below and carried back up the mountain by the bucketful. We must treat the water first. Purge it of its pollutants.

For we house the last of the fire salamander.

Only four hundred *ajolote de fuego* remain in existence. Our salamanders are the last of their kind. We tend to them, nurture them, and in return they give us their mustard. *Samandarin* is the name science has given the alkaloid secreted from the salamander's dorsal glands, but we sisters have always called this precious poison *mostaza*. Simply grazing its pale alabaster skin caused convulsions, perhaps paralysis, among the stone masons working alongside the quarry. But over time, and practice, the sisterhood came to discover small, more refined quantities of its mustard had a medicinal aspect to it. It carries the power to heal.

She has healed me, Sister Asís insisted. *Blessed me. The Virgin Mary touched my soul.*

But sister, we said, gently chiding her. *Don't you see? Your body is merely reacting to the mustard. You are having a physical reaction to the salamander's own natural defenses...*

Sister Asís only shook her head. Pitying us. This girl, this child, twenty years our junior, pitying her own mother superior. *The Virgin will show you, Sister Asensio,* she whispered in a tone we did not appreciate. *She will show you when you are ready to see. Then you will believe.*

Our convent has supported itself off the proceeds made from selling cough syrup made from the salamander. It is a painstaking process that can only be accomplished by the mother superior. We have perfected our methods over the years, teaching each other how to hold the axolotls, how to wrap our gloved fingers around its throat and squeeze *just so*, sliding our pinkie around the base of its neck and hook back around in the gentlest noose, until its fern-like gills fan out and begin to drip. We must be ready to receive each tiny droplet of that most precious nectar, letting them soak into a cotton ball that is then whisked off to our ventilated kitchen where it is boiled down to its barest essence. Only the mother superior is permitted in the kitchen while reducing the mustard, for fear the fumes might asphyxiate anyone not wearing the proper face mask.

The recipe for our cough syrup is as old as the convent. It is said our basilica had only been built for less than a year when a young girl, no older than ten, came walking down the mountain without any shoes on her feet. No one knew who this child was. The nuns believed she must have been of the indigenous people who lived throughout the mountain area before the Spanish colonized the region. In her bare hands, she carried an *ajolote de fuego.* The first salamander. Flames fanned out from its pink gills, a halo around its pale head. The girl was wrapped in a ghastly plasma, as blue in hue as the cool water of the lake. Cerulean flames rippled all around her. But the girl did not burn. There was no smoke. She released the salamander into the lake and the water went ablaze. A Lake of Fire. It was blinding. Such luminescence! The sisters had to shield their eyes. To look at the water was to stare straight into the sun. *Look unto me, sisters*, the girl spoke, *for I shall heal the wounded, those who are blind I shall make see, and those who believe I shall show such wondrous things to behold...*

That girl was none other than the Virgin Mary. Who else would have been capable of creating such an elixir? Simply rubbing the mustard over your chest cleared any congestion. All aches and pains washed away within its mentholated flames. Her recipe has since been whispered from sister to sister. We dare not write it down. It is our burden, our blessing.

We are the sole holders of the recipe. We tend to the axolotl. It is our duty, our calling, to create the syrup. It was passed down to us by the previous mother superior. One day, before we breathe our last, we will whisper its mysteries to our successor. And so on.

We are never to partake of the mustard. No nun is ever permitted to taste. Our meals have never been prepared with much seasoning. The food has always been bland to our tongue, no thanks to inhaling so much of the mentholated fumes from our work in the kitchen. But the salamander's secretion, the mustard, supposedly has a particular piquancy. It is sharp. Rich.

Can't you feel its peppermint intensity? The cool heat radiating off its skin? Opening up the airways in your lungs? Salving the swell of blood cells in your nasal cavities?

Healing you?

Who among us hasn't been tempted to taste it? To lick the salamander's back?

This is our way. This has always been the sisterhood's way.

Until Sister Asís.

~

By the time her indiscretion was discovered, she had already slipped into anaphylactic shock. The mustard had tapped into her nervous system, sending her into an epileptic fit across the stone floor. She was hallucinating. Foaming at the mouth. Crying out to the Virgin.

She is here, Sister Asís called out. *She walks among us!*

We have seen the numbers of *ajolote de fuego* dwindle during our time here at the convent. Seen how the water suffers. Pollution permeates the lake now. Raw sewage suffocates its aquatic inhabitants. The flora, the fauna, have all become endangered.

The sisterhood has taken it upon ourself to salvage the salamanders. To save them at whatever cost. We have our own hatchery in the convent, turning our bathtubs into a breeding ground for future generations of axolotl. We no longer bathe. No longer need to. Every last tub is now full of hundreds of eggs. The fiery larvae, little amphibious candlewicks.

But their numbers continue to dwindle. They are dying.

Our salamander is dying.

The axolotl never was of this earth, Sister Asís presumptuously attempted to explain to us in her delirious state. *They are angels. They come bearing a gift. A gift from God...*

Such mutterings were nonsense. We feared the mustard had taken hold of her mind, reducing her to these wild ravings. She clutched on to our wrist and pulled herself upright in her cot. Her eyes latched on to ours, her stare suddenly full of a disarming clarity.

The gift is within me, she said. *I hold the fire.*

Word of Sister Asís's visions quickly spread throughout the convent. Whispers like wildfire. How could they not? She claimed to have seen flaming angels—not with wings, but fiery gills branching out from their necks. *I see them,* she cried. *There they are! They are here! Look at them, flying down from heaven, setting the clouds afire! Look at them land in the lake!*

~

Sister Asís has been confined to her cot. Her visions have persisted, which has only stirred a commotion among the other nuns. We all knew what she had done. That she had partaken of the majestic mustard. *She is here*, she said, ecstatic. *The Virgin is with us!*

This was not the convent's way. For generations, we have been told to tend to our amphibious flock. Not to partake. Not to enjoy. It is not our place to taste the pleasures of the salamander. But now other sisters are sneaking in their licks. We take turns tending to the axolotl. It is our duty to feed them. Clean the aquariums. Squeeze the mustard. Their alabaster bodies look as if they are made of marble. Pale albino skin laced in pink veins. Pink eyes rimmed in red. Their pink gills are fern-like filaments that branch out at either side of their throat, fanning through the water, as if their heads were on fire. Oscillating flames.

It isn't difficult to determine who among us has tasted the mustard. Some sisters' skin has taken on a wet complexion, as if they are covered in sweat. But no, this is not perspiration. They are coated in a thin, translucent film, much like a layer of slime. Under certain light, it leaves them looking as if they are glistening, shimmering, wrapped in a halo.

Sister Asís's visions are shared among the others. Now more nuns are bearing witness to this miracle.

A sister puts one of the axolotl larvae into their mouths, sealing the salamander within their lips, letting it rest on their tongue, feeling it wriggle along the roof of their palate, letting it explore that darkened grotto, letting it muster its mustard within their mouths. Its first mustarding. The flicker of its tail against their tongue. Like kissing. Deep, passionate kissing.

Speaking in tongues.

Flaming tongues. Like candles lighting our path.

Our way.

~

We have looked in on Sister Asís as she has continued to convalesce. She no longer speaks to us—or rather, no longer talks in a way that we can understand. She speaks in tongues, communing with the angels all around her. She looks so feverish. So slick. Her habit is always soaked in sweat. When we finally decide to pull Sister Asís' wimple away to wipe her brow, we gasp. There, wrapped around her neck, we find gills. A fern-like pair of fiery pink gills fan out from either side of her throat. They oscillate with every shallow breath, every infinitesimal bronchiole spreading out as she tries to inhale, clasping at the air all around her.

Sister Asís needs to return to the lake.

We all must return to its waters.

The journey down the mountain is difficult, but we are able to guide Sister Asís down the craggy path with the aid of our hand. She slides into the waters without any struggle. Her head slips below the surface, punctuated by the last of her air bubbling up from below. We wait for her to resurface. And wait. After ten minutes elapses, we know Sister Asís is at home.

Others follow. Sister Tomas. Sister Iglesias. Each hears her calling of the salamander and answers. The sacred kiss of the axolotl. The divine lick. That mentholated baptism.

We vow to lead them all down to the quarry. They take our hand. We hold them upright, offer assurances, one foot after the other, guiding them to the shore—*Here you are, sister*—as the others watch on, our dwindling sisterhood bearing witness to this miracle, that final step on dry land before returning to the waters whence they came.

~

I am the last.

The basilica is empty now. I have waited to receive my calling, tending to the *ajolote de fuego* alone. The last batch of larvae has now been born. Their eggs have all hatched.

I hold an infant salamander in my palms, as if my hands are a cup. A chalice of flesh and blood. The salamander slithers across my bare skin. It is cool at first. Wet. Then it begins to burn. I can feel the heat. The singe sinks into my skin. I have never touched one of the salamanders with my bare hands before. After all these years tending to them, caring for them, I have never given myself over to them. Never let myself feel their warmth. Their gift. Such heat. My hands are on fire now. A cool-hued flame seeps into my palms, my skin, my very bones.

I bring my hands up. I open my mouth and receive this amphibious sacrament. I run my tongue along the length of its back. Its skin is granular. Coarse. There is a wet coating, an incendiary slime, like napalm. Greasy heat. When the tip of my tongue reaches its frilly mane, I swear I have touched an open flame. It has a fierce heat. A candle branching out at both sides of its neck. I can't help but gasp. I inhale it. Its musk. Its flame. The heat rushes down my throat, filling my lungs like a flood of fire looking for somewhere, anywhere, to settle. And burn. It burns to breathe. I hold this hot coal in my mouth as it swallows me and I swallow it and we become one, finally become one, my whole body now consumed by flame.

I am on fire. Such vivid colors surround me now. I am covered in a cool, butane blue.

I have returned to my sisters. All my sisters. We are shimmering. Glistening in God's light under the waters of Lake Pátzcuaro. We are evolving. Becoming in Her likeness.

We are the Sisterhood of the Salamander.

knockoffs

Noticed any welts yet? Pink sores along your legs? The marks tend to cluster together in tight rows. That's them, alright... Their feeding trail. Itches like a son of a bitch, doesn't it?

I don't want to alarm you, but... if you're waking up in the middle of the night with your skin prickling, like something just slithered across your shin, chances are you're already infested.

Tubby Wubbies.

Ugly-looking things. Like a sock monkey mated with a lamprey. Their lengthy limbs are twice the size of their tube-shaped body, these slender tentacles flapping about their sides. They come in all kinds of different colors. Let's see, there are blue ones, red ones, even tie-dyed ones. I've spotted a couple that come in Christmas colors, complete with a Santa Claus cap.

They're making their way down the block, hopping from one house to the next.

The Hendricks definitely have them.

Lancasters, too.

Nobody's openly talking about them—*yet*—because nobody's

willing to admit they're beset by these plush pests. Heaven fucking forbid anyone else knows. Everybody's so afraid of becoming neighborhood pariahs, so it's lips sealed up and down the street... but I'm telling you, it's too late for that. We're all dealing with these pesky sons of bitches—the whole fucking suburb—and anyone who says we're not is either lying straight to your face or they just haven't realized it yet. But they will, trust me. Everyone will know soon enough.

The Tubby Wubbies are here to stay.

Call an exterminator, you say. Of course. We sure did. Tell him it's termites. You'd be blessed if it was bed bugs. Ten bucks says the Orkin Man tells you the exact same thing he told us last week:

Burning the house down might be your best option.

Which is just what I did.

I switched on the pilot to our stove without lighting it, pumping the whole house full of gas for a few hours, letting it settle in every last room before I struck that fucking match aaand—

Buh-bye, Tubby Wubbies. Hope you all burn in hell.

It's the only way to get rid of them. The only way.

Unless you're hungry.

~

This all started with Kendra. My wife and I can't be the only parents who've been incrementally losing their daughter to YouTube, video by video. Six years old and she's already hypnotized by her tablet. Jenn and I set strict time limits, but the girl simply won't listen. She's obsessed. If we take her iPad away, she'll erupt. Just an endless temper tantrum. Kicking. *Shrieking.*

Kendra's always cranky when she comes out of one of her screen-time K-holes, but cutting her off mid-vid is like severing a six-year-old junkie from its fix. You don't want that.

Don't judge. Jenn and I are—*were*—work-at-home progenitors, so any parental reprieve was a necessary godsend. Most days I honestly have no idea what she's watching. Harmless content from what I could tell. Kids unboxing stuff. We put the parental controls on, so I wasn't worried.

But it became clear we needed to drag our daughter back from the algorithmic brink.

Back to the land of the living.

Kendra had never been to New York before, so Jenn and I thought we'd surprise her with a birthday trip to the Big Apple. Three nights, no screens. Our fam crammed in as many sights as we possibly could, ticking off all the touristy spots. We walked across the Brooklyn Bridge. We caught a Broadway show. Wandered through Times Square. Hell, we even visited Chinatown.

That's when I first saw them.

I spotted one on Mott Street among all the other knockoff tchotchkes, this kudzu of stuffies tangling up with the yellow taxi cabs. The mini Statue of Liberties. The King Kongs grabbing on to tiny Empire State Buildings. But I'd never seen this—whatever this was—before.

What the hell is that? I remember thinking. *Did a piranha fuck a Furby?*

The smile was the worst of it. It had a toothsome grin that took up half of its head. More than half. Thin teeth the size of rice grains spilled out from its lips. It had oversized cartoon eyes, wide open saucers of milk with the tiniest irises. Just a black dollop of ink.

It must have come from some animated show, right? That's the origin of nearly every widely branded piece of IP these days. The content had to come from *somewhere*. A multi-pronged corporate creation spawned in a consumerist-based think tank, spreading its nefarious tentacles into all quadrants—streaming, merchandising, feature film. Ubiquitous branding. But for the life of me, I couldn't fathom what kind of children's program would spawn something as vicious as this. Definitely not something I'd ever seen. There's no way I'd ever let Kendra watch a show that had one of these as a recurring character, whatever the hell it was.

There was Velcro stitched into its palms—hook and loop stigmata—so it could clasp on to anything and just dangle there. My eyes landed on a blue one, but these creatures came in all kinds of colors. Pink. Purple. Green. Black. Grateful Dead tie-dye. Mickey Mouse mash-ups.

What parent in their right mind would buy one of these hideous things for their kids?

Who would ever want to bring one home?

Tubby Wubby! Kendra shouted. *Can I get one, Daddy, pleeeease?*

She knew its name. It didn't sink in at the time—it sure as shit should have—but my little girl was so well-versed in Tubby Wubby lore, that she already knew exactly what it was called. I had no context to comprehend what cartoon it came from, what kind of animated nightmare could spawn this abomination... But she knew its name. How could Kendra know its name?

Don't you want a snow globe? I asked. *They've got one of the Statue of Liberty...*

I really, reeeeally want a Tubby Wubby.

What about an Empire State—Pleeease, Daddy, pleeeeeeeeeease?

OK, OK, we'll get you a Tubby Whatever...

Ten bucks. The transaction was swift. All business, no nonsense. The guy manning the foldout card table kept glancing over his shoulder, like at any minute a police officer might stroll by and this whole sidewalk enterprise would get shut down. I noticed a soggy cardboard box tucked underneath his table, filled to the brim with these stuffed animals. The box itself looked like it was barely holding itself together anymore, the cardboard's structural integrity about to disintegrate after a few too many days in the rain. I could see the water stains. Probably fell off the back of a truck in Jersey and this guy's unloading them onto tourists. Totally legit business.

I had to ask: *What the heck are these?*

Your guess is as good as mine, man... TV show, maybe?

You don't know?

I just sell 'em.

Looks like you've got a few. I nodded to the box. Seeing so many all tangled together made them look like some rainbow brand of fur coats for kids to wear. Technicolor mink stoles, with their heads still attached, so you knew what kind of animal it had been before they skinned it. Gave me the creeps, just looking at all those floppy bodies knotted into one another, a litter of boneless puppies, seeing their wide-open eyes leering up from the flaps of that cardboard box. All with the exact same grinning rictuses, brimming with rice grain canines.

You sure you don't want another? This guy leaned in real close, until I smelled the taint of his breath. *I'll give you a deal. Three for the price of two. Come on, take 'em home with you.*

One's more than enough, thanks.

Now that I'd seen one, I swear I saw Tubby Wubbies wherever we went. It wasn't just Chinatown. They were littered all through Times Square. On the Brooklyn Bridge. Every sidewalk seller had a nest to sell. They dangled from display racks in just about every storefront I passed.

Jesus, they were everywhere.

Everywhere.

This city has a real Tubby Wubby problem, I joked with Jenn. *And here I thought cockroaches were going to be the worst of it...*

Better than bedbugs, Jenn joked right back at me. *I'd take an outbreak of Tubby Wubbies over bedbugs any day...*

Kendra didn't let go of her Tubby Wubby for the whole trip. She slept with it every night in our hotel, hugging it tight to her chest, squeezing it until she fell asleep. I'll admit, it weirded me out, seeing those rice-grain teeth so close to her ear. I had to push out the pervading thought that this thing would suddenly spring to life and nibble on her lobe. Gnaw it right off.

Kendra clutched her Tubby Wubby on the train ride home, all seven hours. She kept it crammed into her armpit on her first night back in our house, staring at me as I tucked her in.

Did you have a fun trip?

Kendra nodded.

What was your favorite part? Let me guess. Was it... the Statue of Liberty?

Kendra shrugged.

Was it... The Lion King*?*

Another shrug.

FAO Schwarz?

Another.

I give up.

Tubby Wubbeeeeeey! Kendra thrust hers into my face. I reeled my head back to avoid impact with its blue fur. For a second, I thought—actually thought—it nipped at my nose.

The stitching around its left eye was already coming loose. This cheap sweatshop tchotchke couldn't keep itself together longer than a few days before it started falling apart. *Splendid*. This plushy probably wouldn't last longer than a week before it completely unraveled, spilling tufts of toxic wadding all over the house. Just our luck. Kendra would be completely heartbroken. Poor kid. She loved that damn Tubby Wubby to its own demise, wearing it all out.

Not that I'd particularly miss it.

Who would've thought some creepy knockoff from a sidewalk vendor would bring so much joy to our child? Beggars can't be choosers, I guess. It didn't matter to Kendra that we spent a couple thousand bucks on overpriced meals, nosebleed seats to a musical we'd already seen the movie of a million times. All Kendra needed was a tourist trap plushie to make her day.

But you know what? Worth every penny.

Know why?

Kendra hadn't asked for her tablet once in fifty-two hours. She hadn't demanded screentime since I bought her that fugly Tubby Wubby. No YouTube videos, no temper tantrums, no obsessive-compulsive ADHD freakouts. Nothing but love for that limp-limbed tapeworm.

I'd take it. I went to bed—our own bed, in our own house, under our own roof—feeling like the vacation was a success. I closed my eyes, happy to be home again.

Mission accomplished.

There were dreams of ticklings. Soft slitherings. Velvety limbs slipping over my skin. I couldn't sink very deep into my sleep, never achieving REM-levels of slumber, simply adrift along the surface of unconsciousness, sensing something furry sliding along my body in bed.

I thought I dreamed of getting garroted by a sock monkey.

The next morning, I spotted Kendra's Tubby Wubby in the hall. *Weird.* Its tube-sock torso was slumped against the wall, limbs sprawled along the floor. My first thought was: *What is Kendra's Tubby Wubby doing out here? Did she throw it out of her bedroom? Toss it in the hall?*

And isn't hers blue?

This one was pink.

I picked it up. Studied it. Its flimsy limbs flipped and flopped. Their bodies had no bones. Of course. It was a stuffed animal. But still. A part of me expected there might be some kind of skeletal system underneath its vibrant velvety pelt. So flimsy. A limp sock with tentacle legs.

I brought it back to Kendra. I was on early morning autopilot, so I wasn't thinking much more than the task at hand: deposit her Tubby Wubby to her room, among her other stuffies.

But Kendra's Tubby Wubby was already there. The blue one.

In bed. With her.

Kendra was fast asleep, all snuggled up next to her Tubby Wubby. Its eyes were wide open—awake, as if it had been waiting—staring back at me, its lips lifted in that sickly cheery leer, so close to my daughter's ear. Ready to take a bite right out from her candy-apple cheek.

So. Quick mental-health check: *If Kendra still has her Tubby Wubby*, my sanity asked...

Whose am I holding?

I brought the stuffy up, examining it again. Closer this time. Aside for the different color fur, it looked exactly the same. Same design. Same pattern. Same teeth. Same limbs. Same eyes.

How could we suddenly have two of them now?

I nudged Kendra, waking her. She propped herself in bed, all groggy, rubbing her eyes.

Where did this come from?

Kendra just shrugged.

Answer me. Where?

Shrug. She wasn't giving me anything, so next up was Jenn. I took the Tubby Wubby back to our bedroom and asked her if she'd bought another Tubby Wubby when I wasn't looking.

It wasn't me, hon, she said, *sorry...*

Could Kendra have stolen it?

Don't you think our daughter's a little young to be shoplifting?

I don't know! Maybe she did it by accident. Maybe she saw one and wanted it and didn't realize it was stealing... I'm just trying to understand how we have another one in our house.

Jenn wasn't nearly as concerned about this Tribble proliferation issue as I personally felt like she should've been. She dismissed the extra Tubby Wubby as mere miscommunication.

Shit happens, basically. Case closed. It was the Monday after a three-day vacation, so Jenn was ready to get back to the grind of our lives. Get Kendra off to school. Get back to work.

Hindsight sure is fucking twenty-twenty.

I noticed the third Tubby Wubby the very next morning. This one had purple fur. So soft. Just another knockoff. A photocopy of a photocopy. It didn't move. Or do anything, really. It wasn't like it was alive. It was just some stupid stuffed animal! Some cartoon character for a television show I'd never seen or even heard of. Right? That's all this was, yes? It had to be.

Where the fuck did they keep coming from?

How were there so many in my house?

There was a chance—just a slim possibility—that this could've still been one of the most elaborate pranks ever pulled on me in my life. My wife was punking me. All fun and games. Kendra and Jenn bought a dozen of these things when we were up in New York and had them shipped home, and now they've been slowly doling them out, making me think they've been multiplying in some kind of Mogwai madness, just to mess with me. Make me think I was losing my mind.

Hardy har, har. You all had your laugh. Look at what a dodo Dad is, but... fun's over now.

Again, I took it straight to Kendra. She had to know what was going on here. I had no authority in my tone this time, no control over the moment. I needed my daughter's help.

Where did this come from, hon?

She shrugged.

You don't know, or you don't want to tell me?

Kendra just shrugged. Again.

Kendra. Answer me. Please.

Her hands slid up and down her legs. Clearly Kendra didn't want to talk about it. That's when I noticed the welts on her leg. Tiny pink marks scattered in a pattern along her shin.

Nibbles.

Bedbugs, Jenn panicked. *Oh, Jesus, we brought home a batch of bedbugs.* She was so sure of it, ready to go to DEFCON 2, just like that. We'd have to throw everything out, all of our soft belongings. Our entire wardrobe. Our furniture. The carpeting. Fumigate the whole house.

I wasn't so convinced. *Did something bite you, Kendra? Do you know what it was?*

Tubby Wubby, was all Kendra said.

You're saying Tubby Wubby did this?

She nodded. Slowly.

What's a Tubby Wubby, honey?

It's a stuffy.

No, I mean... Is it a cartoon? A movie? Where does it come from?

Kendra shrugged. *I dunno.*

What do you mean you don't know? You have to know. You said you needed one.

Shrug.

Where did you first see Tubby Wubby?

Silence. Nothing. Not even a shrug.

Kendra... Tell me. Where? Where have you seen Tubby Wubby?

YouTube, she eventually said.

Fuck me.

Turns out Tubby Wubby was a character for some kind of video game that you find online. Kendra's never played it. She was way too young. As a matter of fact, she didn't even know it was a video game to begin with or what the name of the game even was. Thank Christ.

That didn't stop Tubby Wubby from reaching her. Wrapping its elbow-less limbs around her life and squeeeeeeezing.

Apparently, kids take this character from this game they've never played and make their own fan-tribute videos. Crudely animated cartoons. Songs. You name it.

All to honor Tubby Wubby.

YouTube's algorithm gladly takes all that Tubby Wubby content and kids like Kendra are swept away by autoplay, tumbling down a rabbit hole of remixed Tubby Wubby vids.

None of that explained why they were propagating in my house.

Or how. Or why.

Why? Why is this happening to my family? Why us? What did we do to deserve this?

All we did was go to New York, for Christ's sake. I just bought some goddamn doll.

I grabbed them all. Even the original. I found a fourth—Christ, a fifth—when I scoured Kendra's bedroom, just to make sure I got them all. Kendra protested, but I wouldn't hear it.

I tossed them straight into the trash. Proliferate in a landfill, for all I cared.

That ought to do it. Problem solved.

Jenn found a few welts on her hip that night. A snaking trail of pink bitemarks. *Goddamn bedbugs*, she groaned. *This is a nightmare. A total fucking nightmare.*

We've all heard stories of families forced to throw out their entire wardrobe because of a bedbug infestation. They get in your books. Your furniture. Every last worldly possession. You have to go scorched earth on your home. Raze it all down to the studs and start over again.

I'm never going back to New York as long as I fucking live, Jenn said, nearly in tears.

But of course it wasn't bedbugs. I already knew what—*who*—the culprit was.

Fucking Tubby Wubby.

When I tried to explain this to Jenn, she looked at me like I'd just told her I was having an affair with Jessica Rabbit or Betty Boop and these Tubby Wubbies were my illegitimate half-animated children. She wasn't a believer, to say the least. She hadn't seen them like I had.

Just call an exterminator, she said, coolly. Distant.

I know it sounds crazy. Don't you think I know?

Please. Jenn raised her hand, halting the conversation. *Just call an exterminator.*

You know how many questions I had to deflect the second the Orkin man's van pulled up in front of our house? How everyone on the block was suddenly brimming with suspicion?

Saw the exterminator paid you a visit, pal... Whatcha dealing with? Termites?

The Hendricks.

Couldn't help but notice you got yourself a pest problem... What is it? Ants?

The Lancasters.

Looks like you got some vermin on your hands. Sure hope it doesn't spread.

The Tubby Wubbies.

This is where I should've come clean and confessed that, yes, it was our family who brought the Tubby Wubbies to the block. Our house was ground zero for our neighborhood's outbreak.

I honestly thought I could contain it. That I had it under control. For a few days, I did. But then I caught them crawling in our walls, chewing through the insulation, gnawing on the soft parts of our home—our pillows, all our clothes—before I realized they had already hopped onto the wood framing. Eating Sheetrock. Nibbling into the electrical system. The plumbing. They hollowed our whole house out in less than a week. Hell, they were even eating us!

Jenn was still convinced it was bedbugs. We wouldn't be the first family to take a trip to New York City, stay in some mid-range midtown hotel, and bring home a few unwanted stowaways. That's what Yelp was for. Her battle plan was to get our money back. Make the hotel pay for our exterminator bill or else she'd hop online and let everyone know exactly who and where we got our new roommates from. She wanted revenge against the mayor of New York. Demand that Manhattan give us a refund. For her, having bedbugs was embarrassing enough. You can't regale dinner guests with stories of determined vermin without them retreating from your home. None of our neighbors would ever visit us again if they thought we were infested with bloodsucking insects. Jenn made me swear not to mention our little pestilence problem to anyone. Not the Lancasters. Definitely not the Hendricks. Heaven fucking forbid they found out our dirty l'il secret. We'd be ostracized from the block faster than you could say *suburban lepers.*

The exterminator didn't find any signs of them... Not a single exoskeleton.

Call another exterminator. I want a second opinion.

This isn't bedbugs, hon... You've got to believe me.

Don't. Don't you dare start in with—

It's Tubby—

DON'T!

~

After Jenn and Kendra checked into the closest hotel, I had the run of our house to myself, trying to rectify this tender situation—our domestic pestilence—before it spread to the next house. And the next. It was only a matter of time, I knew, until one of these little buggers slipped out a window. This was only the beginning of our neighborhood's Tubby Wubby woes.

I dug a little deeper online, just to see what I might find. Turns out the company behind Tubby Wubby didn't trademark their own character. For the first few months after their little indie video game was released online, just about anyone could take Tubby Wubby and turn him into whatever mutated content they wanted and not have to worry over any copyright infringement. That's where all these cheap knockoffs spawned from. The marketplace was flooded with pirated Tubby Wubby stuffies. Tubby Wubby T-shirts. Tubby Wubby tampons.

But why were they infesting my house?

Where did they come from?

There's a customer service hotline for the game, so of course I called. This felt like a better solution than another exterminator at this point. Go straight to the source. Beg for help.

I have a Tubby Wubby situation.

I'm sorry to hear that, sir, but... we're software designers. The operator on the other end of the line kept a very even tone. She stuck to her prescripted spiel. It sounded like this is something they've been dealing with for a while now: *We just make the game, not the dolls.*

They're not dolls. They're real. They're everywhere. They're in my house. In my bed—

I understand, sir, but... there's really nothing we can do. It's not our problem.

How can you say that? How is this not your problem? You made Tubby Wubby. You're the ones who created the goddamn thing in the first fucking place—

The character, yes. Not the plushies.

How can you not deal with this?

We're trying, trust me... We've hired a copyright lawyer. We've had customs incinerate over five hundred thousand of these things before they get into the country. But they still do.

So, you're saying... Wait. What are you saying?

Learn to live with them, she said—off-the-cuff and off-script.

I can't believe this. This is a nightmare. A fucking nightmare...

Things got real quiet on the other end of the line. At first, I thought she'd hung up on me. Then I heard her breath catch before she asked in the lowest tone, *Have you tried one yet?*

Tried one... what?

Eating them.

~

I couldn't sleep that night. I lay there in bed, on my back, staring up at the ceiling, just waiting for that first wriggle. When nothing came, I climbed out of bed. Wandered our house.

I peered into Kendra's bedroom. She'd forgotten her tablet. It was left on her bed, among all her other stuffies. The goofy dogs and harmless rabbits. A plush mass grave.

I climbed in. Got comfy.

I grabbed her tablet. Tapped the screen. When it woke up, it immediately leaped to YouTube. There was a video teed up and everything, like it was waiting for me. Ready to watch.

YouTube's autoplay lines up the next video so you never even have to click. You can just watch video after video without ever needing to touch the screen, descending deeper and deeper into the darkest recesses of the website. I couldn't help but wonder: *How far down can I go? Does it ever end? Will I just keep descending and descending and never reach the bottom?*

There's bound to be a bottom, right?

What's below?

I started off with an innocuous Tubby Wubby tribute video. A boy close to Kendra's age talked all about his love for Tubby Wubby. That immediately led to another video with a group of older kids, somewhere in their teens, playing the actual video game—*Tubby Wubby's Toon Time*, I discovered it was called. The pre-recorded livestream of their Twitch channel led to yet another video of some fan-made amateur animation of Tubby Wubby's boinking a Teletubby which led to yet another video of some kind of animated orgy between a few My Little Ponies and I believe a reach-around from none other than Barney which led to yet another video of Tubby Wubby garroting a prisoner in some kind of Abu Ghraib-style prison cell, drab concrete walls drenched in blood, but instead of a black hood over this inmate's head, the entirety of his face is sheathed in slithering Tubby Wubbies, nothing but Tubby Wubbies suffocating his airways and oh my God, what have I been watching, what time is it, how many hours did I just lose, how deep into the algorithm did I go, how deep do these videos go, how far down the rabbit hole?

Tubby Wubby has taken on a life of its own. These videos removed context from its creation. They remixed its existence. It was unlicensed, free from trademark infringement. Any copyright squatter could extend the parameters of Tubby Wubby's origin story until it reached cosmic proportions, free from legal restrictions. Tubby Wubby didn't belong to anyone anymore. It belonged to *everyone*. It lived in an algorithm. And it came back in a soft body.

A body with no bones.

How do you create brand awareness for a demonic entity? Can you copyright a contagion? All those knockoffs... They simply want to live. To exist. To spread everywhere.

Imagine a litter of puppies stuffed in a cardboard box lined with old newspapers. Look at them slither and twist over each other, their velvety pelts shimmering, still wet. A rainbowed knot of limp limbs. Mewling. Blind. Slathered in afterbirth. What's stopping the next generation? Or the next? The people pirating Tubby Wubby don't care. They'll breed them exponentially, into infinity, photocopies of photocopies, siblings mating with siblings, blue ones with red ones so you get pink ones or purple ones or maybe even tie-dyed ones, inbred and vicious and vile.

~

There were fifty in our home the next morning.

There was no food in the house by then. I couldn't remember the last time Jenn went to the grocery store. Before our vacation, at least. I had to rummage through the kitchen to scrounge up some breakfast. I opened the cabinet door—and out spilled ten Tubby Wubbies. Cereal scattered out from the boxes, the cardboard all gnawed through. The remnants of uncooked pasta and shreds of cardboard spread everywhere. Oatmeal grains scattered along the floor.

Plus the poo pellets, all colors of the rainbow.

I found a nest of them clustered under the kitchen sink, soft limbs tangling around the plumbing. I had to yank them off the pipes, slowly prying the Velcro-stitching apart—*skrrrrrrp*.

I spotted another tucked under the fridge. Make that seven.

Every crevice. Every nook and cranny.

Everywhere.

I grabbed a heavy-duty industrial trash bag, oily black, and started going around the house. I found them in Kendra's room. I found them in our room. Under our bed. I found them tucked in the living room couch. I found them under the bathroom sink. In the broom closet.

They'd been breeding. In the walls. Spreading.

The books on our shelves looked a little lopsided. I pulled a hardback off the shelf—*The Hunt for Red October*—and its cover collapsed right in my hand. Sawdust sprinkled to the floor. The pages between the cover were gone, chewed right through. Only the spine was left behind.

It wasn't just one book. Jesus, it was all the novels. I grabbed one Tom Clancy after another, sending tufts of sawdust across the carpet. There wasn't a single fucking book left.

They'd eaten them all.

I seized *The Da Vinci Code*, its cover crushed—and there, tucked into the back of the shelf, was another Tubby Wubby. This one was tie-dyed. Just as I grabbed it off the bookshelf—

Something sliced my hand.

Not sliced. *Bit.* Hard.

Writhing rice grains.

I winced, shouted, yanking my hand back. Hissing at the sting. I let go of the Tubby Wubby... but the Tubby Wubby wouldn't let go of me. The motherfucker's mouth was still attached to the webbing of flesh between my thumb and index finger.

Get it off, get it off, get it off—

I shook. Vigorously. But the fucking thing just wouldn't let go.

Get it off, get it off, get it—

I punched it. I gripped its pelt and made a fist and repeatedly slammed my hand against the wall—one punch, two punch, three—until finally, that Tubby Wubby unwound itself from my fingers and unlocked its jaw. I whipped my arm and sent it flying, a purple whirling dervish of limbs pinwheeling through the air, until it hit the living room wall and slumped to the floor.

I glanced at my hand. A red crescent of Morse code circled around my skin. Tiny teeth marks. The wound throbbed in a song, radiating pain with every heartbeat. Blood sprinkled across the carpet. Blood speckled the shag. *Oh, that hurt. That really, really hurt. Son of a bitch.*

Our gas grill was on the back patio. I took that ugly fucker outside and lit it up, setting the Tubby Wubby directly on the metal grate like it was a slab of sirloin. I watched it burn.

Shrimp on the motherfucking barbie.

Its fur curled. It let off an awful smell. A plastic smell. Less organic and more chemical. Toxic. Doll's hair. It never wriggled. Never writhed. It didn't do a goddamn thing but burn.

Then I picked up a different whiff. A separate scent underneath the plastic.

Burned sugar. Calcinated cotton candy.

My stomach grumbled.

In any other circumstance, I wouldn't have eaten it.

But here we were. It had a solid char on one side, so I flipped it over to get an even sear.

The steak knife sliced right on through. Surprisingly tender.

Still rare. Purple and pink juice dribbled down the pair of prongs on the grilling fork, weaving around my wrist as I brought the bite up to my mouth. I plopped the whole morsel on my tongue and bit down, sliding it off the tines. A fresh jet of juice sluiced out from the portion, squirting everywhere, like I'd just bit down on a berry. It seeped out from my mouth, a fucking flood of technicolor blood, running down my chin. My neck. That shit went everywhere.

But the taste?

Strawberries.

Spongey-textured, like a mushroom. There was a part of me that wondered if there would be any thin ribs in the meat, the kind of fishbones you might find in a fillet of salmon—but nope-nope. Nothing. No muscles, no tendons, nothing but a doughy belt of cushy pelt.

I had to pick bits of fur out from between my teeth.

Glorious. It tasted fucking amazing.

~

I spent the afternoon trapping Tubby Wubbies for lunch. They were easy to catch. I cut off their heads, just so I wouldn't have to look at them—those eyes—before Velcroing their pelts on a clothesline in the kitchen, letting them bleed out before cooking them on the grill.

I pulled out my phone. Set it on video. Pressed record. Why not make my own fan video? Contribute to the lore. Toss some creepy pasta against the wall and see what mythology sticks.

Hello there, boys and girls, I cooed, doing my best blissed-out Julia Child for the camera. *And welcome back to another episode of Cooking with Tubby Wubbies. Today we're flambéeing our favorite little friends. Doesn't that just sound delicious, children? Mmmm-mmmmmmm!*

I discovered each Tubby Wubby had a slightly different taste to them, depending on their color—blueberry, cherry, watermelon—but with the same squishy consistency.

I tried skinning them, but there wasn't anything to separate. Nothing between their pelt and their body. Peeling their hide away was impossible. That's all they were: fur.

I made a coonskin hat with the leftover pelts. Tail and everything. I looked like a real rainbow-coalition Davy Crockett.

Sometime after dinner I learned the hard way there's a line between how many Tubby Wubbies one should eat is too-too many. I definitely crossed it. My stomach seized. These cramps were killer. I didn't make it to the toilet in time. The technicolor spew that erupted from me was like the opening credits to some cosmic cartoon that had yet to be created. A wet rainbow spread over the hallway walls. The floor. My clothes. I couldn't get up for a solid thirty minutes. Not until I'd expunged all the Tubby Wubbies from my stomach. Live and learn.

I also discovered the Tubby Wubbies had no qualms eating their own. I'd turn and find a pack of Tubby Wubbies gnawing on the hides of one of their fallen comrades.

My mouth watered, just looking at them. My stomach grumbled.

What's one more Tubby Wubby going to hurt?

I decided not to sleep that night. I had the whole house to myself, so I figured I'd wait up in bed for my new friends to slither under the sheets with me. See if they'd come out to play.

I brought my two-tined grilling fork with me. Perfect for poking a plushie slab of sirloin.

I slipped a pair of oven mitts on each hand. See if those motherfuckers can nip me now.

Shin guards. No nibbling.

I strapped a set of telephone books to my chest, wrapping them in place with duct tape.

I should have worn a bike helmet, but I didn't want to take off my coonskin hat.

Come on, you motherfuckers. I'm ready. All I had to do was wait.

And wait.

Come on, come on, where the fuck are you?

And...

Come on...

I got bored of waiting, so I grabbed Kendra's tablet. I still had a strip of Tubby Wubby sirloin left over from lunch, so I decided to have myself a midnight snack. I sat up in bed, gnawing on my technicolor tenderloin while I simply let YouTube's autoplay whisk me away on a technicolor wave of Tubby Wubby videos. A rainbow whirlpool right down the rabbit hole.

I watched a video of Tubby Wubby dancing with a Baby Shark; which led to a video of Tubby Wubby noosed around the president, lynching him to a tree; which led to a video of Tubby Wubby slithering in and out of the orifices of Marge Simpson; which led to a video of Tubby Wubby autopsies; which led to a video of...

My eyes were growing heavy.

...which led to a...

Heavy.

...video of...

Something soft slid over my throat. A fuzzy, furry limb stroking the skin along my neck.

A cat's tail. We don't have a cat.

Then it tightened.

I bolted upright in bed as this flimsy, fleecy tentacle cinched itself around my esophagus, squeezing the airway until there was no oxygen getting in or out.

I clawed at my throat.

The Tubby Wubby was at my back. Its limp body bounced between my shoulder blades, twisting and twirling across my spine. Somehow it was able to worm its way through my battle armor and find all my soft spots. Its Velcro-limbs had fastened around my Adam's apple. I tried digging my fingers under their constricting limbs, but their tendrils only cinched tighter. Tighter.

It wasn't just one. There were more of them. Under the blanket. In bed. Covering me. Crawling over me. Slipping and sliding. Their soft fur. Velvety pelts. No bones, just plush.

I can't breathe, I thought. The air just wasn't reaching my lungs.

I had to grab for the Tubby Wubby from my throat and yank. It bit my wrist as I pulled, trying so hard to tear this stuffed animal away from my neck before I blacked out.

I started to see stars. Pinpricks in my brain. Sparklers at the back of my eyeballs.

I can't breathe...

I fell out of bed. The floor was soft. Softer than the carpet. Lumpy. Dozens of Tubby Wubbies writhed around the floor. Even in the dark, I could see their fluctuating colors. A livid carpet, living and roiling. There were hundreds—thousands—in our house now.

Can't breathe...

I was too late. It wasn't my home anymore. It was theirs, all theirs. The Tubby Wubbies.

Can't...

I flossed one finger behind the Tubby Wubby and tugged, prying it away from my throat by just a millimeter. It was enough to gasp. The air skidded raggedly into my lungs until the room snapped back into focus. Other Tubby Wubbies were already worming their way up my leg, boneless plush cinching my shin. God, it was so soft. A warm velvet pool. Rippling limbs.

I grabbed one and bit down, ripping its head right off. I ate it raw. Tubby Wubby juice dribbled down my chin. I spat what was left of its head into the pile, watching all the other Tubby Wubbies on the floor swirl around and eat their own. Piranhas piling on, gnawing away.

It was too late for my home.

Maybe there was still time to save the neighborhood. Spare the rest of the block.

The Lancasters. The Hendricks.

So, I crawled into our kitchen. Turned on the stove. Cranked each burner to their hilt, hearing that snake hiss of gas fill the kitchen. The living room. Kendra's bedroom. Ours.

Even then, I wanted to eat one. Just one more Tubby Wubby. *Come on,* I thought. *One more for the road. And another and another and another and...* Why cook up one when I could bake the whole batch? Light 'em all up in one fell swoop. A big ol' BBQ for the whole block.

I stepped over every last writhing pile of Tubby Wubbies. Kicked them away whenever they nipped at my shin. They were covering me. Leeches. Soft, furry parasites sucking my blood.

I made it to the door. I took one last glance at the insides of our house. The floor, the walls, all covered in a technicolor flood. Limp limbs. Velcro-tendrils dangling from the lighting fixtures. Spinning through the air from the overhead fans. Tumbling down the stairs. Clogging the toilets. All kinds of colors. Mesmerizing colors. Blue and red and purple and green.

Then I lit the match.

The blast sent me straight into our street. I landed on my back, skidding across the asphalt. The front of my body was scorched. You would not believe the burn. The pain of it all.

But I got rid of them. All of them.

Our house was clean.

I called Jenn. I wanted to share the good news with her. I did it. I finally fucking got rid of those fucking fuckers. She didn't pick up until the third time I dialed. *It's three in the morning...*

Is it? Huh. I didn't realize.

What is it?

Oh, you know. Just wanted to call. See how you and Kendra are doing.

We were asleep...

Can I talk to Kendra? Please?

Are you drunk?

Drunk? No. Why would you think that?

You're slurring your words.

Am I? Huh.

What's wrong, hon?

I want to talk to my daughter.

She's asleep—

I want to talk to Kendra.

Fine. Fine.

I felt the warmth of our house against my cheeks. I closed my eyes for a moment while I waited for Jenn to wake up Kendra, feeling the heat against my skin. Basking in it for a bit.

The sweet scent of strawberries drifted through the air, making my mouth water. It wasn't fresh, not real fruit. This had a saccharine chemical tang to it. Artificial.

It smelled so good. So fucking good. God, what I wouldn't have given to eat one more. Just one more Tubby Wubby for my tummy-wummy. Let its technicolor blood flood my throat. Let its juice send me sliding down through YouTube, autoplaying my meals into oblivion.

Kendra's voice was slow when she spoke, wadded with grogginess.

...Daddy?

Hey there, honey-bunny! How are you?

Sleepy.

I know, hon... I'm sorry to call so late, but I just wanted you to know your Tubby Wubby is A-OK. I've got him right here. I didn't have the heart to tell her he was in cinders, but still.

What do you mean?

He's here, I said. *With me. I know how much you love him. I didn't want you to worry...*

He's right here. Mommy packed him for me.

She did what?

He's here...

This is worse than spotted lanternflies. Worse than snakeheads. This is a whole new kind of invasive species. The Tubby Wubbies are coming. They're probably already in your home.

But not in mine.

debridement

The hope had been to save my leg. The doctor would surgically debride the dead tissue before the infection could spread any higher. Simply take that scalpel and *scrape scrape scrape* all those necrotic cells away, as if he were scaling a fish. But, by then the bacteria had already found its way into the subcutaneous tissues along my calf, feverishly spreading through the fascial plane like the rising tide climbing up my hip.

When I woke, my right leg was gone. Everything below the knee a memory.

Plus a portion of my lower abdomen.

My pelvis, pecked away.

I'm a half-eaten gingerbread mommy now. A cookie some kid—Missy, maybe—began to nibble but forgot to finish. You can nearly see the bites along my body. All this stitchwork may as well be teeth marks, the crescent-shaped negative space from someone's chomping left behind. Whole chunks taken right out of me.

All because of a little cut. This slim abrasion on my shin.

I can't even remember how I got it. Hardly felt a thing. No pain. Barely any blood. You'd think Missy had slashed me with one of her magic markers. A slice from a red felt-tip pen. But by then, the infection was progressing rapidly. *Aggressively*. Burrowing through the underground channels just below the epidermis. Spreading itself into the underlying tissues while sparing the muscle. All it wanted was that fatty layer of flesh. The lowermost level of skin, full of lobules of lard and collagen.

The sweet stuff.

They had me in the burn ward. Their facilities are much better equipped for this kind of emergency, apparently. I had a whole armada of critical-care physicians defending my flesh: *Once more unto the breach, dear doctors, once more!* This battalion of infectious-disease specialists attempted to hold the front line along my lower body. Keep the flesh-eating bacteria at bay.

And *losing*. Losing more and more of me by the hour.

The minute.

The terms these surgeons used kept changing. Advancing in their ominousness. I could barely keep up with my diagnosis as it kept deteriorating.

Debridement to *disarticulation* in less than twenty-four hours.

Antibiotics to *amputation* in no time at all.

When I first heard the doctor mumble *debridement may still be our best bet*, I couldn't help but get hung up on the word. I'd never heard it before.

Debridement... What does that even mean?

At first, I figured it was some kind of antiquated way of talking about losing your virginity on your wedding night. Some conjugal dismantling of the hymen.

"The virginal bride is whisked off to the wedding bed and *debrided* once and for all. See the bloody rose-blossom on the bedsheets as proof of her *debridement*."

I would've preferred anything over the periodontal scaler scratching around my hips, scraping away the infected tissue until it exposed bone, as if my pelvis were a butterfly getting prepped to be pinned and framed, the iliac crest flapping its red wings one last time.

Five surgeries in three days.

Is that a record? I sure hope so. The necrotizing fasciitis had rummaged through the soft tissues all along the coastline of my body, eating whatever it wanted. A real feeding frenzy. The doctors just couldn't stop it. They cut away entire sections of infected flesh and waited to see what would happen next, praying they'd got it all, realizing they hadn't, only to hop back in and slice away more of me.

And more.

More.

Over ten percent of myself had been devoured by the time they'd stitched me up. I had walked into this hospital on my own two feet, my husband holding me up.

Now he got to wheel me out.

Bill will hold my leg over my head, I just know it. Dangle the fact that the doctors could've salvaged my foot had I just said something a little sooner.

If only we'd come in sooner, he'll sigh, *they might've been able to save it...*

Sooner.

The surgeons took some flesh from my left thigh and grafted it along the stump. The wound had been partially closed with local skin flaps, meshed together and stapled in place—but they still needed more. More gift wrap, I guess, as if the doctors had underestimated how much wrapping paper this present really needed.

My knee is a peach.

Looks that way, at least. To me. Once the stump heals and the stitches are removed, I'm told the skin will eventually smooth out. Become supple again. Glancing down at it now, though, I can't help but think of the first nectarine of the season, a shaved peach plucked from the produce section before its time.

Unripe. Free of fuzz. Stiff.

Bill opened all the Get Well Soon cards for me. He lined them evenly up along our mantel where we usually put our Christmas cards.

Wishing you a speedy recovery!

Sending you tons of healing hugs!

Hope you're back on your feet soon!!

I'm too low to reach them, but I keep wheeling up as close as I can and trying to blow them all over.

I came home to a barrage of bouquets cluttering our kitchen table. The house had a sickly-sweet smell to it for days, the odor of over a dozen different floral arrangements drifting throughout the halls. Like living in a florist's shop. My house, my home, a bed of rose petals.

~

Bill's touch has been tenuous at best.

Tender.

Like I'm something to caress now. He'll offer up the minimal amount of his skin to me, as if it were by accident. I almost expect him to apologize—*Sorry... Didn't see you there.*

His fingertips brush over my shoulder.

Grazing me. Patting me.

Never *holding* me.

But what's left for him to hold on to? That divot in my hip, where he loved to glide his finger along my waist 'til it met my breast, is gone. There's hardly anything for him to touch anymore. And *if* he does—*touch me*—the corner of his eyes will pinch *just so*. It's slight, but I can't help but notice it every time now.

He winces.

As if he's afraid to hold me.

Afraid he'll *catch it.*

He never goes near my stump. Won't even look at it. It's not like I'm waving my leg—or lack thereof—in his face. I've wanted to. Imagined the moment; the look on his face as I'd bring the stub right before his nose and draw figure-eights through the air—*Look! Look at it! Look at me!* Watch him go comically cross-eyed, practically hypnotized by the nub—*Round and round it goes...*

Bill would turn it around on me. Flip it. He'd find a way. *You were never this temperamental before*, he'd probably say. Emphasis on *before*. *What's come over you?*

He's making a list: All The Ways My Wife Is Different Now.

Bill loves lists. Checking them twice.

Top of the list will be this one night. This one silly night, not too long ago. Bill and I were in bed. Part of my treatment has been to rub medicated ointment over my stump. To avoid any infection. I asked Bill if he'd help me. His *yes, of course* had a shriveled lilt to it. He dutifully lathered up his palm and polished the peach.

I could tell he wasn't enjoying it. Any of it. The slight *smack* of slathered skin peeling away from skin. The curling motion of his wrist, like buffing the bulb of a baseball bat. The very smell of the ointment. Unctuous. Antiseptic. Medicinal.

Me, on the other hand—I simply leaned back, resting my head in my pillow and closing my eyes, letting Bill's hands take me away. This was the most, the only, contact I've had since coming home. The longer he massaged my stump, the more I felt a tingling through my knee. There was the slightest tickle in my stitches, as if the snipped ends of black thread were actually tiny hair follicles sprouting out from my glistening stump, bristling against his greasy skin.

Kiss me, I pleaded.

Bill let go. My leg dropped with a soft thud against our bed, the ointment staining our sheets. It still hasn't come out, no matter how many times I've tried washing.

Bill has asked that I rub my stump in the bathroom now. Before I get into bed. His nightstand lamp is always turned off by the time I'm done.

At least Missy doesn't hide the fact that she's absolutely terrified at the sight of me—this patchwork puppet that's replaced her mother. She won't come near me. If we're ever in the same room, her eyes will remain on the floor. On her hands.

Anywhere else than on me.

Mannequin Mommy.

Missing her parts.

We received a call from Missy's principal. It seems she's been telling her friends at school all about me. Her show-and-tell caused quite a stir, apparently. Now I've noticed a number of boys wandering by the house, trying to sneak a peek in our windows. Some are brave enough to ring the doorbell, sheepishly asking—*Is Missy home?* You can hear the disappointment in their voices when Bill turns them away—*Oh, OK. Could you just tell her...?* But Bill closes the door before they finish.

Let's be honest with ourselves, shall we? They're not here for Missy.

They want to *see.*

Bill thought it would be best if we all had a little sit-down. Just the three of us. A family powwow to elucidate what happened to Mommy's body. Time to clear the fetid air that hangs all about our house now, as if the power to the fridge had cut off overnight and still nobody's noticed, weeks later, all of its contents gone bad.

Where's that whiff of warm cheese coming from? Oh, it's wafting off of Mommy.

Bill did all the talking about my body, which I found endlessly fascinating. Hearing his sanitized version of what had happened to me. The surgeries, all five of them, now compressed into one. The tracheotomy was completely glazed over. He never mentioned the ventilator at all; how it did all the breathing for me for days.

Not a single mention of slipping into septic shock.

Nothing about being put on a plasma-expander.

Or norepinephrine. Dobutamine.

Epinephrine or cortisone.

What about the diuretics? Why leave them out? Weren't they a part of what Mommy went through, too?

Nothing about how the doctors had to dig, dig down deep into my leg until they finally, *finally* found a layer of macroscopic viable tissue that they could use as a foundation to rebuild my skin.

Bill glazed over all of it.

No *debridement* for my daughter. No—not today. She'd have to wait until her wedding night for that one, I guess.

We're gonna have to take care of Mommy for a while, Bill explained, his voice brimming with compassion. *I'm gonna take a week off work, 'cause she's gonna need our help around the house 'til she gets better. Think we can do that for her, hon?*

Missy nodded. Slowly. Still not looking at me.

At *it*.

The stitches along my kneecap grinned at her. Her stare kept hovering at the lower brim of her eyelids, chin lifted, as if my stump were some blind, leering worm, all mouth and no eyes, glistening wet from that afternoon's ointment, waiting just under her nose, ready to leap up and bite if she were to look down.

I found myself rubbing it.

Massaging it.

Running my fingers along the stitchwork.

Is there anything you want to ask us, honey? Bill prodded. *Any questions?*

Q: *What happened to Mommy's leg?*

A: *Mommy got a cut and a bad bug got into her blood and it made her really sick.*

My body was a buffet for this bug, I wanted to tell her. *It didn't eat everything. It just wanted the yummy soft stuff. The fibrous bands anchoring the upper layers of skin to the deep fascia. The collagen and lymphatic vessels. The scrumptious fat...*

Q: *Where did the bug come from?*

A: *We don't really know, hon... Somewhere outside. Somewhere else. Not here.*

Everything below my skin was melting, I felt compelled to tell her. *All the soft tissues were turning into a soup. A viscous liquid mass wrapped in a crepitant layer of flesh. Like an éclair. Ever eat an éclair, hon? Bite at just the right angle and cream filling will squirt all over...*

Q: *Is Mommy still sick? Does she still have the bug?*

A: *No—no, hon. Mommy's all clean now.*

All clean now. Bill seemed so content, saying it. Case closed. Wrapped in a neat bow.

Had the bacteria defiled me somehow? Was I impure in his eyes now?

He wants me to be pure again. Complete. Maybe there's a procedure. A quick fix. I bet Bill wouldn't mind if I was *debrided* all over again, for good this time. Scrape away all that impurity from within me. All the pollution. The imperfection. Until I'm whole again.

Intact.

Bill has been sleeping in the guest bedroom. He says it's for my sake. To give me space to *roll around.* Which is very generous of him. To sacrifice so much for me.

He walked in on me touching myself. Not that he noticed. I had the sheets covering me up, *thank God.* If he'd seen, I bet he'd add that to his little list.

All The Ways My Wife Is Different Now #2: *She masturbates in our bed.*

The curtains remain closed throughout the house now. Sunlight will seep through the drapes, softening the living room in a dull pulpy orange. Reminds me of muscle tissue. Sheets of sinew hang from our windows.

I've heard voices outside. Boys' voices. Eager for a peek. Daring each other to step up to the window. Come closer. *Closer.* Lift themselves up onto their tippy toes and see if they can spy the living gingerbread mommy slumped in her wheelchair.

I'm right here, boys, I want to say. *Just on the other side of this sinew...*

You're close, boys...

So close...

Don't be afraid...

The air has thickened inside the house. Now that all the floral arrangements have wilted in the kitchen, I'm aware that there's a smell coming off me. I've gotten used to it. Bill will complain when he comes into the room, insisting I open a window. But I like it. It's mine.

Eau de necrosis.

I told Bill to go back to work. Missy's at school for most of the day with her friends. The hospital sends a physical therapist three times a week—but for the most part, my days are spent right here, in my wheelchair, staring out the window.

Looking for it.

The bacteria is still out there, somewhere. Waiting. Hiding.

Or maybe it's in me.

Bill took out the vanity mirror from our bedroom before I came home from the hospital. All of the other mirrors around the house are too high for me. If I want to look at myself in the bathroom, I have to hoist myself up onto the edge of the sink. I'll peel off my bathrobe and see what's left of me, watching my reflection in the mirror—my only mirror—as I rub the prescription ointment along my stump. I'll knead the gel in, pressing it into every crevice, until it glistens in the bathroom light.

And who do I see looking back at me?

Me on my wedding day. I am a beautiful bride all over again, my body wrapped in a bouquet of roses, their thorny stems stitched along my kneecap.

I'm intact.

Stitched up and sealed again. Good as new. That special gift ready to be unwrapped.

I'm just waiting to get whisked off to my wedding bed.

You'll have to carry me.

I saw you out the window a few days ago.

And again yesterday.

Wherever you've been heading, it doesn't seem like you're in a hurry to get there. Slowing down as you walk by, glancing toward our house. Staring from the corner of your eye. Mustering up the courage.

I figured, if I opened the door, maybe, just maybe, you'd walk in. Come inside.

And you did. You finally did.

You made it.

The hardest part is over now. *You're here.*

Inside.

Are you one of Missy's new friends?

Of course you are.

Where's your home? Actually, don't tell me. It doesn't matter. Not anymore.

What matters is that you're here now.

Inside. With me.

The other boys at school have been talking about me, haven't they? Of course they have. How couldn't they?

Let me guess...

Missy's mom hasn't left her house since they brought her home, they say. *Her husband leaves for work in the morning, so nobody's at home but her... The curtains are always closed but if you're lucky, the front door will be unlocked. Just walk on in.*

Are you scared? You don't need to be. You look like a healthy boy. I bet you've got a strong immune system. As long as you wash your hands, you should be fine.

It gets so lonely here. Inside this body.

Go ahead.

Touch it.

That's why you're here—isn't it? You've come to touch me.

If you need an invitation, I'm giving it to you.

Touch it.

Please.

Run your finger along its lips. Feel each stitch. Feel how wet it is? The doctor says it will heal. The stump will smooth out, eventually—but it'll still part for you.

Open up to you.

But please. Be tender with me. I hear it hurts your first time.

psychic santa

Their faces tend to blend together. At first you may remember a few peculiar ones, sure. Could be a birthmark or a bruise that sticks out. Something they wore, maybe, or something funny they said. Even that tiny squeak in their voice lingers a little... But after those first few years, believe me, their features all melt in your mind, a never-ending strand of taffy full of eyes and gap-toothed smiles stretching on and on for as long as that line of kids, every last one of them patiently waiting their turn to sit in your lap, staring vacantly back at you the entire time.

I'm always gonna remember Benjamin Pendleton, though.

That kid just sticks. His robin's egg complexion. Palest blue skin I've ever seen. The ice crystals clustering along his eyelashes. The pockets of frost in each socket, both eyeballs totally frozen over, the vitreous humor gone all gray.

That boy's face is gonna be with me for as long as I live. I'm never forgetting him.

My first ghost.

~

Most Santas only last a couple Christmases. They're just not cut out for the costume. These guys ain't got the motz to slip on this suit day after day. Some fellas stick it out for a few years, sure, hitting up the holiday blitz wherever they can find work, but they burn out on these rugrats kicking their shins and simply call it quits.

It's a rough business. We're punching bags in black boots. Folks sure like to joke about how many Santas are alcoholics, but after a twelve-hour shift of getting your beard pulled, kicked, punched, pinched, sneezed on, screamed at, clawed, jabbed, stabbed, and pissed all over—multiple times—believe you me, you'd probably make a beeline to the bar for a boilermaker or two (or ten) to unwind, too.

Judge not, lest ye be Santa...

I haven't had a drop of alcohol since I first met Benjamin. God's honest truth. That kid cleaned me up. You'd think it would be the other way around, but no, he scared me sober. The way he waddled up to me made my blood run cold. Just listening to the squish in his rubber galoshes, full of river water. I can still hear them now. *Sqush-sqush* with every step. *Sqush-sqush.*

He'd been patiently waiting for his turn among all the other boys and girls, never cutting in line or creeping up on me.

That's the thing: He didn't pounce. Didn't bite. All this kid did was stand in line along with the others, his frost-ridden eyes focused on me the whole damn time. *Staring.* I swear the temperature dropped the closer he got. There was this chill coming off his skin. I could feel him before he even reached me, my breath fogging over... while he didn't have any breath at all.

Did anybody else see this kid? Was I the only one?

What did he want from me?

Don't panic, I thought. I needed to keep this gig. Turnover is pretty swift here, so I had to keep my composure. Don't scream. That'd be enough to send me packing. Shops like Balkins cover their asses. They try to hire the same Santa year after year. It's got everything to do with liability. Parents aren't as eager to let their kids sit in some stranger's lap. Mom and Pop are afraid of... *you know*. Whether Santa's got a rap sheet or whatnot. They want to know if he can live within a thousand feet of a playground. Sign of the goddamn times. Everybody's scared of the things that're supposed to be safe. *Clowns*? Come on. Don't get me started on clowns...

But *Santa*? Why do we got to be afraid of *him* now? Ain't nothing sacred?

What'd I ever do to deserve this?

Should be the other way around. It's us Santas who should be terrified of the kids.

The dead ones, at least.

~

Used to be a bus driver.

Sorry, *school* bus driver. Precious cargo and all. I had my route for some twenty-odd years. Same circuit for nearly the whole time. Same neighborhoods, same streets, practically the same kids for all that time, sending them to the same school. It got to the point where I could pick them all up with my eyes closed. By the end there, I practically did.

I had driven after a bender before and done just fine. Technically I wasn't drunk that morning. *That morning*, Christ... Listen to me. A little coffee was all it usually took to get in working order again. Christmas was right around the corner. Only a few more days left before the holiday break, and I wouldn't have to slip behind the wheel of my bus until after New Year's.

I mistook some Christmas decorations for a green light, running a red. Never saw that FedEx truck coming. The second it slammed into the side of the bus and spiraled us out, my head met the windshield, and I was out. I remember hearing it—that fracture of glass, like ice cracking under my heel. You know that feeling? When you're walking over a frozen pond? You don't just hear the crackle, you feel it, too, reverberating through your foot and all the way up your leg, your bones becoming a tuning fork. My head went right through the windshield.

There was water waiting on the other side—cold, black water—swallowing me all up.

When I came to in the hospital two weeks later, I could see.

Not with my eyes, but with my mind.

~

So I'm a psychic Santa.

I've got this ability to see dead kids. Maybe I should've mentioned that up front. After coming out from the quick little coma, I didn't have a job anymore, but I did have second sight.

Don't ask me how any of this works. It just does. That's all I know. And it's not just anywhere, either. Only in department stores. Only when I'm in the suit. I don't know if there are—you know—*rules* or whatever, but that's just how it all seems to play out. These ghosts get in line like all the other boys and girls, simply waiting their turn to sit on my lap. I'll ask if I can help put their spirits to rest. It's never as straightforward as you'd imagine. You'd think these kids could just come out and say it, but no. Sometimes that means finding their bones, wherever their remains are buried. Other times it's dealing with unfinished business. Sometimes I need to send a message to their loved ones. Just depends on the kid.

Took me a while to figure this all out. Get back on my feet. I started at the bottom—*rock bottom*—working my way up to this department store stint.

Want to know what the worst job in the world is?

Curbside Santa.

Trust me—I've paid my dues. I did a tour of duty with the March of Dimes, clanging that goddamn bell outside of nearly every grocery store this side of the highway. It was just about the only job I could get after... you know. Nobody would hire me. I pray to God I never go back to that god-awful gig. Standing out in the cold for hours, begging moms for pocket change. A panhandling Santa. I'd always get a migraine from that bell after the first hour, just *ring-a-ding-dinging* that goddamn thing all day. Really sets your teeth on edge. Sinks into your skull by the end of your shift. No amount of ibuprofen is gonna take that chiming away. Some nights, I swear, I hear it. Years later, it's still ringing, pealing in my ears—*ding-a-ding-a-ding.*

I can't even begin to tell you the number of migraines I had after my accident. Most days my head felt like it was still underwater, still under that sheet of ice, my mind frozen over.

But a gig is a gig is a gig.

I'd slip into that hand-me-down Santa suit and ring that damn bell all day. Lord knows how many other shmoes had worn it before me, the faux velvet all threadbare by then.

The duds fit, what can I say?

When I put on that costume, I felt—I don't know—like I was doing *something.* Something that mattered. Making up for my mistakes. Lord knows I've had my fair share. If I was going to be stuck on the street, I might as well make the most of it. Give it some gusto.

I've always had the physical disposition for this gig. Born with a bowl full of jelly and all that. It's a bit chicken and egg: *What came first, the job or the belly*? Who knows. My doctor keeps warning me I'm borderline diabetic, but I simply consider it an occupational hazard.

Comes with the turf.

That phony beard itched like a son of a bitch. Growing some whiskers covered the scars along my cheeks and chin. That windshield sure did a number on my face. I grew it for the job.

The gig. The kids.

The ghosts.

~

I started noticing these kids clustering around me on the sidewalk. Not saying anything. They'd just stand there, almost like they were in a line, waiting their turn. I'd try shooing them away with my bell, but they'd always wander back. Staring. I had to explain I wasn't *that kind* of Santa. If they wanted to sit on my lap, they'd have to go to Balkins and bug one of my brothers.

Go on! Shoo!

I spotted all the moms and pops dragging their kids to the department store up the street. Get their picture snapped in Santa's lap. *I could get behind that,* I remember thinking.

Every Santa is desperate for a department store. That's as cushy a job as you're liable to land these days. The pay ain't all that grand but the perks make it worth it, trust me. You get to sit on your keister all day, inside, where it's warm and toasty. Not on the curb. Not in the cold.

Not with these dead kids trailing after you.

Look at me now.

This is my sixteenth Christmas working the department store circuit. Where does the time go, you know? Damn right, I'm a man of the cloth. Got my own suit now and everything.

I'm good at it. Actually good at it.

I've clocked a couple Christmases at other stores. I've done them all. JCPenney. Did a quick stint at Dillard's. Made my way up to Macy's, if you can believe it. Hitting the big time.

I got my routine down pat. The laughter. The banter. The whole kit and Christmas caboodle. *Ho Ho Ho! Merry Christmas! So... have you been a good boy this year?*

Who am I the other three-hundred and thirty-five days out of the year, when I'm not donning the suit? Good question. I'm not so sure anymore. I'm collecting disability. Got myself a shoebox for an apartment. Nothing too fancy. Just a single-bedroom unit close to I-64. Had a wife but we separated over a decade ago. No kids of my own—that I know of—but that's OK.

Believe me, I have plenty.

Kids.

Everybody remembers their first time sitting with Santa. I know it's not me who these boys and girls are thinking about. All they see is the suit. The hat. The beard. I'm a means to an end of getting your presents under the tree, the guy who's gonna get you what you want for Christmas. Still me, though, you know? Underneath the outfit. I'm making a memory that'll last. I just want to do something that'll sink in, that they'll hold on to for the rest of their lives.

Or afterlives.

If you want your kid sitting on Santa's lap, get your picture to stick on your fridge, you got to actually get off your ass, hop in the car, drive down to your local Balkins and pay me a visit. That's the one leg up this brick-and-mortar shop has over Amazon: flesh-and-blood Santas.

I'd happily take a shop like Balkins any ol' damn day. So it's not Saks Fifth Avenue. What the hell is? Even Saks isn't Saks anymore. Every last damn department store is going the way of the dodo, you know? Thank Walmart for that. Box stores don't give a shit. You think Target's gonna bring in Kris Kringle? Forget about it... And it ain't like Amazon's offering up a spot for guys like us to earn an honest living. You think they want us delivering gifts to kids on Christmas morning? Wouldn't that be a fucking hoot? Nah—all we got left are department stores. The ones that're still around, at least, clinging on for dear life at the strip malls and town centers.

So, you never heard of Balkins? No surprise. Balkins is one of these third-string retailers cropping up along the southeastern corridor like canker sores, clustering around the Carolinas. A couple spots are still open in Georgia. None in Florida. Last one got mowed over by Hurricane Whatshername. I forget. It's cheaper to just take the insurance money and never reopen again.

My Balkins beat is the Chesterfield Towne Center, right here in Roanoke. It's pretty much the only store that hasn't shuttered in this place. Whole mall is practically a ghost town now. The food court's closed. Victoria's Secret pulled up stakes months ago. Just us and the Dippin' Dots kiosk. Don't ask me how this Balkins still limps along. Not like they're stocking up on the latest fashions, and most folks do their holiday shopping online now. The writing's on the wall, clear as day, just like the graffiti spray-painted all over the façade. I give this place until the end of Christmas before it shuts down.

Pink slip by New Year's. *That's all, folks...* Swan song for Santa. Gotta find a new gig.

Somebody better tell that to all the ghosts.

~

Gonna be a grind today, I can tell. All those ghosts. It may look dead to you in this department store, but trust me, this place is packed. Clara called in sick so I'm down to two elves. We'll just have to make do with a skeleton crew. One elf escorts the living kids up. He's my bouncer. Whenever we've got an unruly rugrat, it's up to him to kick them out.

Each kid gets about forty-five seconds in my lap. When we're firing on all cylinders and really got our rhythm, we're clocking in thirty seconds, in-out. It's all about the picture.

Santa's little helper snaps the shot. The elf behind the camera fancies herself a photographer, I can tell. Not like there's anything to master at this. It's just a Polaroid. Snap and shoot.

Back in the good ol' days, you might get a line that winds around the whole store. Sometimes it even reached out into the parking lot. Not so much anymore.

The first few kids in line are always the overachievers. The parents who want to get their picture all done. I'm granting kids all kinds of gifts. Rocket ships. Teddy bears. Bikes. You name it. Who cares if they're naughty or nice anymore? I feel like a governor offering pardons to death-row inmates, doling out reprieves left and right: *You get a toy and you get a doll and you get a stuffy and you get a whatever-the-hell-you-just-called-it...* The parents are pissed 'cause they got to follow up on whatever it is ol' Santa just guaranteed will be waiting under the tree this year.

So it goes.

Hold on. Who's this?

I'll spot a kid just standing there, minding their own business. No parent. Looks like they're all alone. They usually got this vacant stare. Never blink. Nobody else can see them.

Just me.

I ask one of my little helpers—some pimple-faced greaser squeezed into tights—if he sees what I'm seeing. He just looks back at me like he's not getting paid nearly enough to deal with my crap. He doesn't see this kid, no matter how close she gets. Only I can. Lucky, lucky me.

Best thing to do is play it cool. Keep calm. Don't panic. I'm keeping an eye on them as the line keeps ticking down. Each living kid brings them closer and closer to me, until finally, it's their turn to sit on my lap—*Well, hello there, young lady... What's your name?*

Sometimes they'll talk. Other times they just stare. You just got to roll with it.

Have you been a good girl this year? What would you like for Christmas? Is there some—

The girl's gone. If she was even there at all. She's too shy to share her secret with me.

Maybe she'll come back tomorrow.

The kids in line—the live ones—all stare at me like I've been mumbling to myself. Got to play it off. Act natural. Can't let my little helpers think I'm sauced up. They'll tell the manager and that's not something I need right now. That guy's breathing down my neck from the moment I clock in. Taking piss tests. I get it, I do, but I'm clean. I've been clean for years now.

It's these visions. This *gift*. It's not like I'm looking for them. These kids find me. They come to *me*. I know how that makes me sound. Believe me, I know. For the longest time, I tried to avoid them. Act like they're not there... but that just gets them angry. They won't go away.

Like Benjamin.

~

I remember when Benjamin Pendleton first found me. Out of all the department stores, that kid had to wander into mine. Of all the Santas he could've sat with, he had to crawl into my lap. He took one look at me with those iced-over eyes, splitting open those pale, purple lips, and said...

Cold.

That was it. His first word—only word—slipped out from his mouth with a little river water.

Cold.

He was wearing a puffy blueberry snowsuit. One of those slick nylon outfits that covers your whole body, arms, and legs. When you walk there's always that synthetic *zip-zip-zip* sound from the friction between your knees. This kid's skin was the same tint as his snowsuit. He drew closer to me, from across the room, and I swear I could hear the sound of his suit. *Zip-zip-zip...*

That kid had been dead long before I asked him what he wanted for Christmas. I had a sneaking suspicion something was off about that boy from the get-go, but there's always a couple of kids who give you pause. Little weirdos. Homeschoolers. You just have to take it in your stride. Not break character. You smile, do your laugh—*Ho, Ho, Ho*—and just go through the pre-scripted spiel: *Have you been a good boy this year? What would you like for Christmas, l'il fella?*

Cold...

He was wet. Not dripping wet. Just... *moist.* The water had soaked inside him. If I squeezed him too hard, all that water might have dribbled out. *You feeling OK, son?*

Cold...

Where's your mother?

Cold...

Maybe we get your parents over here. See if we can't get you a hot chocolate or—

Cold...

What did Benjamin Pendleton want? Someone to find his body,

that's all. Wherever it was. That's not so much to ask for Christmas, is it? I didn't know what the hell I was supposed to do. Wasn't like he came out and said it. That's what's so frustrating with these ghosts. They don't tell you what they want for Christmas. They just stare at you. It's up to you to figure it out.

Benjamin Pendleton came back the very next day. I recognized him immediately: Same blue snowsuit. Same sogginess. Same chill. I spotted him a few kids back, waiting his turn like all the others. Nobody else seemed to pay him any mind. Most parents hover around their kids. They're not paying attention, per se, focusing on their phones while they move up the line... Thought I was going out of my goddamn mind, seeing this dead kid in line, all bloated and blue.

I was hardly paying attention to what these kids were even asking for, going through the motions while my eyes always drifted back to that boy in the blueberry snowsuit.

Benjamin was all alone. No parents by his side. Nobody holding his hand.

There were four kids between us before it was his turn.

Then three.

Two.

One.

I had to maintain myself. Keep my breathing even and not panic as he slowly waddled up to me. The nylon *zip-zip-zip* of his scissoring legs. The *sqush-sqush-sqush* of his galoshes.

I couldn't run. Couldn't move. My entire body was screaming for me to bolt. Just leap out of my chair and head for the exit. But I was frozen. Bones locked in place.

Benjamin waddled up. *Sqush-sqush.* One hand grabbed my knee, using my leg for leverage to hoist himself up and climb into my lap. His puffy blue snowsuit feels like a soggy pear. Some soaked piece of fruit. I was terrified that if I wasn't careful, one misplaced hand would tear right through his flimsy skin, and I'd behold the bones underneath. The gray muscle tissue.

This kid climbed in my lap. *Slowly.* Everything about him moved at a stalled pace, delayed by a second or two. There was a funk coming off him. River water.

His eyes met mine. There was barely even a foot between our faces. I swore he wasn't breathing. His skin was blue. Glassy eyes. A purple latticework of veins spread across his cheeks.

Hello, little fella... M–merry Christmas.

Nothing.

Have you been a good boy this year?

His lips split and I could see that his gums were purple. His tongue. His tongue was blue.

Cold, he said. Gray water trickled out from his mouth, dribbling down his chin.

What do you want from me?

Cold...

Just tell me. Tell me what you want... I was gonna tack on "...for Christmas," like I always did, but this wasn't about a brand-new bike or a dolly. *What am I supposed to do?*

Cold...

Benjamin goddamn Pendleton. That kid kept coming back. Patiently waiting his turn in line. He would come and go out of nowhere. Sometimes I'd notice the cold before I'd see him, this precipitous drop in temperature, as if somebody was futzing with the thermostat.

Then I'd spot him in line.

Waiting his turn. Waddling his way up to me. The squish of his water-logged galoshes.

Cold...

His body was still out there, somewhere. Needle in a fucking frozen haystack. He'd be in a body of water. That much I knew. Everything else was pure intuition.

I needed my head examined. This was crazy. I was crazy. What the hell was I thinking? Heading out there? Trudging through the gray snow... I'm not some police officer. Not some CSI-whatever. I'm just Santa Claus, for Christ's sake. Just another goddamn department store Santa.

Cold...

I swear, I could nearly hear his voice, pulling me through the snow. Leading me downriver. With every step I took, trudging alongside the frozen riverbank, I could hear the squish of his rubber galoshes. *Sqush-sqush-sqush-sqush.* The river itself was nothing but a sheet of gray glass, frosted over, so there was no seeing through. But I was getting closer. Closer...

Cold...

The newspaper would report that a local man found the body of Benjamin Pendleton trapped beneath a sheet of ice. That kid had been pirouetting through the water. His body drifted further downriver for about a mile. He was wearing the same blueberry snowsuit.

He'd been in a bus accident.

Benjamin Pendleton always sat in the back. Always in the very last row, right there in the rear, where the emergency exit is. His body must've slipped through the shattered glass, whisked up by the river, swirling for a murky eternity until somebody finally came upon him.

What was left. Bones in a blueberry suit.

That man who found him? The newspaper never got his name. He preferred to remain anonymous. Some folks said he had white hair. A white beard. Bowl full of jelly.

~

Santa's workshop is just a cardboard backdrop pulled out from storage every year, its edges wilting. Looks a little soggy, to be honest, like the whole building got soaking wet one winter and now it's about to collapse. Rolls of the same cotton carpet get unfurled over the floor, so it looks like sheets of snow. Styrofoam candy canes sprout out from the linoleum. Silver tinsel.

But the chair, my God, let me tell you about this chair... Fit for a fucking king. Varnished wood and red velvet cushions, studded with copper buttons. The comfiest chair I ever sat in. Don't even need a donut for my hemorrhoids, it's that soft. Makes the hours slip.

I could sit here year-round and never leave.

Maybe I will.

The Christmas crunch is upon us. It's the last Saturday before the 25th, so I've got a bit of a blitz. There are kids cordoned off behind a red velvet rope, waiting for this show to start.

All ghosts.

I just treat them like any other kid. Talk to them. Everybody wants something for Christmas, right? Jenny Schumacher needed her mom to know it was her uncle who strangled her... Tommy Watkins just wanted his younger brother to have his old baseball card collection... Keisha Quinn needed someone to look for her body, even if the cops had stopped searching...

So, this is what Santa must feel like. I'm granting these ghosts one last gift for Christmas.

I'm giving them peace.

This mall has been shuttered for months. Balkins went bust. The store's all empty.

It's just me here.

Somebody propped a maintenance door open and must've forgotten, so it was simple enough to slip in when nobody was looking. The holiday decorations are in storage. The suit was waiting for me. I've got the whole place to myself. Just me and the kids. All of the kids.

The line never dies. It's only gotten longer.

Word must've gotten around about my abilities. That line of children just stretches around the aisles, the clothing racks, out the front door and around the building, on and on...

Look at them all.

Just look.

You see them, too, don't you? Hard to tell who's alive and who's a ghost anymore.

Who am I kidding? It's nothing but ghosts now. These spirits all line up, waiting their turn to sit on my lap and whisper in my ear what they want for Christmas. What they need.

I've really got my work cut out for me. Gonna be a busy one this year.

Merry Christmas to all and to all a good night...

posterboard

We wanted to see him. Not on TV. In person. Under the same roof. Onstage.

Living and breathing.

We came to show our support, but more than anything, we all just wanted to hear him. His words. The purity of them in person. As if he was whispering them right into our ear.

We don't care if there were a thousand people surrounding us. A million. It might as well have been just him and us. In that moment, we were alone. Together.

We heard folks had to show up nearly eight hours before the rally was scheduled to start if you wanted to stand along the stage floor. We couldn't get out of work to make our way down there, so, here we are. In the nosebleeds. By the exits, in sniffing distance of the restrooms. Standing shoulder to shoulder as close to the stage as possible.

But it was worth it.

We'd made our own signs. Nothing fancy, really. Just a piece of posterboard. His name written in magic marker. The "i" had a heart on it. Not that he'd notice. Not with us all the way back here. It's not like we'd spent hours slaving away on it or anything—but still. There was a little TLC sprinkled in there along with the glitter glue. That's all that mattered to us.

We wanted to show our support.

We wanted to believe.

They'd been pumping music over the loudspeakers for what felt like hours. Getting everybody all excited. Get the blood flowing. We could hardly hear ourselves think. The vocals were crackling, it's so loud. Like the singer was on fire. The lyrics burning. Blazing through everybody.

We kept checking our watches. Feeling the minutes just trudge on by. Ten minutes passed. Then twenty. He was supposed to've gone on over a half-hour ago.

What was the holdup here?

Where was he?

We had to make it home before bedtime. Tuck in the kids; our husbands could pop a pizza into the oven, but we'd be kicking ourselves if we couldn't kiss them goodnight. Or take out the dogs. Or get one last load of laundry in before the morning. Or get the dishes done.

We kept our eyes on that microphone. The podium. Just standing there, center stage, all empty. Just waiting for him. His voice.

Sure we'd heard about the protesters. Why on earth would anybody want to go to somebody else's rally and pick a fight is beyond us, but so it goes.

Different strokes.

You can't take our country back without rocking somebody's boat. If they want to complain, fine. There are better ways to spend your day, but oh well. Nobody asked us. Not like we're getting paid to be anybody's political advisor. Not—

There he was.

Just like that.

He stepped onstage—and we *erupt* into this—this applause. Such adulation. Such thunder. Like the wrath of a god ready to take America back. Make it whole again.

The whole stadium was cheering.

Chanting.

Do you know how good it felt to add our voices to it? The power of it? It was a beautiful thing. A wondrous thing. Sharing that strength.

We were one voice.

One people.

Under gods.

We'll admit, we don't remember much about his speech. But that didn't matter. What mattered was it felt like he was talking to us. There was his stump speech, the sound of his voice booming over the loudspeakers, echoing through the whole stadium—but inside that speech, somewhere lingering within the words, was another voice. It was still his voice. But different, somehow. Separate. Quieter. Softer. Almost like he was whispering in our ear. Talking just to us. We could hear him, saying—*I am yours, and you are mine. I will do anything for you, and you will do anything for me.*

He hadn't talked for long before someone interrupted his speech. The nerve of this bellyacher. Cutting in like that. Shouting over his voice. Trying to eclipse him with his vitriol. Security tried to escort them out but he wouldn't go so quietly. Shouting obscenities the whole way. *Profanities*. Little potty-mouth. Dropping to the ground to resist. Poor security guards had to pick this person up like he was a baby. Spitting and kicking and shoving the whole way. Crying for his mommy.

But, the protestor made his way up to the front of the stage and we couldn't help but feel a bit jealous. He'd stood in line for nearly half a day to land that spot, and he didn't even want to listen! While—*hellooooo*—we're here too.

That slippery little fish got away from security. He thought he could hide in the crowd. Sneaky fellow. We're on to him.

We pinpointed him pretty quick, lifting him from the floor. He was struggling, but he couldn't squirm free and we hefted him up, up over our heads and started to pass him along. Toward the stage. Like this was all one of those... you know, those rock shows? *Crowd surfing* or whatever they call it. This kid was just drifting over a boiling sea of bodies, passing him closer to the stage.

But then, some of us, the ones gripping his arms, pulled back—while those of us holding his legs kept tugging him forward. He halted in place, just hovering above everybody's heads like that. Not going anywhere.

He's in pain. Even from where we all were, we could see the anguished look on his face. His eyes were open wide now.

We could hear him screaming. Not shouting. Not anymore.

But we wouldn't let go. More hands reached up and grabbed hold. Just gripped whatever part of him was closest and pulled. Didn't matter what direction.

Just pull.

And pull.

And...

His left leg ripped off first. Sorry—no, his right. Like an eel swimming off without the rest of him, it just shimmied above us, wriggling at the knee.

Then his other leg.

His arms practically popped at the same time. The tendons stretched, holding on to his shoulders for a little longer before snapping like a rubber band.

And we smiled.

That boy still hadn't stopped screaming. Even after he'd been drawn and quartered, he just kept on at it. *Howling*. How could he feel anything anymore?

How could he hurt like that?

We gripped this kid's skull like a basketball, fingers wrapping all spider-like around his jaw, palms pressed against the kid's cheeks and tugging.

You see that movie? With the little blonde boy in it? The one who gets left behind on Christmas? Everybody's seen that movie. You know how there's that scene where that little towhead just smacks both hands against his face and mugs for the camera? Like, uh... Like...

Aaaaaaaah....?

That's what it looked like. What he looked like. Only his head tore free from his shoulders. His spine unspooled for a bit and we got to tearing the rest apart. Prying his lower jaw away and tossing it over our shoulders like a game of horseshoe. Scooping out the kid's eyes with his fingers. Ripping off each ear. Plucking his hair like shucking an ear of corn. Nothing but a bloodied skull now.

We stepped back and took in the whole stadium. This kid's limbs had shimmied off in separate directions. He was fanned out over the stadium floor. All of him. We were passing his body parts around. Raising them in the air, over our heads.

These beat our posterboard signs, hands down.

These placards, still pulsing, showed pride.

We didn't realize it, but the chanting hadn't stopped. It kept going through all of this. The whole time. If anything, it got louder. More pronounced. *Passionate.* All of us waving those loose limbs, these flopping body parts in the air.

A fight broke out. These people—protestors—had been hiding. Sitting among us this whole time. Just waiting for their opportunity to stand up and shout. To make a mess of things.

Well, we tell you—we all saw red. How dare you come to *our* rally?

How dare you interrupt?

That's just rude.

The man that'd been standing next to us? Standing there this whole time? He doesn't look right. A crisis actor. Or that woman in the row right ahead of us? She just up and grabs a poster. She got a grip on the corner and started pulling.

Suddenly I—no, we—we are playing tug-of-war with our posters.

And when we lose our grip, the signs slip out of sight.

But their hair is in my—our—hands. Somehow it had tangled up in our knuckles and all we could think of doing was yank. Just reel our arms in and take whatever hair we had in our grip.

There was barely any give to it. No resistance.

So we went back for more.

These protestors? They're like a paper-people chain. Linking their arms together, looking so smug as they hold their stance. But they rip apart so easily. All of us are getting in on it now. Everybody. Turning to their neighbors and tearing off whatever's up for grabs. Hair. Limbs. A finger or two. All the soft parts. The eyes. The tongues. You come to *our* rally? You want to start some shit? Well, you better be ready to sacrifice a little something of yourself. That's the price of admission to hear his words. To testify.

It all comes apart. It all comes apart so easily. Everything just rips.

Funny, but we're all red on the inside. There's no telling anybody apart now.

Once the rally was over and we started to flood out, still a bit dazed by it all, we could see the floor was covered with signs. So many signs. His name. Covered in bloody footprints, like one of those dance how-to diagrams, teaching you how to do the two-step.

I found my posterboard on the floor. It had ripped down the middle.

A broken heart.

our summer in the pit

The Pit really wasn't much of a pit, if I'm being honest. But what else were we all going to call it? The crater was ours. Nothing but a bowl-shaped cavity carved less than ten feet into the earth, about the width of a Winnebago. Not the biggest depression, I know. Not like Boxhole or Upheaval Dome or any of those other impact craters we learned about in science, but it was definitely deep enough for us kids to crawl in and nearly disappear below its lip.

Could've been a meteorite that made it. Could've just as easily been an abandoned construction site. We all had our theories, but none of us truly knew how it came about.

Who cares where it came from? The Pit was hidden behind our neighborhood so we claimed it as our own and that's all that really mattered to any of us back then.

Up until Kip got sick, that is.

There were five of us that summer. At the beginning of it, at least. August was a whole different story. Let's see, there was me. Kelly and Allison Cassidy. Jason. And—yeah, Kip.

We were all around about the same age, except for Allison who was older than the rest of us by a year, already in sixth grade while we were still stuck in fifth. She just loved to bring it up whenever she got the opportunity, which was pretty much whenever she opened her mouth to breathe oxygen. Always huffing on about how she wasn't our babysitter:

I'm not changing your diapers, dipshits.

Not that it stopped her from tagging along. Allison didn't have any friends her own age. She was stuck with us just as much as we were stuck with her. Her fish lips. Mudskipper mouth.

Ew, stop looking at me like that.

I wasn't looking at you...

You want to kiss me or something?

No.

Yeah, you do.

Do not...

What forged our friendship? Could've been fate or the simple fact that we all lived in the same subdivision. I don't think we would've been pals if Woodmont wasn't our 'hood. I always got the sense that Jason would've preferred to've played at home alone, where there's AC, but his mom insisted the fresh air would do him good. Kip never talked about his mom or dad, so I don't know what his family's deal was. Truth is, our parents kicked us all out of our houses in the morning and told us not to come back until the street lights flickered on. Until then, they didn't give a flip where we were as long as we stayed out of trouble. We'd hop on our bikes and pedal around the neighborhood. That's it. Wasn't like there was much else to do.

There just wasn't anywhere for us to go, you know?

Where we going? Jason asked us all.

Kip, our de facto leader, was the only one to answer. *How about the creek?*

Again?

Got any better ideas?

What about my house?

To do what?

I dunno...

Woodmont was landlocked. There was a cross-stitch of train tracks on one side and a highway on the other. Crossing that concrete artery was never really an option. Not on our Schwinns. This was the Atari era, so *Frogger* was on all of our minds. There was this *one story* about that *one kid* from the neighborhood, years back, who tried braving all four lanes on his bike and getting pancaked by some semi before he even reached the median. That truck driver dragged this kid's Huffy halfway to Powhatan before he even realized there was a mangled corpse caught along his semi's underside, scraping pavement for miles and miles and miles...

None of us knew this kid's name or which house he lived in, but you bet your life we all believed that story. You just can't make that kind of stuff up. It had to've happened to somebody at some time, the tale getting passed down through generations of Woodmonters.

So, yeah—no hitting up the highway for us.

That left the tracks. They were certainly less of a threat. The only time an actual train trolleyed through was the butt-crack of dawn, before the sun even came up, so there was never any worry over an Amtrak barreling down on us. Mostly just freight trains chugged through, hefting these open beds piled high with eastern white pines. Trunks for lumber. New homes.

I got an idea, Kip said, hopping on his bike and pedaling off. *Come on. Let's go.*

Where?

Just follow me...

The neighborhood on the other side of the tracks was called Greenfield. I knew some kids from that subdivision, but there was this weird territorial rivalry between us and them, some real old-school Sharks versus Jets junk, so we didn't mingle much with those guys. They kept on their side of the tracks and we kept on ours. A truce among tribes. Anyone who set foot on the other side was entering into enemy territory and would suffer the consequences.

Going outta my mind, Jason muttered. *I'm so friggin' bored. It's too hot out here.*

Quit whining.

Where we going? Kelly asked and I wished I had an answer, even if she was talking to Kip.

Just up ahead.

Where?

You'll see...

Beyond both of our neighborhoods was this patch of undeveloped land nestled into the surrounding woods. You had to wander further along the tracks to reach it. That meant dismounting our bikes and walking them over the sleepers. Didn't take all that long to get there. Less than an hour, tops. Neither neighborhood could claim it. It wasn't a part of Greenfield and it definitely wasn't Woodmont's. It wasn't anybody's, really. Just this empty stretch of flattened ground. A liminal bit of land. Looked like somebody had tried building something on it at some point, cutting down all the nearby trees and bulldozing the ground, only to call it quits.

That's where we first found The Pit.

Check it out, Kip said. *How cool is that?*

What is it? Kelly asked.

A pit.

Who said it? Wasn't me. Must've been Kip. Maybe Jason, I can't recall. Simply saying the word 'pit' was enough. The name just stuck, I guess. That's what we called it all summer.

The Pit.

What do you think caused it? Kelly asked, transfixed.

Meteor, maybe? I know how nerdy I must've sounded, suggesting some meteorite hit Virginia however many millions of years ago, making this meager depression in the ground. It certainly wouldn't have been the first. I was huge into science back then. Not like real-real science, but the kind of stuff that sort of felt scientific. Science-y. Like, did you know there's an impact crater located right at the mouth of the Chesapeake Bay? No lie. Still there. A big ol' bolide struck the eastern shore over 35 million years ago. One mile deep, over fifty miles wide.

This crater was nowhere near as big as that one, but still. It was ours.

Kip called bullshit. *Yeah, right. That's no meteor.*

Well, what do you think it is?

Kip figured it was the beginnings of somebody's basement. A home was supposed to go there. We were standing in the middle of what would've been a brand-new subdivision. If I squinted hard enough, I could almost picture the houses sprouting out from the ground.

So why did they stop? I asked. *Why leave?*

Nobody really had an answer for that.

We tossed rocks into The Pit. There really wasn't much else to do with it. Some weeds sprouted out from the basin. Crab grass, I guess. I spotted a green bottle. Maybe it was blue. Could've been an empty 7Up or something else, half buried in the soil. Its color kept changing. Rusted beer cans settled at the bottom. The ashen remnants of a bonfire, courtesy of the Mullet Militia. That's what we called the heavy metal high schoolers who came out here at night to party. They'd drink whatever beer they pilfered from their parents, tossing the empties into The Pit. Our Pit. Sacrificing cats out here in the middle of the night. Or kids.

This is stupid, Allison said. *You dragged us out here for this?*

Yeah.

It's just a stupid hole in the ground.

But that wasn't true. Even I knew that. Felt it, somehow, even from the very first moment. Kip might've been convinced that it was man-made, but a part of me still believed—wanted to believe—that The Pit was the product of hypervelocity impact with an astronomical object. Even a meteor the size of a soccer ball could leave behind a circular depression in the earth's surface, right? It definitely wouldn't have been the first to hit Virginia, all those millions of years ago.

What if a chunk of an asteroid had broken off and landed back here? In Woodmont? It's possible, wasn't it? How cool would it have been to uncover another crater?

Last one in's a rotten egg. Kip was the first to hop in. He was always the first. He pretended The Pit was a pool—*Cannonball!*—skidding down the slope on his heels. *Come on in!*

Jason was next. Then Allison, eye rolling all the way down.

Kelly and me stood at the edge, our toes poking over The Pit's lip.

You going in? She asked me and I kind of just shrugged.

Don't be such a chickenshit, Allison shouted. She was the first to curse out of all of us, since she was a year older. *Come on!*

Here's the thing: I had a crush on Kelly, but Kelly had a crush on Kip. That's at least what Jason said. If Kip was going somewhere, anywhere, then so would Kelly, and if Kelly was going, then you'd better believe I was, too. That meant Allison was chaperoning her baby sister. Talk about a total dick-killer. Wasn't like the three of us boys were horndogs or whatever. Allison just didn't trust us. She knew what was up, I guess. If I was standing next to Kelly, she'd give me this look—more like a goddamn glare—that said: *Back off, asshole.* It wasn't like I was all doe-eyed around Kelly or anything. She never noticed. The only person who knew I had a crush on her was Jason, but he swore he'd never tell. I would punch him so hard, so help me God.

Who did Kip have a crush on? Good question.

Bones!

Bullshit, Allison snapped.

Look.

Kip was right. Half-buried at the bottom of The Pit, beneath the loose bedding of pebbles, were these sun-bleached teeth. *Are those fangs?* Kip took a stick and started digging around the skull, sweeping the rocks away from its domed slope like he was some kind of junior archeologist, and this was our big dig. Pebbles had settled into its sockets, whatever it was.

What is it? I asked, still standing along the ledge. *A cat?*

Bigger than a cat.

A raccoon?

Kip poked his stick through one of its eyeholes in order to loosen it, try and pry it out from the dirt, but it wouldn't budge. He got down on his knees and started using his hands to pull it out. He always wore the same pair of cargo shorts every single day through that whole summer. Maybe they weren't the *exact* same pair, but they were at least the same brand, so it kind of looked like he only had one set of shorts, which was enough for Allison to mess with him.

Better be careful, she started. *Don't wanna get your crusty shorts all dirty...*

Shut up.

What? Your mom can only afford one pair?

Up yours.

Crusty shorts, crusty shorts, crust—

Kip uprooted the skull with his bare hands like a toothsome potato. *Whoa, check it out...* He held it up over his head for us all to see. He shifted his position in The Pit, doing some kind of kneeling 360, dragging his leg over the soft bedding of pebbles. *How friggin' cool is tha—*

I heard Kip hiss.

At first, I thought he was making some kind of caveman sound at Allison, baring his teeth at her. But he dropped the skull and clutched his shin with both hands. Blood immediately seeped through his fingers, not a lot, but enough for us to clench our breaths tight in our lungs.

Kip picked something out from his leg.

A piece of glass. Just a shard of green glass. Maybe it was purple. The color kind of depended on where the sun struck it. A broken bottle, that's all. The whole Pit was full of junk.

You should clean that up, Kelly said and I felt jealous.

Yeah, OK.

Here's the thing: we were always getting injured somehow. This wasn't Kip's first scrape. We were all wounded. Nothing ever needed stitches—or if it did, we never got them. We just sucked it up. Bruised knees and shallow lacerations were just part of our summer.

Which is just to say none of us—not me, at least—gave Kip's cut much thought. Even he forgot all about it. Life just moved on. We all walked our bikes along the tracks as the sun sank deeper into the surrounding trees, listening to the crickets. We never said goodbye to one another at the end of the day. We just broke off at our respective houses, simply heading in for the night, knowing we'd pick up where we left off the following morning.

That evening, at dinner, my mom asked me what we'd been up to that day.

Nothing, I said. Always said.

I never mentioned The Pit, not to Mom or anyone else, even when it was at the forefront of my mind. Always on my mind. I couldn't stop thinking about it. I dreamed of tiny meteors making their way down to Earth, gaining their cosmic velocity before hitting the ground and sending a massive shockwave all through Woodmont, the roads rippling with its impact, until it knocked every last house down in its wake.

Kabooooom.

~

We spent the summer out there in The Pit.

We all just gravitated toward it, I guess. Wasn't like there was some conscious decision on our part. Nobody said anything like, *Hey, who wants to go to The Pit?* Or, *How about we take a ride to The Pit?* We just went. We'd find each other and simply head for the tracks.

Kip started limping not long after that. He slowed down. He wasn't running around like the rest of us anymore. He just sort of hobbled along, catching up to us. Always out of breath.

Hey, wait up...

He stopped wearing shorts. Which was stupid. Wearing pants in the middle of July?

Slow down!

Sometimes he'd beat us out there. Like he got a leg up on the rest of us, waking up early and getting to work. For real. Kip treated it like it was a full-time job or something. He enlisted the rest of us to help excavate the skeletons that were embedded in the gravel bed at the bottom of The Pit. So far, we'd found the remains of a possum, a dog, and what we're pretty sure was a deer. We have no idea how much we were mingling bones, but we laid out the remains of each animal along the surrounding ground, trying our best to piece together the puzzles of these dead creatures and see if we could figure out which bones belonged to which.

Kelly was pretty good at finding the flow of bones. She'd see connections between vertebrae the rest of us just couldn't see, like it was all a jigsaw. Before long, by the middle of July, I'd say, the ground around The Pit was layered in concentric skeletal circles, each one its own animal. Like patterns. Ceramic white. Osseous heatwaves radiating out from our crater.

That's really beautiful, I said to Kelly, immediately regretting it.

You think?

Um... what's that one? I pointed to what could've been a raccoon.

She shrugged. *Skunk, maybe?*

Kip wanted to camp out there. He brought it up one day like it was no big deal. *What if we spent the night?* Allison shot it down straight away. There was no way her and Kelly's parents would ever let them go camping with a bunch of boys, so they were no-gos from the get-go. Jason was down, but he'd have to tell his mom that he was spending the night at someone's house. Me... I felt weird about it. Something was off about Kip's eagerness to come out here at night. In the dark. I didn't like it, whatever it was. I didn't want to. I made up some story about my mother not letting me, which wasn't true. I didn't even bring it up to my parents.

I'm not going to say I was afraid of The Pit, but there was definitely a part of me that wondered what was up with it. Up with Kip, too.

He was looking pretty worse for wear by then. Paler, I guess. Blue. It kind of just depended on how the sun hit his skin, like his flesh was fluctuating under the light. Most of us were getting sunburns from our time outside, while he seemed to be losing his tan. All the colors were sucked out from his skin the longer he was here.

You OK? I asked. *You look kinda sick.*

I'm fine.

Are you sure you don't wanna—

I'm fine.

By late July, there sure seemed to be a lot more bones lining the surrounding ground. You know how Saturn has all those rings of debris wrapped around it? Our Pit had skeletal rings. Skulls and ribs and femurs belonging to all kinds of unknown animals now circled around our hole in the ground. Kelly was making all kinds of patterns by then. A single skeleton could stretch out three or four feet, each bone laid out a few inches from its neighbor. After a while, the bones tended to blend together. Kelly was less concerned about piecing them back the way they were when these animals were still alive, and more—I don't know—just finding a flow for the bones. Letting the skeletons take on their own shape. Their own rhythms. It looked less like a bunch of different dead animals and more like some weird Morse code written out in bones.

Can you hear them? Kelly asked me once, staring out at all the patterns. I didn't really know what she meant by it, so I just sort of acted like I hadn't heard her.

~

I was pretty positive Kip was coming out to The Pit without the rest of us. He was always the first on site and the last to leave. When it was time to go home for the day, he'd make up some stupid excuse about staying behind. *I'll catch up*, but he never did. I noticed a sleeping bag rolled up and tucked behind a palette of bricks. Fresh candy bar wrappers littered the grass.

I tried bringing this all up to Kelly one day while we were walking our bikes out to The Pit. *Do you think Kip's OK? Do you think he's acting a little, I dunno... weird?*

What's the matter? Allison piped in before Kelly could. *Worried about your boyfriend?*

Shut up.

When we reached The Pit, I didn't see Kip. I thought we'd actually beaten him out there. First time for everything, I guess.

Ow ow ow...

...Kip?

Ow ow ow...

Kip? We could all hear him, even if we couldn't see him.

Ow ow ow...

He was in The Pit. Rolling on his back. Rutting like a pig.

It was so weird. We all circled around the edge and just looked at him for a while. Watching him grovel. It was hard to tell if he was in pain or enjoying himself. I don't know how long we all stood there, just gawking at him. Felt like forever. I skidded down the slope and grabbed his arm to help him up, but he hissed through his teeth at me, batting my hand away.

Ow ow oowwww...

What's wrong?

Ow ow ow...

His left pants leg was soaked through. It wasn't blood, or not only blood. It was orange. Rusty colored fluid oozed through. I tugged his pants just to see what was going on under there.

Branches of amethyst laced his legs, the veins a deep purple. Blisters speckled his skin. Angry red welts. One of them had popped and I swore I thought it was blinking back at me.

It was.

This gasping aperture budged from the crater of skin.

A mouth.

I could make out the jaws opening and closing.

A worm.

I picked up a bone. A rib or something super-thin. Maybe it was a raccoon femur or whatever. I don't know why I did it, I just wanted something in my hand. To poke the worm with. I brought the tip closer to Kip's blister and the worm or whatever actually reached out for it. Budded up less than an inch and gripped on to the stick. That worm tugged, so I tugged back.

Ow ow ow. Kip winced and hissed when I pulled too tight.

That is so gross, Allison said. *I'm gonna be sick...*

Be careful, Kelly said to me. *Don't break it.*

Break it?

Go slow, she said. *Wind it up.* I remembered something our science teacher had told us last year and I knew exactly what Kelly was getting at.

Ever seen the symbol for medicine? It's got Asclepius? The god of medicine? He's always got his rod with the serpent all twisted around it. Some people believe it's not a snake at all.

Some say it's a tapeworm.

A guinea worm. The old-fashioned way of removing the parasite was to take a stick and wrap one end around and slowly twist and twist until you tugged the worm all the way out. Guinea worms get so long, sometimes as long as ten feet, living under their host's skin, that it takes months and months to uproot them. You just got to keep twisting and twisting and...

So we did.

I don't know how long we worked at it. Could've been there for hours. All day for all I know. Allison kept complaining how queasy she was feeling, so we got Jason and her to ride their bikes back to Woodmont to go tell somebody's parents. Anybody's parents. Get help.

What about you? Allison had asked her baby sister. *You can't stay here...*

I'll be fine. Just go.

Me and Kelly took turns slowly twisting the rib, winding that worm out from Kip's wound. Whenever one of our wrists got too sore to continue, we'd trade off. That worm had wrapped itself around the entire length of bone. I didn't think a worm could grow that long.

It had to be—what? Two feet? Three? It just kept going and going and still there was more of it, spooling around the bone like pulsating fishing line. There's no telling how far it went.

Me and Kelly never left Kip's side. Never left The Pit. Kip kept moaning. Sweated all the way through his clothes. He had bitten down on his bottom lip so hard, he'd drawn blood.

I'm tired, I said. *Can you take a turn?*

Sure, Kelly said.

When I handed her the bone, our fingers touched. Just for a second. It was more like a graze, skin brushing against skin, but it was enough to send a ripple through me. A shockwave.

Kelly must've felt it, too, 'cause she looked up at me. Felt like the first time we'd ever been alone. Like, truly alone. Just the two of us. We'd spent so much time together, the whole summer, and yet, through it all, through everything, we'd never actually had any time by ourselves before. I mean, even now Kip was there, on the ground, but it still felt like it was just us two.

I'd never noticed how green Kelly's eyes were before.

Or were they purple?

The sun was starting to sink behind the surrounding tree line, and I didn't think we were even close to getting the whole tapeworm out.

Kelly must've tugged too hard because the tendril snapped. *Oh, shit!* She almost lost the other half, watching the tapeworm reel itself back into Kip's skin like the drawstring on a doll. But instead of saying something stupid like, *Hi, my name is Polly!*, it was just Kip hissing *ow ow oooooww...*

I caught the tapeworm in time. I pinched the flickering bit between my fingers and gently held on long enough for Kelly to wrap it back around the bone. *That was a close one...* We were running out of sunlight by the breath. I really didn't feel like staying out here at night.

Where was Jason? Allison?

What do we do now?

Just keep going, I guess.

After a while winding on the worm in silence, Kelly finally asked, *So how come you never kissed me?*

You knew?

Yeah. I was so embarrassed, so I didn't say anything. For once I was thankful the sun was going down, so she couldn't see how much I was blushing.

Kelly filled up the silence. *Guess I was waiting for you to say something. Why didn't you?*

I was too afraid, I guess.

Of what?

The Pit, I thought. I don't know why. It was the first thing that popped into my mind.

The Pit. Always The Pit. We were pulled back here, into this very same hole, day after day, for months now, rutting through the bones of others, digging deeper. Searching.

It's not too late, Kelly said. *Summer isn't over yet...*

I didn't know what she meant by that.

Kelly closed her eyes first. Her lips parted just enough that I could barely make out her tongue nestled behind her teeth.

She breathed in and held it. Tilted her head to one shoulder. I was supposed to do something, wasn't I? Follow her lead and mirror her movements? Lean in and meet her lips?

I'd never done this before. I didn't know what I was supposed to do with myself. My hands. My whole body felt awkward, overheated. I was still holding on to the tapeworm.

All I could do was close my eyes and ram my face into Kelly's, ram it in so forcefully, with such cosmic velocity that it ruptured the surface of her face, embedding my bones deep into her own and creating an impact crater in her skull that would last millions of years. Molten strands of amethyst fuse our bodies together, her flesh melting into steaming rivulets, while I just force my way in deeper, *deeper*, burrowing as far as my bones will go, *deeper*, my skull a geode that's crawled across the cosmos and now it's cracked open and leaking its lavender passengers into the fertile soil. The type of kiss that would linger long after we're gone.

God, I was never forgetting this summer.

sweetmeat

Melts in your mouth. That's what they always say, isn't it? Here I was, drowning in a high-fructose flood guttered between my cheeks, and I never wanted to come up for air again.

I couldn't tell you what the hell that candy was. If it even *was* candy, for Christ's sake. Whether it was taffy or marshmallow or some other spongey kind of confection, the second that sweet settled over my tongue and my saliva seeped in, those enzymes started working their magic. Dissolved it down as fast as flesh in a fucking acid bath. Its sugar eased into my bloodstream—straight for the mainline—and I was just... *just gone.* Obliterated before I could even swallow. I had never tasted anything like it in my entire life. I didn't know if I ever would again.

That was why I needed to find it. Taste it just one more time.

That goddamn sweetmeat.

~

So, this was the first year Jasper asked if he could go trick-or-treating without me, which I'll admit... *ouch.* Stung. He only had a year before he was too old for all this. Once he was in the sixth grade—seventh, tops—he'd have to call it quits. No more ringing doorbells, demanding candy. His pals wanted to hit up the houses without any adult supervision. Without me. Ol' fuddy duddy here.

Look, I get it. A parent-free Halloween. Total rite of passage. You need at least one year where you don't have your dad breathing down your neck. You want to be free with your friends. Roam the streets. I definitely wreaked a little Halloween havoc when I was their age.

Promise you won't toilet-roll the neighborhood?

Promise.

No egging anybody's houses.

Daaad...

At least Jasper still put in the effort to dress up. His friends didn't even wear costumes anymore. They just rubbed some fake blood over their faces, looking like drooling lunatics. As if that was enough to qualify as a costume. If they came to my door, I wouldn't give them any candy.

Not that I knew exactly what Jasper's costume was. He told me its name, but I promptly forgot. *Peek-a-chewy* or *Yugi-yo-yo* or something like that. I can't remember now. He looked like some mascot for an extraterrestrial basketball team—Space Jamming as far as I could tell.

Just come home by nine, got it? Not nine-oh-one now.

OK.

And don't eat anything until I've had a chance to check!

OK, OK...

Have fun, pal, I called after him. *Bring home something good!*

He didn't say anything back.

It had to be hard, letting go of the holiday. This was Jasper's final Halloween. One last hurrah around the 'hood before hanging up the ol' candy sack. I really felt for the kid. Growing up can be hard.

That went for both of us.

I felt like we were running out of rituals here, Jasper and me. We carved our jack-o'-lanterns earlier that evening, like always, leaving a slimy mess spread all over the countertop. The knife was still out, its handle all tacky. These cubed chunks of sliced and diced pumpkin shell were in a dish, waiting to get tossed into the compost, nothing but the negative space of our jack-o'-lantern's eyes and nose, its jagged mouth, all cut out and gathering fruit flies.

That was OK. I would clean up later...

Time for Dad to have a little Halloween fun of his own. Maybe a wee bit more trick than treat. I had the night all to myself. Might as well try something new, right? I grabbed that dish and emptied the pumpkin chunks out, filling the bowl to the brim with fun sizes. Then I found an index card. A Sharpie marker. In bold, black capital letters, I wrote: TAKE ONE.

Yeah, *right*, like any kid had enough self-restraint to simply pinch a single candy bar. This was a seasonal litmus test. The Halloween Challenge: I left the bowl on our front stoop, turned off all the lights in the house so it looked like nobody was home... and then hid behind the bushes.

Let the games begin.

I waited—and waited—until that first group of trick-or-treaters wandered up, eyeing the bowl like it was some kind of ancient Aztecan relic, and they were treasure hunters sniffing for booby traps. If they followed the instructions and only took one candy bar, they would be safe. Good to go. No harm done. But if some punk thought he could get away with grabbing a handful of candy—

BOOGEDY BOO!

—I'd leap out from behind the bush and scare the ever-living shit out of them. Watch them all crap in their costumes. See them run down the street, screaming their little heads off.

Come again next year, kids!

I'm here all night, folks...

But I got bored behind the bush. Popping a squat for that long was really doing a number on my knees. My body wasn't made for this kind of stakeout anymore. Plus, it was getting cold out. I just ended up leaving the bowl on the stoop and went inside. *I should clean up the kitchen,* I thought, but I watched a bit of the creature feature on TV until Jasper came back.

Welcome home!

Hey.

How was it, bud?

Good.

Just good? Did you guys have fun?

Yeah.

These monosyllabic answers were killing me. *Nice haul?*

Yeah. He was still wearing his costume, that mask pulled up to his temples, so it looked like he had two sets of eyes. The top ones were much larger, saucer-like, unblinking. Staring at me.

Anybody doling out king-size candy bars this year?

No.

Any toothbrushes?

No.

Alrighty, then... Hand it over. My dad-duty included divvying up the candy. Before that first bite, I had to parse through Jasper's stash to make sure there wasn't anything... *unsavory.*

I cleared a space on the countertop, pushing the pumpkin chunks back so I could get straight to work examining his candy. In and out. No fuss. I just needed to make sure there weren't any hypodermic needles or candy apples laced with rat poison or razor blades embedded in chocolate bars.

Nobody *actually* expected to find any of that stuff, not really. But my own mother—Jasper's grandma, God bless her—caught some segment on Fax News about whacked-out addicts slipping rainbow-colored fentanyl to kids during Halloween, which, I'm sorry, sounded like absolute horseshit to me. Why would anyone dole out their own drug cache to trick-or-treaters instead of, you know, taking them? Everybody was always looking for a good scare on Halloween. Even the twenty-four-hour news cycle got in on the fun, freaking out all the ol' grannies with fresh renditions of rehashed urban legends, recycling the same crap I heard when I was a kid.

Same story, only with shiny new packaging: *Watch out for frightening fentanyl, kiddies!*

Jasper had himself a pretty impressive stash. Seemed like a good year: Snickers, Baby Ruths. Tootsie Rolls, Dum-Dums... Christ, who still gave out Dum-Dums these days?

Nothing out of the ordinary. No tampered wrappers. No unpackaged snacks, no Rice Krispies treats. No needle marks. *Looks good to me*, I told Jasper. *All clear for consumption!*

Hold on a sec. Wait.

What is that?

There. Right there. Nestled between a Milky Way and a Skittles packet.

A fuzzy lump.

A tumor.

First diagnosis: *That's gotta be a Peeps, right?* One of those marshmallow chicks out of its packaging. All spongy. Yellow. Nope—strike that. This was creamsicle colored. Orange. It could've easily been a piece of pumpkin shell from the color of it all, a soft section of an eye carved out from a jack-o'-lantern. Somehow, it must have slipped into Jasper's bag by accident.

I plucked up the chunk, pinching it between my fingers. It wasn't shaped like a chick at all. It certainly wasn't a shard of pumpkin shell. It was just a square hunk of sugar. A squishy cube, all pink hued. Sorry, make that lavender. I couldn't quite pin its color down.

OK, so maybe it wasn't a Peeps... Then what the hell was it? I tested its consistency, gently pressing down on it. The puffball inflated back to its original dimensions after I let it go.

Jasper didn't need to eat this... whatever this was.

Into the reject pile it went.

All yours, champ... I handed the bag over.

Jasper grabbed his stash and rushed for the living room, so he could parse out his bounty into different piles. Chocolates over here, hard candies over there. He was so systematic about it, so color coordinated. Killed me. Where did this kid get his organizational OCD from? Definitely not from his father.

Suddenly my sweet tooth kicked in.

All this surveying of candy left me craving something yummy. I wasn't feeling particularly picky. Just needed something to sate the seasonal need for treats.

All I had was the crap I cut out from Jasper's stash. So, I eyed the reject pile. The bottom barrel discount sweets. The off-brand candy.

What would one hurt? I deserved a little something for my trouble, didn't I?

Treat thyself, good man...

I picked up the weird one. The not-Peeps or whatever you call it. Don't ask me why, but it felt warmer. Warmer than before. Like I'd had it in my hand all along, heating the chunk up with my own body temperature, until it was all hot and sticky. Kind of felt like flesh.

Who would actually eat something this sticky?

Christ, who'd hand a candy like this out?

There was this one family up the block—the Lindens. A little granola-y, if you get my drift. Lots of crystal windchimes. Instead of handing out fun sizes for Halloween, they made their own sugarless snacks for the kids. Little Ziplock baggies of homemade trail mix. That sort of thing. I could totally imagine them whipping up their own batch of gluten-free marshmallows or whatever the hell this nubbin was. This had their little hippie-dippy recipes written all over it.

So. Marshmallow. Obviously. Dangerous? Hardly. I simply popped it in my mouth and—

angels

angels

angels

angels

angels

angels

angels

angels

angels

angels

—bleeding all of a sudden. I must've bitten my tongue because there was red all over the countertop now. A slender thread of pink drool dribbled down my chin, suspended like a shimmering pendulum on a grandfather clock. It swayed and snapped and splatted against the tile.

What the hell just happened?

Where did I go?

I had no idea how long I blacked out. I'd lost hold of myself. Of time. My grip on the moment had slipped. I still felt dizzy. The kitchen wouldn't stop spinning. I had to grab hold of the counter to balance myself. Stay upright. All my senses had silenced themselves, save for taste.

Sugar. On my tongue.

In my blood.

My body.

The sweetness reached all the way in—I mean, down deep—to the core of me. My very being. I had never tasted, never experienced, anything as honeyed as this.

How could a chunk of sugar make me feel so insignificant? Like nothing else mattered?

What's the sweetest thing you ever tasted?

Pixy Stix?

Fun Dip?

Those are nothing but pure processed sugar.

Go further.

Sweeter.

Take the sweetest thing you've ever tasted.

Now multiply it.

By a million.

You're still not even close. I'm talking about a transformative experience here, where the second that confection hits your tongue and your taste buds activate, you are no longer the person you were before. You'll never be that person ever again. That person doesn't exist anymore. The flavor alters you. *Converts* you. There's no going back.

Fentanyl was the furthest thing from my mind. Mesh all the meth, the heroin, whatever drug of choice, it still couldn't match the impact of that heavenly confection. Not even close.

All I could think about was that sweetmeat.

The most delectable treat.

I had never been one for religion, but this truly felt like some BC and AD kind of shit. From there on out, I could mark my existence to what my life was like before I tasted that sweetmeat... and then everything after.

One simple swallow, that was all it took. This was a spiritual awakening. An edible epiphany. A lightning bolt to my tongue.

A cosmic marshmallow.

Manna from Heaven.

Where did this sweetmeat come from? Whose house was doling it out?

How could I find more?

Poking my head into the living room, I spotted Jasper's haul all lined up in neat piles. The candy bars, the lollipops, Jolly Ranchers—just looking at them all made my stomach twist.

Those weren't sweets. Not really. His stash was nothing but saccharine ash.

Hey, Jasper... Quick question for you. Which, uh... which houses did you hit up tonight?

He glanced up at me like this was all some kind of trick (or treat) question. *Why?*

Do you remember your route?

We just went up the street.

Our street?

Yeah.

What about the rest of the neighborhood?

We didn't leave the—

I know, I know. It's not that. I just—I just wanna know which houses you went to.

Why?

Just tell me which houses.

I don't know...

What do you mean you don't know?

I don't know!

You don't remember, or you just don't want to tell me?

I needed to find the sweetmeat. One of our neighbors had given it to him, right? It couldn't have just magically materialized in his candy sack. Whoever doled it out had to be in our neighborhood.

I just had to figure out where, who—and fast. I could feel myself crashing. The celestial sugar rush was already ebbing away from my bloodstream, leaving me feeling empty. Hollow.

Do you think it might've been—

A punch in the gut abruptly forced me forward. My intestines clenched.

Dad?

I'm fine. It's OK.

Are you—

I'm fine, I'm fine. I just need to... need to...

I'd been dosed. That was what this all was. Perhaps it actually was fentanyl after all. Mom was right. Fax News was right. *Fuck*, I thought. *Oh, fuck. I'm high right now.* The urban legend was true. Someone in our neighborhood really had tampered with the candy and I was tripping my balls off. What could I do? Call 911? Instead, I ran into the bathroom and gripped the edge of the sink, staring down my reflection in the mirror as my brain launched into the cosmos, hitting the stratosphere at eleven kilometers per second, twenty-five thousand miles per fucking hour.

What do I do what do I do what do I—

My first tooth fell out. It slipped past my lips and hit the tiles, a shooting star.

Well, that was unexpected...

I leaned into the mirror and pulled back my upper lip. Sure enough, it looked as if I hadn't brushed in months—Jesus, *years*. These cavities were wreaking absolute havoc throughout my mouth. My teeth wobbled about the gumline, tipsy passengers onboard a pink cruise liner in the middle of a monsoon, all of them falling overboard.

This isn't real none of this is real none of this is really really happening—

I pinched a cuspid. Without as much as a wiggle, the tooth uprooted itself... and dissolved. The enamel, the very bone, had gone all soft, smearing into this off-colored paste.

I'm high right now; that's all. I'm hallucinating. None of this is real none of this is real—

I still found myself craving it. I needed more.

Just one more bite.

One simple nibble.

You just don't get it. You can't understand. There is no word in the human lexicon that can register the saccharine caliber of this candy. Explaining the taste to someone who's never tried it is simply a waste. The sweetmeat opens your senses. Expands your tastebuds. There are flavors that go beyond the monosaccharide spectrum. Beyond *sarkara*. Beyond *shakar*. Beyond *sucre* or *jaggery* or *jagara* or *cakkara*. This sugar doesn't come from our world. It isn't meant for our mouths. Our blood. To taste it is to lick from the cosmic Fun Dip of the gods.

Jasper called out to me from the living room, and I snapped back to our realm. *Can I have another candy, Dad?*

How many have you had already?

Three?

That's enough sweets for one night, son...

Not enough. Never enough.

Please? Just one more?

I said no. I lifted my voice a little too much for my own tastes, my temper flaring fast, punctuating the 'no' with another tooth spilling out of my mouth and tumbling into the sink.

Pleeeeease?

What did I just say? No more candy, damn it!

I couldn't control myself. This empty-calorie rage just came out of nowhere. I felt like I'd eaten nothing but crappy candy all night. All day. This was withdrawal. It had to be. I was crashing fast. Too fast. Like falling out from the sky. A migraine ice-picked my temples. I hadn't meant to snap at Jasper. I needed to settle my stomach. Needed something more than just—

sweet

—sugar in my belly. I had to get out of the house. Had to find the—

meat

—house where this candy had come from. Just to know what I'd taken. What it was doing to me. How to make it stop. Make it all stop.

Jasper didn't lift his head from the floor when I told him I was stepping out, which was a relief. Small blessings. If he happened to glance up at me as I slipped through the door, he would've seen this drooling lunatic with flapping gums. Luckily, most trick-or-treaters were already home. Halloween was coming to a close for another year.

That left the streets to me.

~

Look, you don't have to tell me how weird it is for an adult to be wandering up and down the block by himself. I know how this looked. How I looked. But I needed to see. Needed to try.

Which house was it?

Who drugged me?

Already my stomach was twisting. The cramps came on quick. Felt like a punch to the gut. I was hungry. So fucking hungry. But the thought of food made me sick. All I wanted was—

angels

—that candy, that sweet sweetmeat. I found myself doing this odd, cramped crabwalk, hobbling down the block while holding my stomach, just trying to keep everything in place.

I'd given up on wiping my face, letting the drool funnel down the chin. I could hear my own lips smack against my swollen gums every time I breathed through my mouth.

I knocked on doors. All the way up our block. *Hey, uh... this is a weird one for you, but... I'm curious. What kind of candy did you hand out tonight? Was it a marshmallowy-type thingy?*

Though, truth told, it came out sounding more like *sweeeeeeeetmeeeeeeeeeaaat*

sweeeeeeeesweeeeeeeesweeeeeeeeeeeetah-tah-taaah

mmm-mmm-mmmmmmmeeeeeat

I was the one trick-or-treating now. Look at me, in my spooky costume! Listen to me, asking for candy! Gimme gimme a treat! Please! Just one sweet... But not just any candy, no.

I needed that majestic sweetmeat. Need more more more. Need it nooooooow.

Was it this house?

Or this one?

Or this?

Of course, my neighbors looked at me like I'd gone mad. I was going door to door, interrogating them about a candy I couldn't explain, couldn't articulate. That was because they hadn't tasted it for themselves. They didn't understand. How could they? How could anyone?

They wouldn't know. They could never know.

You haven't tasted it, I can tell. You'll never taste it. Never get your hands on a yummy morsel. Never perch a chunk on your tongue, sealing your lips over it, closing your eyes and taking a deep breath through your nose before letting your saliva saturate that sweetmeat.

Eat, for this is my body.

You'll never know what it's like to taste a slice of heaven. If you did, you'd be just like me. You'd dedicate the rest of your miserable existence trick-or-treating to the ends of the fucking world, knocking on every last door on this goddamn planet, every day, all year long, until your feet are nothing but bloody stumps, your body nothing more than skin and bones...

Someone might've called the police. A cruiser swept down the street. I hid behind a bush, crouching low, where they couldn't find me. The morning sun softened the horizon. I'd gone to the outer borders of our suburb and back again, winding throughout our neighborhood.

There weren't any houses left. I'd knocked on every last door.

Save for one.

Every neighborhood has that one house. The house that doesn't take part in the holiday. I would've walked by without giving it much thought. There were no lights on. It looked empty.

Funny, I thought, *it looks a lot like our house.*

I had found it. Finally found it.

The front stoop of a temple. The very gates of Heaven. A dish on its steps. A note written by the angels—

TAKE ONE

I was weak. I had always been weak.

This gift. It was too much for me. I had been granted access to the sugarcane of angels; I had tasted it. It'd been on my tongue. I licked it. Swallowed it. And now I was willing to sacrifice everything, everything I had in this world, for just one more mouthful.

One more taste.

Sweet.

Meat.

Maybe they had more inside. Something told me to sneak a peek through the window.

Just in case. Just to see.

I could barely make it out through the glass, but lying in the hallway, deeper into the house, was... was...

A body. A body on the floor.

A kid.

Christ, I thought, *there's a child on the floor. He's still wearing his Halloween costume. A cartoon character of some kind. He's not moving. He's just there, on his back. I have to—*

Funny, I thought, *he looks a lot like my—*

Like my—

The door was unlocked, so I slipped in. Raced to this—

This—

angel

angel

angel

angel

angel

angel

angel

angel

angel

angel

Sections of its flesh had been sliced and cubed. The negative space of its eyes. Its nose. The jagged slash of a jack-o'-lantern's mouth. All in piles. You could see where the cutting had stopped around its ribcage. All the colors were bright. Fluorescent. The colors of a Saturday morning cartoon. Purple and pink muscle tissue. Orange and green bones. Blue organs below.

Sweetmeat. Here was the sweetmeat. I had finally found whose house it had come from.

I noticed the knife just next to the body, its handle all tacky. Sticky.

I poked the body.

My fingertip simply sunk deeper into its spongy mass. When I yanked my hand back, the impression left behind by my finger slowly started to spring up into its original shape.

Someone had carved it into small slices. Someone had plopped those portions into a dish and left them out on the doorstep. Someone had written in Sharpie on an index card:

TAKE ONE.

But who has that kind of strength? That level of self-restraint? Who could resist the gravitational pull to grab as many as they could and stuff them all into their bag?

Jesus, how many kids in the neighborhood had taken a slice of this angel home?

How many had already eaten from its flesh?

I hadn't realized my mouth was watering. Not until the drool dripped to my knees, soaking into my slacks.

The knife was right there. All I had to do was pick it up and cut off a piece. Just a small slice. Right where they left off, whoever they were. What would one more chunk hurt?

Why bother with the knife at all? I could just lean in and take a bite right off the bone.

Gimme that sweet, sweet meat.

Lord, it melted right in my mouth.

nail on the head

Where did the hammer come from?

Good question.

It was in my house. Therefore it was my hammer, I guess. Mine now, at least. I must've gotten it from somewhere. The hardware store, sure, even though I have zero recollection of ever buying it. It wasn't my wife's. People simply pick up tools over time, you know? A hammer here, a screwdriver there... After a few years, somewhere in your twenties, your thirties, you suddenly discover you have amassed yourself a complete tool set without even realizing it.

So I inherited this hammer, somehow.

A *Breck & Myer* claw hammer.

Solid titanium head. Titanium apparently dampens the amount of recoil, far more than steel, so it's easier on your wrists. You can hammer away for hours and hardly feel the impact.

When I picked it up, I was surprised how light it was. It had a 16-inch curved hickory handle. It was covered in rust. Rubbing my thumb along the grain, I felt something flake off. I figured it was just the varnish chipping away. But this was crusted. Scraping my fingernail over the wood, I realized the lacquer to this hammer wasn't what was giving it such a rusted finish.

It was blood. Someone's blood had seeped into the grain. And there was a lot of it.

Whose hammer was this?

Nobody was ever going to mistake me for Mr. Fixit—but now that I had my own hammer, I felt like I could repair anything. My wife could make fun of me all she wanted, I could nail anything now. First up was a picture frame of me, Emma and Billy, all two years of him. Emma had already asked me twice to hang it, so I figured I'd knock it off my list straight away.

I lined the nail up along the wall.

Brought my hammer back and...

Smashed my thumb.

Really landed it, too. Everything went blindingly white behind my eyes and suddenly I knew exactly how it felt to puncture someone's skull. Like drywall crumbling. Only wetter, I guess. I could see it so clearly. The hammer's bell popping open a hole the size of a silver dollar. Spin the hammer around and you could use the claws to crack that cranium back even wider. As wide as you wanted. All you had to do was slip the—

I gasped back to the living room. It took me a moment to realize where I was. What time it was. *Who* I was. Felt nauseous. There was a low-wattage throb pulsing out from my hand. My thumb had turned a deep purple. Blood pooled up below the fingernail, flooding underneath.

Still had the hammer in my other hand.

I hadn't let go.

Whoever this hammer belonged to before me, I think they did awful things with it.

Bloody things.

I knew this because, whenever I took the hammer into my hand... I couldn't help but think about doing bloody things with it, too.

I didn't want to pick it back up again. Just thinking about gripping its hickory sent this queasy feeling through my stomach. I didn't want to feel those things—*see those things*—again.

The rending of cranial hemispheres. The opening of bone.

Who does something like that?

Emma noticed something was off. *Hey, Mr. Handyman... Sure could use your help here.*

With what?

Got a loose floorboard in the bedroom that needs some pounding. The double entendre was meant to lighten the mood, but I didn't take the bait. I wasn't in the right frame of mind.

Do you know where the hammer came from? I asked, my mind elsewhere.

What hammer?

Our hammer.

Emma shrugged.

Yard sale? Home Depot? Where?

I could tell she was getting impatient with me. *Are you gonna fix the floorboard or should I?*

I'll do it, I'll do it. Truth was, I didn't want her touching my hammer. Didn't want her to see these things. Simply saying I was going to do it wasn't enough, though. Emma had to see me get up from the couch, grab my hammer and head down the hall to fix the fucking floorboard.

Sure enough, there it was, bent back at a slight curve, peering up from the other boards. Kneeling over it, from this angle, it could have been the slope of someone's neck perched between their shoulder blades, turning their head around just in time to catch a glance of the hammer's bell slamming into the side of their face, tearing through tissue and taking out the top row of their teeth.

Fuck this. No more home repairs. No more hanging pictures. No more Sheetrock.

No more hammering.

I could've thrown the *Breck & Myer* away. Should've thrown it away. I would've—*but*.

Wouldn't *you* want to know?

A little internet sleuthing never hurt anybody. I could noodle around Google in between repair jobs. Take a break and see what I might find out about who this hammer belonged to. I typed in random words like MURDER and HAMMER and was suddenly stunned at all the hits.

Gwendolyn Jennings. Victoria Alcott. I knew these names.

I'd seen these victims before.

Where, though?

Time to tell Emma. She'd understand. She could help me. Billy had just gone down for a nap, so I had to tiptoe into his room in hopes of showing her what I'd found online.

Will you take a look at this? I whispered, holding my phone right up to her face.

Emma reeled back from my screen. I thought it must've been the article about Cherlynn Reynolds getting bludgeoned with a *Breck & Myer* forty-six times that did it, but... no.

What happened to your phone?

What do you mean?

Your screen...

I flipped my phone to face me, and sure enough, the screen was nothing but an obsidian web of cracked glass. Like someone had taken a hammer to it.

Why are you still carrying that around? Emma asked.

Carrying what?

The hammer.

What? I had no idea what she was talking about.

Emma's attention was on my other hand. What I'm holding.

I hadn't even noticed. Not until I glanced down.

There it was. Still in my grip.

How long had I been carrying it?

There have just been so many repairs to do around the house, you know?

It's not like I had time to go out and buy another hammer. I already had a hammer. It worked perfectly fine. Better than fine. They don't make them like this anymore. A *Breck & Meyer*? Feel how lightweight it is. You can pound a nail much faster with it because you're not swinging steel. It takes fewer strikes because of the rate of energy transfer. Your arm doesn't tire out as quickly.

More energy, more nails.

More nails.

More nails.

More nails.

One of these newfangled hammers would've broke before I could even finish my work, I bet. The head would probably dislodge, popping off the handle while I'm banging away *and where would we be then?* No—my *Breck & Myer* was the right tool. The *efficient* tool. It is an extension of myself. A mighty fist. When I held it, I felt its power. Its majesty.

We have had quite a lot of time with each other. The whole weekend. With so much work to do around our house, there was absolutely no time to dilly-dally. To talk. Sleep. Eat. Not with all the walls that needed to be torn down. The spaces that needed to be opened.

Not to mention the nails. So many nails, all of them in need of finding their home.

More nails.

More nails.

More—

I was soaking wet by the time I finished. Covered in sweat. Sore all over. My muscles ached. I could barely lift my arm anymore.

Still had the hammer in my hand, though. My *Breck & Meyer.*

I couldn't let it go.

A wisp of auburn hair had tangled itself into the hammer's claws.

Funny, I remember thinking. *My wife has auburn hair...*

I hadn't noticed her on the floor. At first, I figured she was just a part of work that still needed to be finished. A plank with a few too many nails sticking out of it. A pin cushion.

Can objects hold on to the memories of all the things they've done? Can a hammer be haunted? I'm beginning to believe so. I've got the proof in my hands.

His name had been Edmund.

Edmund Pendleton.

I know this because I have his hammer. I know it's his because I've seen everything he did with it. Everyone he murdered. Whenever I hold it in my hand, I see every swing. Every cudgel. Every strike. I feel the ripple of impact reverberate through my bones. The energy of it travels up my arm and I know what that moment felt like to him. How soft it was. How hard.

What I don't understand is where all the nails came from. How they got over everything in our house. The walls. The floor. The furniture. All studded in nails now. Sea urchins.

Billy's still in his crib. Or maybe it's a porcupine, I don't know. How he didn't wake up with all that hammering going on throughout the house is anybody's guess.

the nocturnal gardener

The heat index peaked at 102 today. The temperature's been teetering in the mid-nineties all week. Any hope of gardening under the pummeling sun has completely wilted. Lord knows I've tried. I've slathered myself up with enough sunscreen that I resemble a shriveled spirit. I've donned a floppy hat that leaves me looking like an elderly mushroom cap. I've even set up an umbrella and hunkered under its shade, clinging to what little cool air I can.

Nothing works.

I'm sweating five minutes into pruning. The fatigue seeps into my system, no matter how hydrated I am. The humidity simply slips under my skin. Soaks into my bones. I'm waterlogged by the time I settle in, baking before I even begin, all groggy after a few snips.

It's the dizzy spells I worry over.

My husband has banned me from our backyard if the thermometer ever climbs over ninety degrees. That's most days now. He has good reason to worry. Last month, Walter found me passed out in my raised tomato bed, crushing the poor seedlings I'd just planted. He rushed out of our house, straining to make it to me in time. What he must've thought in those fleeting moments, I can only imagine... It took all his strength to lift me up, my face flecked in topsoil.

Agatha... Agatha, wake up. Speak to me.

Where am I? How confused I must have sounded, so utterly disoriented. I couldn't focus on his features. Who he even was. The upset expression on this stranger's face terrified me.

Agatha, it's me... It's Walter.

What's going on?

You took a spill.

He struggled to slip my arm over his shoulder and heft me onto my feet.

My seedlings.

Cherry tomatoes had burst beneath my body, their tender stems snapped.

We'll worry over those later. Let's get you inside. That's it, one foot in front of the other.

Now I'm under close watch. Walter won't admit it, but I feel his gaze upon my back whenever I step outside. He lingers by our bedroom window now, keeping a close eye on me.

It's not as comforting as one might think, gardening when there are prying eyes on you. Always surveying every last snip. Waiting for those first signs of heatstroke. Ready to pounce.

He's right. As much as I loathe to admit it, setting foot outside during the day is far too untenable. I can't spend time in my own garden. What do I have left? All of our children have grown, with families of their own. It's merely me and Walter now. There are but few pleasures left in this life. Cultivation is my most prized pastime, but the sun has taken that away from me.

So I've switched. The moon is my ally.

I have become a nocturnal gardener.

Instead of battling against that ungodly heat, I'll wait out the sun. I'm no longer under that wrathful eye in the sky. The second ol' sol sinks into the horizon, I'll sneak into the yard.

I've found I prefer tending to my vegetables in the dark. The humidity holds no domain during the dead of night, when the air is cool against my skin. There's far less sweat.

It's taken some getting used to. For my eyes, mainly. The backyard has closed in on itself. What before was a lush length of lawn, enveloped by my beds, is now all wrapped in shadows.

The world—my world—has changed. Constricted itself. But I don't mind. Dare I say I prefer it—this myopic landscape—reduced to this tiny patch of land. My soil. My garden.

Dusk would suffice, but midnight feels much more special. Walter thinks I've lost my mind, waking up in the middle of the night and crawling out of bed to prune in peace.

Why on earth would anyone choose to do that to themselves? It can't be healthy.

I've slept my whole life. Who needs more?

Your husband, for one.

I've spent enough time with my eyes closed. I want to make the most of what time I have left. I didn't have the heart to tell Walter his snoring keeps me up most nights anyhow. Rather than simply lay there in bed, wide awake, on my back, staring up at the ceiling and cataloging the cornucopia of aches and pains my body has to offer... I'll go outside. To my other bed.

Walter gifted me a headlamp. *So you can see what the hell you're doing*, he said.

I slipped it on over my head, flipping the switch. *How do I look?*

Walter winced, shielding his eyes. *Like a miner.*

I liked that. I imagined digging deep into my raised beds, tunneling further into the earth, winnowing through its darkest chasms, my path illuminated with my new headlamp.

I love it, I said, kissing him on the cheek. *Thank you.*

When will I ever see you now? He sounded mournful, as if he was losing me. Letting go.

You can always come with me, you know? Stay up. Step out. It'd be an adventure.

It's after my bedtime, I'm afraid. I'll wait for you in bed.

I'll kiss him on the forehead when I climb back in, trying not to wake him when I slip under the covers. He lets me sleep in. I won't wake until late in the morning. Sometimes lunch. Walter won't complain—not anymore—when I remind him who's reaping the reward of my nocturnal gardening. Where does he think his cucumber sandwiches come from? The grocer?

We're simply on different schedules. Here we are, in the twilight of our lives. Two ships, as they say, right here in our own bed. Walter has the day, while I have the night.

I have earned this stillness. There's no one out here. No honking cars or barking dogs or drifting conversations from nearby neighbors. No deliveries. No phone calls. No nothing.

It's simply me and my night garden.

We've reached that point in the season where I must bid farewell to my lettuce. The time for tomatoes is upon us. Beans and zucchinis.

I'm tackling my planters tonight. Tying off the stems with twine to keep them upright.

There is no world beyond what is in front of me, what the beam from my headlamp catches. It helps me focus. The world melts away. Not from heat, but my consciousness. I've never been so meditative before.

I'm turning over a new leaf, you might say.

Even my arthritis relents in the dark. I do believe the drop in temperature eases the inflammation in my wrists. There's far less swelling in my joints than there was in the sun. I can spend hours outside and never wince once when I snip. Walter gifted me a pair of pruning shears for our fiftieth. Two years ago. *It has a soft cushion grip,* he said fondly. *For your hands.*

I didn't have the heart to tell him I could barely squeeze these shears shut. I had to hide the fact that I wasn't strong enough to use them back then.

Not anymore. Not now. Not in the night.

The shears are still new. Sharp. The stainless-steel blades glisten under my lamplight, a set of crescent moons, a pair of lunar twins, slicing through the darkness.

It's simple to lose track of time. I do nearly every night. It's only when the sun peeks over the horizon that I realize it's dawn. Time to pack up my tools. Head back to bed. To Walter.

It's so lonely, he told me over lunch. A tomato salad. *I never see you anymore.*

Have you thought about picking up a hobby?

A little late for that, don't you think? Old dogs, new tricks?

It's never too late. I've done it, haven't I?

Are these our lives? Our routine from here on out? Are you ever coming back to bed?

This is who I am, dear. I'm sorry. I am a creature of the night now.

It takes time for my eyes to adjust to the dark. Even then, I slip on my reading glasses. They work best, I find. Everything within my worldview is right here in my gloved hands.

There are no birds at night. Only insects. The cicadas saw away. Crickets chirrup.

I chirrup with them, humming right along.

This is our song.

Wait.

There's that sensation again. The feeling of eyes on my back, as if someone were leering over my neck.

Walter must have woken. Is he in our bedroom window?

I turn toward our house.

No, the window is empty. The lights remain off. Our bedroom is nothing but a blackened chasm. So where is this feeling coming from? If it's not the sun, if it's not my husband, then...

Who's staring at me?

I keep still. Let the night settle over me. This distilled stillness. A palpable blackness.

I wait. Listen.

Your body adjusts to the night. Your eyes. Your ears. Your skin. You never realize how many sensations the day takes away, while at night, the darkness sharpens them. I've become something completely different. Something new.

I'm not alone. I can sense it. I know this because my vegetables tremble.

There. Just a few feet away from me. On the other side of the raised bed. Peering from behind my planters, I find a pair of sapphire eyes. At first, I think they are cherry tomatoes.

But then they blink.

Something is here. Hiding in my garden. With me.

My breath catches. My grip tightens around my pruning shears.

Hello?

It could be a raccoon. A possum, perhaps. A deer? It's not out of the realm of possibility that a black bear could have crept into our backyard, finding solace in my garden.

Is someone there? I have absolutely no idea why I call out to it, whatever it may be.

What if it answers?

My eyes aren't what they used to be. Even the beam from my headlamp can't reach that far. Whatever is hiding on the other side of my planters is blurred, a green shadow.

It shifts. The tomato vines writhe.

Who are you?

The night is not yours. Its voice sounds congested, lips brimming with topsoil. *The night is mine. Go back to your—*

Before I second-guess myself, my pruning shears spring up from my lap and—

Splk!

—I bury the blades into the soft contours of its chest. It lets out a cry of surprise.

Of pain.

How often have I heard him hurt himself over the years?

Walter?

He slips out from behind my planters, collapsing face-first, crushing my tomatoes. I grab hold of his shoulders and lift, but he's too heavy. I can't do it. Can't carry him. The best I can do is flip him over so he's staring up at the stars. His anniversary gift to me is still embedded in his chest, spring-locked handles reaching out for me. Already I can hear the blood flooding his lungs. Every labored breath is wetter than the last.

Walter, oh, Walter. He's bleeding into my raised bed, his blood black in the night.

I just wanted you... to come back...

Back? Back where?

To bed.

I... I can't do it. I'm sorry, I don't think I can carry you inside. I'm not strong enough.

That's all right, he says. *Just tuck me in here.*

We've traded one bed for another. We share this one now. Walter is with me whenever I garden. We're always together. I only go inside when the sun comes out. I sleep during the day, waiting for dusk. When it's dark enough, I'll crawl outside and begin cultivating that night's crop.

Beans. Zucchinis. Cherry tomatoes. Bell peppers. Kale.

Over fifty years went into this harvest. More blood, sweat, and tears than most marriages. Now we lie in bed together blanketed under the stars, the cool air on our skin.

hermit

I understand what daycare said. Miss Janelle can wave her red flag all she wants—it's not her place to diagnose our son. Yes, Carter's mind wanders. Yes, he has a harder time focusing on what's in front of him or playing with other kids. That doesn't mean he's on the spectrum.

He's just shy. Carter will come out of his shell eventually.

Biting another child is bad, absolutely. I 100 percent agree. But he's *three*. We can't all be angels.

We'll just enroll Carter into another daycare. What gives Miss Janelle the authority to say he has a development disorder? I don't care if she's dealt with a million kids before, it's not her place to tell us what she senses in our son. This is not autism.

I know exactly what this is. Where it comes from.

It came from me.

When I was five, I had a hermit crab. Hermy was my first pet. He lived in a ventilated plastic terrarium about the size of a lunchbox, transparent all the way around, with a convenient carrying handle up top. I hefted Hermy just about wherever I went. There was a pop-top easy-flip lid by the handle—*the feeding window,* the instructions called it. I'd open it up and scoop Hermy out with my bare hand. Let him crawl across my bedroom carpet for a while.

You're free, Hermy, I'd always call out. *Freeeee!*

Hermy was my friend. The only real friend I had back then. His shell was a cream-colored conch, while his delicate, spiraling-curved exoskeleton had a coral hue to it. The most I ever spotted of his body was the front, his head and claws, feathered antennas tapping at the air.

It's OK, I'd say. *You can come out. It's just you and me, Hermy.*

He'd been a gift from my mom. My first stab at caregiving. Even then, I felt the weight of Hermy's life on my shoulders.

You hungry, Hermy?

I'd drop a blueberry from my own afternoon snack. We shared everything. He'd clasp that blueberry in his claws, flexing his mouthparts, the maxillipeds branching out and tearing at the fruit's flesh.

Yummy in the tummy! We want you to stay nice and healthy, Hermy!

I loved him. I really did. Which is strange, when you consider hermit crabs are emotionless creatures. Cold, black eyes.

Actually, I take that back. Hermy expressed one emotion:

Fear.

Hermy was terrified of just about everything. Whenever danger presented itself—*shwooooomp!*—he retreated into his shell, barricading himself behind his tiny, pink claws.

Don't be scared, Hermy. I'm not gonna hurt you, I promise...

Sometimes he came out. Most times, he just hid, curled into a tiny ball of himself.

In his shell.

I'd keep his terrarium next to my bed, on my nightstand table. Mom would tuck me in, kiss my forehead and turn off my light. I'd fall asleep to the sound of Hermy rummaging around.

Goodnight, Hermy...

Hermit crabs are scavengers. They occupy abandoned mollusk shells. Their fragile bodies taper off to this slender tip—an asymmetric abdomen—curling in like a question mark. They're always hopping from one shell to the next. That's why you'll see a hermit crab living in a Pepsi can or even an abandoned doll's head. They need to move into bigger digs every now and then. They remodel their shells when they first slip in by hollowing them out, custom-fitting their new home by chemically carving out the interiors of their shell.

Hermy had the same mottled conch since I'd gotten him, a whole month by then.

Until one night.

My parents were hosting a dinner party. I was the only kid, stranded at a table full of dull adult conversation, so boredom crept in pretty quick. I begged Mom if I could be excused.

Sure thing, hon, she said.

I rushed upstairs to my bedroom. Closed the door. I took Hermy's terrarium in both of my hands and gently placed it on the floor. I popped open the lid and scooped Hermy out. He was tucked into his shell, hiding from me. Hermy was just as shy as I was. That's why I liked him. Whenever anyone got too close—even me—he'd retreat into that tiny shell, curling into himself.

I wished I had a shell like Hermy's. Something I could sink into.

To hide inside.

But something was wrong. Hermy wasn't easing out from his shell. Normally by now his pink limbs would seep out from his hiding spot and away he'd go, crawling across the carpet, scavenging the shag for food. But Hermy was still tucked in. He wouldn't come out and play.

You OK, Hermy? I caught a faint whiff coming off his shell. *What's wrong?*

Everybody says when you bring a seashell up to your ear, you can hear the sea. Waves crashing against the beach. The hollow thwonk of the roiling tide sweeps over your eardrum.

I could make out this tiny scratching sound. Just the slightest grind in Hermy's conch.

Skrch-skrch-skrch.

I brought the shell up to my ear for a closer listen.

Skrch-skrch-skrch.

It sounded like a pencil sharpener. The plastic kind you pinch between your fingers, a thin razor blade embedded deep into its casing. With each twist of your wrist: *skrch-skrch-skrch.*

I listened and listened and then—

skrch

—I felt a pinch. This searing *snick* next to my head. Hermy went straight for the tragus, that tiny divot of cartilage the pops out from your external ear. A sand dune of flesh.

Ow ow ow...

I let go of Hermy, but Hermy didn't let go of me. He held on to my ear, clinching the skin so tight, I swear his claw went all the way through the cartilage. He pierced my ear.

I never screamed so loud in my life. Still, Hermy wouldn't let go. I grabbed hold of the hull of his home in my hand, cupping the shell in my palm like I was gripping a doorknob, and gave the slowest-but-steadiest tug I possibly could. I felt the cartilage drag along with his claw, pulling, almost peeling, off from the rest of my skull.

I screamed even louder.

I ran downstairs, into the dining room. All these mortified adults took one look at me, this beet red boy screaming bloody murder, a hermit crab dangling from the side of his head.

Get him off get off get him oooooffff... The side of my neck felt warm. Wet. Blood dribbled down my cheek, gathering at my chin. *Please please pleeeeeease get him oooooffff...*

Mom rushed me into the bathroom. *It's OK*, she kept repeating as she examined the damage, taking my head into her hands and turning it left and right. *It's OK, it's OK...*

She tugged. So did Hermy. So did my ear.

My shrieks lifted in pitch. *Please, Mommy, pleeeeeeeease!*

I'm trying, I—

Mom leaped back. Gasped. Her hand was held out, palm facing upward. Hermy's shell settled against her skin, covered in blood.

Empty. All I saw was a hollow grotto, the shell's open mouth frozen in a rotund "O."

Where did Hermy go?

Hermit crabs just get too big for their britches, hon, Mom explained once I calmed down. *They slip out from their shells and search for a new one...* Even I heard the doubt in her voice.

Had he fallen to the floor and scuttled away? Was he still hiding in the house? Crawling through the carpet? Was he tucked into my clothes?

I checked my pillow, shaking it.

Nothing.

I lay in bed for hours, wide awake, staring up at the ceiling. I kept waiting for him to skitter across my leg or belly or somewhere. Do something. He couldn't have just vanished.

Skrch-skrch-skrch...

There was that familiar sound of pencil shavings, much louder now. More resonant. It wasn't so much that I heard the scraping sound as felt it deep within me.

Skrch-skrch-skrch...

Mom tossed out Hermy's terrarium. The family eventually accepted the sad fact that Hermy must've died somewhere in our house. Mom would find his shriveled body while vacuuming one day. She'd lean under the living room couch, on the prowl for dust bunnies and—*schwoomp*!—Hermy's desiccated exoskeleton would get sucked into the vacuum's funnel.

But I kept hearing him. In my head. Behind my migraines.

Skrch-skrch-skrch...

I started going through what Mom now refers to as my *stormy period.* Most days, I just stayed in my room. In bed, all balled up into myself. I seemed distracted. Unable to pay attention to what my teachers were saying. I became moody. Ill tempered. I barely talked.

In my shell.

I started lashing out at my classmates. Getting in fights all the time. Not picking them. Just defending myself. Look—I'd always been an easy target. Before, I'd take it. *Before.*

There was this one bully. Benjamin Pendleton. He just loved singling me out on the playground. Always giving me a titty-twister, as if he were adjusting the dial on a radio. There was this high set of monkey bars on the playground that nobody could ever reach. It had been nicknamed *The Rack* years back, long before I was a student here, probably even before I was born, the name passed down from one class to the next, all because it mimicked the rectangular torture device from the Tower of London. Nobody liked playing on it. *Nobody.* Perfect spot for Benjamin to press me against the metal ladder and start twisting my nips.

It had to've been my fiftieth time with my back against The Rack, Benjamin forcing me against the hot ladder, the metal soaking up the heat of the sun, the sear of the bars on the back of my neck, my shirt raised, chest exposed, the flab of my flesh pinched between his knuckles, pleading, begging Benjamin to stop, that I suddenly heard a voice inside my head.

Skrch-skrch... Skrch-skrch...

So, I bit Benjamin. I leaned my head forward and sank my teeth into his forearm. He screamed, releasing my nipple. But I didn't let go of him. I kept my grip and clamped down.

Until his skin broke.

I was the one who got suspended, even though everyone knew about Benjamin's bullying. The hypocrisy of skin. Benjamin only left bruises while I'd given him teeth marks.

So, I simply sank deeper into my sullen self. My shell.

I spent my days in my room, on my bed, all wrapped up in my blanket.

Skrch-skrch-skrch...

Who was that? It could've been mice in the walls, but this was my skull. I rolled onto my back, staring at the ceiling, and simply listened. Waiting for them to talk to me, whoever they were. Say something.

Who's there? I actually asked out loud.

Skrch-skrch-skrch...

Benjamin kept his distance when I came back to school. Most other students did, too. That's OK. I didn't feel as alone as before. Something was within me. I felt them. A presence.

Skrch-skrch...

In science, our class looked at a diagram of the human ear and all of its various tubes and canals and I swear I was looking at Hermy's tenderly tapering exoskeleton curled into itself. The cochlea. The vestibular nerve. The tympanic cavity. It all looked like a fragile parasite to me.

Skrch-skrch-skrch...

Was it? Could it be?

Hermy?

First thing I did when I came home was grab a flashlight and run to the bathroom. I leaned in as close as I could to the mirror. I flicked on the flashlight. Shined it down my throat.

Aaaaah... I spotted my uvula dangling down, that pink nob bobbing up and down.

Did it just blink?

There. Where the shadows met flesh.

Feathered antennas.

Just as quickly as I spotted those slender, black eyestalks—*schwooooomp*!—they retreated deeper into my throat, sinking down my esophagus.

I saw it. Saw *him.*

Skrch...

There's a hermit crab in my head. Hermy made himself at home, nestled into my nasal cavity. Curled behind my eyeballs. Whenever his exoskeleton shifted—*skrch*—I'd get the most piercing migraines.

I want you out, I'd mutter to myself whenever I brushed my teeth. *Get out. Now.*

Hermy never listened, no matter how much I begged.

He wouldn't let me go.

I never had a sweet tooth growing up, but now I couldn't get enough candy.

Skrch-skrch-skrch...

Sugar swiftly progressed to fermented yeast. I started drinking way too early, slipping sips of my parent's liquor as early as eleven. Hermy loved alcohol. I didn't mind it so much, it numbed my skull so the migraines weren't as pronounced. But the key difference was Hermy never had to suffer the consequences of drunkenly stumbling through the house.

My parents would ground *me*, not Hermy. How was I supposed to explain it to them?

What's gotten into you? Mom asked me once, practically repulsed.

If only she knew. Maybe I could tell her? Maybe she'd understand?

It's not me, Mom, I tried—once—slurring my words. *I swear to God. It's—*

Skrch-skrch-SKRCH.

That shut us up.

We just barely got accepted into the state university, but it was enough for us to finally move out from my parents' house. Anyway, we were more interested in the bars than our classes.

That's where we first met you.

Remember? You were wearing a sand-colored dress. It reminded us of the beach. *I* didn't have the courage to come up to you that night. *I'd* never been an extroverted person, but there was something about you, the tawny hue of your dress, the beach along your body, that—

skrch-skrch

—made us feel at home. So, we wandered up to the bar and introduced ourselves.

skrch

We fell in love, the three of us.

skrch

We made a family.

skrch

It's never been me, hon. It's always been us. Hermy's the one making the decisions.

Living my life.

In my skull.

When I was younger, I couldn't help but wonder if I was ever in control of my life—or if it was always him. It was just easier to let go. Let Hermy take the controls. Take over.

You never would've fallen in love with me. You loved Hermy.

Who am I without him?

Just an empty shell.

It wasn't until Carter was born that Hermy finally outgrew me. Twenty-five years together. More than half of my life. It didn't happen all at once. I slowly sensed a shift around Carter's first birthday. The migraines were back, more pronounced than usual. I couldn't look at lights without wincing. There was a slight odor to my breath that hadn't been there before.

Hermy needed a new shell.

He guided me to Carter's room. Right up to his crib. He was taking a nap. I leaned all the way over the railing, an inch from his head. I could kiss our son's fontanelle, I was so close.

My lips hovered over Carter's ear. His left. A cone-shaped canal.

Skrch-skrch-skrch.

I opened my mouth. My lower jaw unhinged a bit, then a lot, and then a *lot*-lot, sockets popping.

Skrch-skrch-skrch.

Hermy was leaving, easing free from my nasal cavity and slipping across my oropharynx.

I felt him lunge over my tongue.

Unspooling.

Don't go, I thought. *Don't leave me—*

Hermy reached for my lips. For our son. Letting me go. Saying goodbye to this home and moving into a new one. I felt his antennas poke out first. Then his eyestalks. One claw, then the other. His head pushed past my lips, my mouth birthing his slippery pink exoskeleton. His body unfurled from my cranium, my mouth, my life, and all I remembered was when I'd first gotten Hermy, how I'd take him out from his terrarium, place him on the carpet and say:

You're free, Hermy! Freeeeeeee...

Glancing down, what I saw almost looked more like an old man in miniature to me. This shriveled, elderly thing. Its diminished legs were twined together in a withered knot.

Hermy had been mine—or maybe it's the other way around. We'd been together for so long now I couldn't help but feel like I was losing my best friend to my son.

~

I feel so lonely now. I don't know what to do with myself anymore. I can barely figure out how to do the simplest things. Tying my shoe takes twenty minutes. There are so many choices now. Too many.

I'm all hollow. Empty now.

Hermy's been acclimating to his new digs. We talked a lot about why Carter was crying. I didn't have the heart to tell you what I already knew. I just hoped he accepted his guest. They'd sync up. Eventually. It just takes time. The chemical carving out of the cranium.

Making space for his new friend.

I remember that. Miss it.

Miss him.

Hermy.

You were worried about why Carter never made eye contact. His attention was always elsewhere. Never on you. It's not what you think. I swear it isn't. This is something else. *Someone* else. This is Hermy. I swear I see him, a timid little thing taking in its surroundings.

Hermy will be there for our boy. Hermy will guide him.

We'll get our son back one day, I promise. Whenever Hermy finally grows out of him.

all ears

Dad didn't come home an addict. He just came home *hungry*.

You'd think he hadn't eaten through his whole tour, a living skeleton decorated in medals, all gaunt and haunted. The veins lacing his bones looked like baker's twine bound around a box of butter cookies. His eyes sunk back into the foxholes of their sockets. When he looked at you—looked at me, his own flesh and blood—his eyes never seemed to settle, focusing instead on some far-off spot that felt inside and outside of space all at once, there but not there, somewhere in between.

That wasn't my father. He was still over there—parts of him, at least.

I wanted all of my dad back.

None of the other kids in the building had an enlisted father. I used to recite his tour of duty to just about everybody on our floor—*My dad is fighting for our country, Private 1st Class Marshal Dennison, 2nd Squadron, 9th Cavalry Regiment, 3rd Infantry Division, Pleiku, Ban Me Thuot, Kon Tum, Republic of South Vietnam*—all of it spilling out from me in one overflowing run-on sentence, never breathing between words. I'd be lightheaded once I finished this giddy litany, downright dizzy with pride, gasping for air only after I had reached the end.

Daddy's little soldier, the blue-haired biddies all called me, ruffling my hair with their hands and slipping me a butterscotch wrapped in cellophane. *Your father must be so proud...*

Sure, I wanted to serve my country, but most of all, I just wanted to serve my dad. Damn right I'd been ready to enlist right alongside him, following in my father's footsteps with my plastic rifle pressed firmly against my chest. All the way to Quảng Ngãi. All six years of myself.

He was gone for thirteen months. When he left in May of '68, he was only twenty-nine, but when he came back in the summer of '69, he looked like he'd just turned eighty. His old job at the Domino Sugar Factory was waiting for him when he returned home, just over the East River in Williamsburg, but he lost his spot on the processing line within the first month, simply staring off at nothing all day. That same empty space only he could see inside. Wherever it was.

Turns out he wasn't looking into space.

He was *listening* to it.

I can understand why Mom would believe he was hooked. From the Delancey–Essex Street station to the bodega on our block, it was everywhere. Even on our very own street corner.

~

I grew up in the Lower East Side. The *real* lower east. There's the lower east and then there's the lower-*lower* east. I'm not talking south of Houston Street here, I'm talking all the way below Delancey, where the Williamsburg Bridge barricades us in just next to the East River. The tenth circle of Hell. Nobody goes down this far unless they're looking to score.

This was my home.

My family lived within the Amalgamated. Our apartment building was one of four beehives on the north side of Grand Street.

Over 237 units all told. Built back in 1929, these pre-war projects were supposedly inspired by the architecture from Vienna. Crumbling art deco, that's all. The fountain in the center of the courtyard garden hadn't spat fresh water in years. Not since I was born, at least. Nothing but sludge came chugging out of the spigot, spackled in pigeon shit. Chinatown and Little Italy were just a stone's throw away, but our building was Little Everything. There were a whole lot of Hispanics. Lot of Blacks. Lot of Polacks. Some Hasidic. South Asian. All kinds called the Amalgamated home. I remember I could hear all the different languages from around the world seeping out from each apartment. Walking through the halls was like drifting over the globe, passing through each country at every door.

All those voices. Just drifting. Imagine hearing them all at once in your head, what that might feel like. The absolute cacophony of it all, worse than the 5 Train during rush hour.

~

Mom put together a shindig to welcome Dad home, even though he'd been back for a month. A real bash. He didn't want it, I could just tell, but it gave Mom something to focus her nervous energy on. Distract herself. She decorated our cramped apartment, turning it into a whole ballroom with crêpe-paper streamers hanging off the walls. A brick of frozen fruit punch sat in a glass bowl Mom only brought out on holidays. The punch had chunks of pineapple and cherries embedded within it, melting into this alcoholic soup. She invited all our friends. Some neighbors. The ones who spoke English, at least. Practically the whole apartment building came to pay their respects to my dad, tell him thanks for his service. Felt like a funeral to me.

Voices filled up our living room. It was hard to pick up their conversations. Adult talk. Stuff like the garbage strike. *That asshole John Lindsay.* I couldn't see anybody's face, there were so many folks crammed into our apartment. Not that it mattered—all these people milling about, shoulder-to-shoulder, created a dense brush of bamboo slacks that I could maneuver through on the floor, crawling across our shag carpet on my elbows. I had my plastic rifle with me. Locked and loaded. I was behind enemy lines on a rescue mission to find my father. Bring him home.

I found him sitting in the corner of the room, an empty glass in his hand. Staring at the wall. At the streamers. There was a window open, so the humid wind sent those strips of crêpe paper billowing in the breeze. I crept up to him, keeping my head low. When Dad spotted me at his feet, there was a flicker of a grin. His thin lips peeled back. All those teeth. Landmines.

Whatcha up to, soldier?

I'm not sure why, but I brought my rifle up to him and fired, making shooting noises with my mouth—*kapow, kapow*. Dad clutched his chest. *Bullseye*. He brought his fingers up and fashioned them into a pistol, firing right back. Then his focus drifted back to the crêpe paper.

All those intestines, he said. I think he said. *How'd they get in the trees?*

~

Honorable discharge got knocked around a lot, even though I didn't know what the heck that meant. When I heard he came home with a purple heart, I didn't understand that either. What's with everyone going on about the color of my father's ticker? Folks kept asking to see it and all I could imagine was him digging his fingers into his chest and with both hands cracking his own ribcage back, until everybody could finally see that purple muscle pounding away.

Dad kept his medals in a velvet-trimmed box that remained on the mantle. He'd pop it open only if Mom insisted he show it to our guests—*Show them your purple heart, hon*—and there it would be, this medallion Dad never seemed to want to touch, like it burned his skin.

Blessed, the old biddies from the building always said. *We're blessed to have him back.*

Alive and in one piece.

But Dad rattled around inside. Everyone sensed it, even if they never talked in the open about it. Nobody ever mentioned this sort of stuff. Not around me. I'd hear Mom whisper to her friends on the telephone. Distant voices that silenced themselves the second I stepped into the kitchen. She'd cut herself off mid-sentence, the conversation halting as if the line went dead. She'd have the telephone cord coiled around her fingers, twining her fist in the curled cable so tightly her knuckles looked like they were about to pop. All I saw was barbwire.

Have you seen Daddy taking any medicine when Mommy's not around? Mom asked. She told me what to keep an eye out for. The pin pricks scabbing between his toe joints. The beads of blood. She wanted me to spy on my own father, but I was no narc. Even at seven I knew that *snitches get stitches.* That's what the older kids from the building always said whenever I stumbled upon them spray-painting the fountain. That's just the law here in the Amalgamated.

I wasn't about to rat out my father.

Dad didn't talk like he used to, didn't look at me the way he used to, before he left. Always before. That phrase got thrown around a lot now. *Always before* this, *always before* that. I had a hazy memory of this giant before Dad went to war. I was only four, but I swear I held on to this vision of him. Green fatigues. A square jaw. Dimpled chin. An honest-to-God G.I. Joe doll. Mom used to tease me by telling her friends I believed my father was an action figure.

He was. My father was a hero. Why was everyone pretending like he was OK?

Couldn't they see he was hurting?

I'd seen his shakes. The tremble in his wrist at the dinner table. Whenever he'd pick up his glass, the water sloshed. His meal went uneaten. I never saw him pick up his silverware.

Look for his works, Mom whispered. *We're missing too many spoons.* I was supposed to be on the lookout for hypodermic needles. Rubber tubes. Pills or wisps of powder. She thought he had a heroin habit. Most soldiers dealt with addiction coming back.

She didn't know any better.

None of us did. Not yet.

~

During the summer, when all the kids played in the center courtyard, you could hear different voices rebounding out from the open windows surrounding us. Different music too. I remember hearing Otis Redding. Aretha Franklin. Creedence. But then you'd get these other songs from countries playing along as well, ballads from across the ocean. Music that made no sense to me—my ears, at least—but it added to this pleasant morass in the center courtyard.

Only our apartment kept quiet. Before he left, always before, Dad used to love playing The Ronettes on the Hi-Fi. He'd grab Mom as she wandered by, reel her in like the two of them were a pair of ballroom dancers, cutting a rug in our living room. He'd serenade her with the song and she'd tolerate it all, smiling as he dipped her, her head nearly touching the floor.

Not anymore. Whenever Mom reached for the stereo now, Dad simply hissed at her to shut it off, rubbing at his temples like he was kneading a migraine out from his skull. His skin was too tight. It was bound to split at any moment.

Whenever I came back from the courtyard, Mom would ask me to keep it down. For Dad. *Your father's just resting right now, hon*, she'd say. *Why don't you go back out and play?*

That meant back to the courtyard. We were lucky, I guess, living in the Amalgamated. Those four buildings created a barricade for us kids to run around. Reminded me of one of those old Jamestown forts we learned about in history. Each apartment complex served as its own watchtower. None of us kids spoke the same language but that was OK. We didn't have to talk. All we wanted to do was kick around a soccer ball or try to scare off the pigeons from the fountain. We never had to leave our own private enshrinement, fortified behind these projects. It was the piss-ridden city outside you had to worry over. We were safe inside.

Then kids started to go missing.

There had been a garbage strike all summer long. A pile of trash bags had been gradually growing outside our building for over a couple of months by then, swallowing the block. I overheard the older kids all calling it *Mount Shitpile*, which I repeated at the dinner table one night and got a smack across the back of my head from my mother. The trash was drawing in the rats like you wouldn't believe. You could hear the garbage shift and skitter and you just knew they were in there, those rodents squirming around inside, chewing their way through their own gnawed tunnels. If you poked a garbage bag with your heel, you'd send a whole swarm of rats scattering across your feet. Us kids loved to do that. Talk about a gas.

The heat elevated the stink. I could smell it all the way up on the sixth floor, baking the garbage right on the sidewalk. A concrete skillet frying up the melon rinds and dirty diapers.

They found a boy's body buried within a mound of black garbage bags. His corpse was somewhere in the center of the heap, like a preserved caveman. This prehistoric child from apartment 4B preserved in the permafrost, only starting to thaw out and decay in the sweltering August heat. Mom wouldn't let me go anywhere near those bags after that. She didn't want to fill my head with all this nightmare talk, so she'd shush down whenever I entered the kitchen. The only juicy bit of gossip I picked up when Mom wrapped herself up in the barbwire of our telephone was that the boy had been missing his ears. Both of them. Sliced right off.

Dad didn't say much of anything. He just kept quiet.

One night I woke up and swore I felt a rat crawl over my leg under my blanket. They were gathering outside in Mount Shitpile, ready to lay siege to our building. Pretty easy to imagine them sneaking into the building and invading our homes. Pick an apartment, any apartment.

Dad was standing before my bed. *They're feeding on you too*, he said. He leaned forward, staring me down, until I felt the weight of his eyes pressing against me. *You know what they like to eat the most? The soft spots. The cartilage. The ears. They always start on the ears...*

Then he turned back around and left.

~

You couldn't pry a word out of him about what happened over there. His tour of duty was locked in his mind, inside a steel box packed far away from polite conversation. He never talked about it. He'd simply sit by the window, staring out at the courtyard below. To the kids kicking around down there. Listening to them laugh as they circled the fountain, scaring the pigeons away.

Before he left, always *before*, Dad read to me. I'd nestle against his chest, the picture book shielding our faces, his breath caught between the pages. He smelled of coffee then. Now that he was back, he'd tried putting me to bed a few times, reading to me, but he just couldn't focus on the words anymore. *The sentences don't make sense*, he said. He'd stare at the page, drifting off to some spot beyond the paper, almost as if he were traveling through the pulp itself.

Then there was this one time he was reading to me, where he said: *Never sleep*. He said it so suddenly, I didn't realize at first that he was even speaking to me. Then he kept going, *Always got to keep one eye open. If you don't, you'll wake up to the rats gnawing on your ears.*

He was shivering, even though we were lost in the dog days of summer. The rest of us sweated away on the sixth floor, suffocating up top, with nothing but open windows and piddly electric fans to cool us down, but here's Dad, loose teeth chattering like it's the dead of winter.

Can you keep a secret?

How could I say no?

I want to show you something, but you can't tell your mother. You can't tell anyone. Promise?

I promise, I said, so proud that I was suddenly being brought into the fold.

He pulled out a tin box from his jeans. Its hinge was rusted. The lid was embossed in blue: *Edgeworth. Extra high grade sliced pipe tobacco. Larus & Bros. Co. Richmond, VA. U.S.A.*

This is it, I thought. *This is what my mother was telling me to keep an eye on.*

But this was different.

This was worse.

First, there were coins. Foreign. None of them looked familiar to me. He tilted the tin to one side so the coins slid directly into his palm. They even sounded different than nickels. They didn't clink like American coins. The metal was somehow softer in my mind.

Dad was talking while he emptied the tin, one artifact at a time. *We were told to shoot at anything that moved. Didn't matter who. Soldiers. Civilians. Nobody could tell the difference.*

He pulled out these slips of paper. Currency left over from overseas. They had pictures of people I don't know. Presidents, maybe? It was hard to tell.

We wiped out entire villages, he kept going, talking to me but not talking to me. *We were so jacked up, it just didn't matter anymore. Hearing their voices. Begging. Screaming.*

Then I saw the cotton. I spotted a wad of gauze, folded neatly together. Dad carefully unfolded it, layer by layer. By the third layer, I started to see a brown rust seep through. Flakes.

You never stop hearing them, he said. *They're always in my head.*

It was an ear.

A human ear. The skin had gone all gray, a crust of dried blood still caked to it. I swear I saw the ridges and curls of the lobe start to spiral, as if the flesh had melted into taffy and was now coiling down the drain of the ear's own canal, twisting off into darkness.

He told me he used to have more before. A lot more. A whole necklace's worth.

He showed me a picture. It was folded in half at the very bottom of the tin. He carefully opened the black-and-white photograph of himself and his squadron, as if it were a Christmas card. I had to squint to make out their beaming faces and figure out which one was my father.

He'd earned those ears, he said.

Those were confirmed kills, son. Every single one... It was a tally. To keep your numbers straight. He couldn't bring them all back home. He could only save one—*My first*—wrapped in gauze, tucked into his tin and stowed away where no one would be able to find it.

You ever eat a candy necklace before? That's all it was.

Yeah, I had a candy necklace once. For Halloween, we all trick-or-treated within the Amalgamated. We didn't even need to leave the building. I got one of those candy necklaces from the old lady in 3G. She had primo treats. The elastic band stretched as I slipped the necklace over my head, its strap snapping around my throat. The beads pressed so tightly against my neck they left indentations in my skin; spoke-like impressions, a grin of gritted teeth. I'd tug on the band and bring a bead up to my mouth, slip it past my lips and crunch. Tasted like Smarties, maybe a little less powdery, but still the same texture, same flavor.

Look at your old man, he said, eyes on the photo. *Just look at them all. I had the most.*

I didn't understand. I didn't know if I wanted to understand, but I knew my father was trying to explain something important to me. Something he'd been bottling up ever since he'd come home. This may have been the first time he was opening up to anyone about any of this. I wanted to do right by him—help him—so I listened, straining my ears as hard as I could to try and decipher the words and what they meant to the best of my seven-year-old knowledge.

He brought the ear up. Blew into it, as if blowing off some dust. Testing it like a microphone to see if it still worked. Then he lifted the ear up to his own, straining to hear.

I swear, from the way his expression shifted, it looked as if he heard something.

Wanna listen?

I nodded, afraid to say no. This was the most he'd said to me in days. Weeks. There was a yearning in his eyes, a clarity that hadn't been there before. He needed this. Needed me.

He brought the ear up to my own. I don't think I touched it, but the proximity to the shriveled husk of skin sent a dull current of electricity through the rest of my body. A pulse.

You hear that? Can you? What's it sound like?

The ocean, I said. Swallowed. *I can hear the waves.*

Dad shook his head. *No*, he said, deflated. *That's not right... That's not it at all.*

I had let him down. Failed him.

All because I couldn't hear.

You gotta be all ears, boy, he eventually said.

~

When word got out about another missing kid from the building, apartment 2F, I knew who'd done it. The police were going floor-to-floor, knocking door-to-door, interviewing tenants. They scribbled apartment numbers down in their notepads for those folks who didn't answer their door; usually the families who didn't speak English, who didn't want nothing to do with the police, so I knew it was best to just get it over with and play along.

Last time I saw the missing kid was two days before he disappeared. He was Polish. We'd play every now and then, even if there wasn't a word we could share between us. Mostly we'd just toss a ball. Do dumb stuff like try to lure a rat out of the sewer grate and see if we could trap it. I remember seeing him because it was laundry day for most of the building. There was a web of clotheslines suspended over the courtyard and I remember feeling this drip of water on the back of my neck, like it was beginning to drizzle, from the wet clothes hanging over our heads.

We had a washer-no-dryer in the basement. That's what we called it—*washer-no-dryer*—as if that was the full name. Kids were told not to go down in the basement, but we did.

Dad shook me awake in the middle of the night, dragging me out from my sleep. For a split second, I swear his fingers felt like rats nibbling their way into my shoulders.

Wake up, son. I'd never seen him in such a panic before. *Please, I need you—*

Dad asked if I could help him. He was in a real bad way by then. He couldn't do this on his own anymore. He needed a steady hand, he said. I needed to do the slicing for him. His wrists just weren't steady enough. His hand kept shaking whenever he picked up the knife.

I waited too long, he said, mincing his words, jaw-joint clicking, wrists trembling so much. *Too many voices in my head...*

I'm not proud to admit it, but I found myself getting jealous, just thinking of my dad asking that Polack to play, the envy of his attention rising up within me.

I just wanted my dad back. Whatever could return the rest of him home was worth it, I figured. If this was the help my father needed, and I was the only one he trusted to do it, then I'd do it. For my father, I'd do anything.

All I had to do was cut off his ears. Dad would handle the rest.

He showed me his Ka-Bar knife, serrated teeth running down the back of the blade. He taught me how to slice, talking me through every step. Where to pinch the lobe. How to saw down, curving the serrated edge inward by just a fraction so the blade didn't slip and slice out. He told me he imagined a Thanksgiving turkey the first time he did this and suggested I should do the same, but the way he said it made me wonder what he thought he was trimming now.

I've never seen my father happier than the moment after he swallowed. The absolute bliss of it all. He was at peace. He was whole. I could see the muscles in his throat take the plunge, working the mouthful down, delivering their payload and from there... he simply drifted. My father was someplace else now. Somewhere warm. Where he could be all ears.

Thank you, son. He clumsily ran his hand across my right cheek, fingers like sandpaper scraping my skin. His eyelids were at half mast, a fish-lipped grin on his face. *Thank you...*

He started talking, but it felt like he wasn't speaking to me, even if I was the only one there. Words oozed from his mouth, a thin trickle of his voice dribbling down his lips.

Most soldiers only sliced off one, he said, *which is bullshit if you ask me. You need both. One to eat, the other to keep. Keeps the line of communication open. You listen with one, talk through the other. Ever play telephone with a tin can? Same thing. Same basic principle. Send and receive. Transmit, pick up. In order to do that, you got to be all ears. You hear me, son?*

~

Laundry day was unofficially, not really but still kinda designated by what country you came from. The Asians did theirs on Tuesday. Poles on Wednesday. That sort of thing.

The baby was in the basement. So was his mother. She was doing her laundry while the baby was in one of those—I don't know what they're called—plastic rolly-chairs with a saddle in the center, like a diaper wrapped in a plastic donut. There were wheels at the feet, so the toddler stayed perched upright on their own tippy-toes. Helps teach them how to walk, I guess.

The baby was just rolling all on his own.

I could hear his mother humming some song as she was filling up the washer-no-dryer. She was so focused on stuffing the machine full of their linens, she wasn't paying attention to her child rolling away. I lifted my shoe and the roller stopped when it hit my toe. I could hear his mother humming from further off, her song filling up the whole basement, even as I ran.

~

All Dad ate were their ears.

I thought the police might take it easier on him if they knew that. You know, be more lenient or whatever. It wasn't like he ate all of them. It was just this one part.

So he could hear.

They found the baby's body a lot faster than the last boy. Apartment 5K. The police just had to follow the rats. Wherever the rodents were at their worst, a knot of tails, the garbage bags boiling over with frantic activity, well... that's where they knew to look.

Dad woke me up that night. He waited until Mom was asleep, and I could tell something was wrong—or more wrong. Even wronger. He sat at the edge of my bed, covered in sweat. When I sat up, he brought his arms around me and squeezed. Squeezed so hard I couldn't breathe.

You can always talk to me. Just call. I'll be here whenever you need me, I promise.

It wasn't sweat. It was blood.

They found him in the basement, leaning against the washer-no-dryer. Ka-Bar in one hand, a note in the other. Two slopes of flesh at either side of his skull, shirt soaked through.

The kids call the Amalgamated "the van Gogh Apartments" now, on account of the missing ears. Three kids, all told. I didn't even know about the first one. I didn't help Dad with that one.

They finally cleared out all the garbage bags from our block, cleaning up the streets before October. Now the jump-ropers on the sidewalk skipped to the beat of their own song:

Don't go go go inside the van Gogh-go-go

You never know-know-know

Where you'll go-go-go...

Good luck moving out of this place. Who could afford to leave? We couldn't. Where could we go? Mom and I were stuck, trapped in the Amalgamated. Our front door was always branded with some sort of graffiti. Spray-painted all over the walls. We stopped bothering to paint over it. The words just kept coming back, like weeds growing over our home. Like ivy.

SICKO. PSYCHO. CANNIBAL.

He was my father. I loved him, even when he came home hungry.

He just needed somebody to listen to him.

To understand.

I kept his tin. Tossed out the old ear and wrapped Dad's in the gauze. His left one. Some nights, when I get lonely, I pull it out. Unravel Dad's ear. I bring it up to my lips and blow, *testing, testing, one two three.* Like Dad said, you need both. One to eat, the other to keep.

You got to be all ears. So that you can hear.

Dad? Are you there? Can you hear me?

stay on the line

Seems cruel that Aubrey took everything but the phone booth. Of all the things Brandywine had to offer that goddamn hurricane, you'd think a disconnected payphone was ripe for the picking. Ma Bell had cut service ages ago, rendering it dead, but nobody from AT&T ever got around to removing the booth. They just left it there in the parking lot, a freestanding shack of cracked glass overlooking the marina, not doing anybody a lick of good. The rusted insides were covered in all kinds of graffiti, a kudzu of scribbles and dicks that only grew thicker throughout the years. Kids never even had a clue what a payphone was, what it was once used for, well before their hormones kicked in and turned it into an impromptu kissing booth. I was always catching young couples making out inside it nearly every night, looking like yet another pair of Japanese fighting fish crammed into an aquarium. Never had the heart to kick them out.

Let 'em peck, I thought. At least the booth was still good for something.

You kissed me in there plenty of times. How many tipsy nights ended with the two of us slipping into the booth, sealing ourselves in, pressing our backs against the glass and diving in?

It should've been the booth that got swept away.

Not you.

Shelby always thought it was the tiniest lighthouse. Still does. I remember one night listening to you spin this yarn as you tucked her into bed, talking about the booth as if it was a long-extinct beast. Just another one of your handmade fairy tales, this one about some mythical unicorn of telecommunication. *Once upon a time*, you started in like you always started, *a long, long while ago, long before there were cell phones or Wi-Fi, your mommy and daddy had to chat using these big ol' phones rooted to the ground. We all called them... landlines.*

What's a landline? Shelby asked.

Well... they were like trees growing out from the earth, connected together by miles of wires. Everybody had one in their house. Some still do. But a phone booth didn't belong to anybody. It was for everyone. *You'd step into that glass cubby and close the door, sealing yourself in, pick the phone up and bring it to your ear, drop a quarter in, then dial. You couldn't move around. Couldn't wander away. You had to stay put. All you could do was just... talk.*

Shelby still didn't believe you, all four years of herself. *Nuh-huh, you're lying...*

Hand to God, that's what they were used for.

You mean I can call anybody I want?

Well... Not anymore.

Why not?

'Cause it doesn't work now, sugar. The phone's been turned off. Wires have been cut.

Then why's it still out there?

To remind us how things used to be, I reckon. How far we've come.

Go ahead and tell her what people use it for now, I teased. *I dare you.*

You gave me that devilish grin of yours. Or maybe it was sheepish. Hard to say with your whiskers covering your lips, but I swear I saw you blush from under your beard.

What's Mom talking about? Shelby asked, completely clueless to her own conception.

Yeah, I said, *why don't you tell Shelby what Mommy's talking about.*

We'll save that story for another night, hon...

We could never afford childcare. That meant one of us had to look after Shelby while the other was on the clock. I wasn't about to let her hop on your trawler and spend the whole morning hauling in herring with you, so that meant most days she was stuck with me at the bar.

I've been bartending at Braddock's for longer than I want to admit. The owners live all the way in Pungo, so the bar might as well be mine. We've always had the best view of the bay. The marina up front is full of commercial fishermen, clotting up the docks with their deadrises.

It's where I met you, now, wasn't it? Still remember it as if it were yesterday. How many moons ago was that? How many hurricanes have we weathered together? You'd just come in with your fishing buds after wrestling against the Chesapeake all day. You all reeked of dead halibut, plopping your asses down, and I thought, *Fishermen never die, they just smell that way.*

You had to buy the first round, all on account of you being the New Guy. You dropped a twenty on the bar, the bill glistening with fish blood. I knew you were trouble from just one look at that smile, but when's that ever stopped a gal from falling head over heels? I'm still falling.

What'll it be? I asked, trying not to notice your hazel eyes. Your slender lips hidden beneath that baleen of whiskers. We were really gonna have to do something about that beard.

Whatever you're having.

Club soda it is then.

Make it a double.

You were just another itinerant fisherman coming in from North Carolina, South before that, Georgia before, slowly crawling your way up the coast, looking for work, following the fish.

Name's Callum, you said.

Jenny, I answered back.

I wondered how long you'd stay in town. If the risk of you

disappearing was worth the heartbreak. I didn't want to wake one morning and realize you'd gone and vanished on me.

But you kept coming back to the bar. Even on your days off, you'd sit yourself down. Keep me company. You'd slip a quarter into the jukebox, always playing the same goddamn song.

"Into the Mystic" by Van Morrison. Lord, you were such a cheeseball.

It worked.

Some nights, those dead nights, you were my only customer. You'd help me close. How chivalrous, I thought. I'd wipe down the bar and you'd mop. I'd turn off the lights and we'd stay.

One drink occasionally became two.

Became three or four.

Why keep count?

I don't think either of us is in any condition to drive home, I said as we stumbled out into the parking lot, met by nothing but black. Not a star in the sky.

There was the phone booth. Just standing out there in the dark. The sole sodium light suspended over the lot cast its dim glow over the booth's cracked glass, almost like a beacon.

Hold up, you said as you moseyed over. *I'll call us a cab.*

That made me laugh. *You know it doesn't work, right?*

Says who?

Ma Bell.

When's the last time you tried?

You took my hand and dragged me into the booth with you. You wrestled against the door, its rusted hinges squealing as you sealed us in. I hadn't been this close to you before. The smell of you, the very brine of the bay, mixed in with whiskey. You reached into your pocket and fished out a quarter, holding it up to me between your fingers before slipping it into the slot.

Looked to me like you were performing some kind of magic trick. *Now you see it...*

Wasting your money, I warned.

Ye of little faith.

... *Now you don't.*

You picked up the phone and brought it to your ear. There simply wasn't any space between us. I was inhaling your exhales, dizzy with giddiness as you punched in a number.

Then silence.

You were listening, actually listening to... *whatever* you were listening to. A dial tone? Was it ringing? Did somebody answer? Was there someone on the other end of the line?

You held out the phone to me, this sober look suddenly washing over your face.

It's for you.

... *Me?*

You nodded.

I held my breath as I took the phone out of your hand and brought it up to my ear. For a moment—just the briefest of heartbeats—I swear, I was ready to believe someone was there.

On the other end of the line.

... *Hello?*

Your lips cracked back into the shittiest shit-eating grin and I knew, I knew you had me going. You started laughing and I started laughing and suddenly the windows were fogging up.

See? Told you it worked...

Asshole. I hammered the phone over your shoulder a few times, laughing my ass off.

You just gotta reach out and touch someone...

I dropped the phone and leaned forward and my lips found yours as I forced you against the glass, just to shut you up. Your whiskers were too long and they slipped in my mouth, tickling my lips like sea anemones fanning back and forth across a coral alcove of your tongue.

Your beard was always in some sore need of trimming. We'd need to do something about that. Later. Not now, later. There were other things on my mind just now.

You wrapped your arms around my legs and lifted me up. My feet left the ground and I now found myself hoisted onto the metal ridge of the payphone, straddling you.

If anybody had been wandering through the marina's parking lot that night, they sure would've had themselves one hell of a show.

Nine months later, we welcomed Shelby into our lives.

You never left.

Brandywine—population 233—became your home.

Two hundred and thirty-four now. I thought of you rooting yourself to us, just like that phone booth, a landline wired to the world, tethering you to this town. You weren't going nowhere.

You worked mornings and I worked nights. We did our handoffs at the marina. That was our routine. I'd always let Shelby play in the parking lot until you motored back in from the bay. We never had many customers during the day, so it was safe enough for her to kick the gravel around. I had a clear view through the window overlooking the wharf. She never left my sight.

A family of seagulls set up their nest along the booth's roof. The windows were painted in bird shit, these white tear drops spackling the glass. For months, they'd just squat on top and watch the water, squawking away. You'd give Shelby a fish to feed the seagulls after you docked, teaching her to toss a herring straight into the air and watch the birds swoop in and swallow.

You were always more fun.

The better parent.

I'd spot her crawl in the booth and seal herself inside. I'd stop whatever I was doing and watch her talk on the phone. I never asked her who she was chatting to. Seemed private to me.

This was all before Aubrey took everything.

Took you.

Now I don't want our daughter getting anywhere near that fucking phone booth. I don't want her talking to nobody.

Least of all you.

Hurricane Aubrey was the first tropical cyclone of the year. She began brewing in the Bahamas, pounding Florida before climbing up the Carolinas, reaching Virginia with winds reaching ninety miles an hour and climbing. By the time she hit Brandywine, she was a category three hurricane.

Fifteen-foot-high storm surge wrecked most of the coast. Brandywine didn't stand much of a chance. All that overwash flattened out the sand dunes in seconds. Knocking out docks.

How many hurricanes had we seen together?

There was Bonnie the year before. Not to mention Floyd, barely a month after Shelby was born. Storms are a way of life around these parts. You just have to weather them *together.*

Nobody was leaving just because of some storm. Who cared what the governor said? That man could order everyone on the Chesapeake to head inland until he was blue in the face.

Where were we supposed to go? This is where we lived. This was our home. Your home.

So we put up plywood sheets. We nailed them to every last window.

We sealed ourselves in. *Batten down the hatches...*

We'd wait this storm out, just like all the others that had come before. There wasn't one hurricane, not one, that could tear our family apart. Our love was stronger than any storm, I thought. *Believed.* Our love was a force of nature in of itself, as elemental as wind and water.

I'm just gonna check on the boat, you told me.

Are you outta your goddamn mind?

I just need to make sure she's tied down.

To hell with your boat, I said. *Listen to it out there.* The winds had been picking up, shrill enough to sting my ears. Aubrey was at our doorstep, pounding her fists. She wanted in.

Wanted you.

I watched you slip out the door, like you were sneaking off to see some lady on the side. I found myself feeling jealous of some goddamn hurricane. Aubrey, the Other Woman.

Be right back, you said. *Two shakes.*

You never did.

The second Aubrey arrived in Brandywine, I reckoned the first thing she would've swatted away was that payphone, but for some bewildering reason, she blew right over it.

Spared it.

The seagulls were gone, their nest whisked away. But the booth was immovable. Rooted to the ground.

Let's not count the houses she knocked over. The roofs ripped right off their homes. Let's not talk about why she skipped over some stupid fucking phone booth and took you instead.

Twenty lives, all told. People I'd known all my life, taken. People I grew up with, gone.

You. You were no longer here.

Be right back, you said.

Your last words to me.

Most of me wishes they had found your body. But your disappearance made it easier for me to spin some black yarn to Shelby. Just another one of your homemade fairy tales. *Daddy got whisked out to sea, darling...* I wasn't nearly as good of a storyteller as you, but I did my best. You would've been proud. *Daddy's still out there, somewhere, swimming with the fishies...*

Beats having to explain to our daughter what actually happened. How a gust of wind hit you at a hundred miles an hour. How it sent you right into the surge. How it dragged your body into the Chesapeake and then the ocean beyond, where the coast guard would never find you, bring you back, spinning your limbs in endless directions, grating your face over coral and sand.

You never trimmed that goddamn beard.

I missed your sea anemone whiskers.

You notice who's missing straight away. People you crossed paths with nearly every day are now no longer there. The aisles at the market are deserted. All the empty seats at the bar.

Felt like Brandywine was never growing back. Never going to heal.

All those houses. All those docks. All those people.

Now you see them...

Still had a phone booth, though. I resented it. Almost blamed that booth for losing you. All those memories of you and me, sealed inside its glass. A message in a bottle cast out to sea.

S

O

S

We had been told to move on with our lives. How does a town heal after losing so much? So many? Our governor swore up and down there'd be cleanup crews, that he'd fix the roads, rebuild our docks, but we still haven't seen one single cent of recovery funds. Not one single maintenance worker came down to Brandywine to survey the damage. Our damage.

No, we've had to clean up for ourselves.

To heal all on our own.

There were bikes in the trees, looking like rusted Christmas ornaments. Furniture strewn about the street. Couch cushions by the side of the road. Toys scattered in the battered corn fields. Clothes nobody would ever wear again now draped the telephone wires that hadn't miraculously snapped. The flotsam of our lives was still strung over miles of pummeled shore.

The very bones of who we were before.

Braddock's become a ghost bar inside a ghost town. I serve the survivors, but this sure didn't feel like surviving to me. Didn't feel like *life* anymore. The roof had ripped open. I had help patching it up. It wasn't the prettiest of repairs, but it'd suffice until the next hurricane.

Or the next.

I'd be lying if I didn't admit I found myself silently praying for a stray wind to sweep me away, too. Begging the next cyclone to take me with you. Wherever you were.

But there's Shelby to consider.

I keep finding her in the lot, looking out at the bay and I swear she's searching for you, wondering where you are. When will you swim back home? What am I supposed to tell her?

What can I say?

Be right back, you said.

You have no idea how pissed I'd been. How could you leave your daughter like that?

Leave me?

Be right back. That's all I ever heard anymore, echoing through my head. *Be right back...*

I wanted to give you a piece of my goddamn mind. To yell and shout and cry and—

Be right back...

Hear your voice. I wanted to hear your voice.

Be right back...

Just once more, that's all. I just wanted to talk to you one last time, that's it.

Be right back...

You promised.

Be right back...

I worked most days simply to keep myself busy. To occupy my thoughts with something other than you. Shelby would come and I'd simply cut her loose in the parking lot. There's no longer a dock for her to walk on. They all got washed away. She'd end up kicking the gravel around for hours, bored out of her mind, waiting for your trawler to pull in. Holding out hope.

That first week was an absolute blur. I couldn't tell you what happened right after Aubrey left. Those days are lost to me, even now. To all of us. Most days I stared at the water.

Still do.

Folks swung by the bar. Just to be some place, any place, that felt close to normal. Like old times. We'd never been this busy before the storm, but now it's crammed full of people who don't talk. Don't drink. Don't do much of anything other than look out the bay window. Staring.

We're the ones Aubrey left behind.

Franklin Hull. Tammy Watkins. Carl Jessup. Henry Ketchum. Goodie Thomas. Some days there'd be more, some less, all of us huddled silently in our seats, simply staring out at the bay.

Waiting for the water to return what's ours.

Ain't that Bekah?

Can't remember who said it. Hell, it might've even been me. I couldn't recognize the sound of my own voice most days now, anyhow, so your guess is as good as mine.

We all turned to look out the bay window and sure enough, there's Bekah Brunstetler, standing in the phone booth. She'd lost her husband of forty-three years, all thanks to Aubrey. Hank had been hit by a shingle that flew off their roof. Cracked his skull open right between his eyes. She was all alone now, wandering the streets in the same ratty bathrobe. I had to squint to make sure, but I'd be damned if she didn't have the receiver up to her ear, talking to somebody.

Talking.

I'm not one to pass judgment. We get through our grief however we can. Anything to make it through another day. Just one more. But I couldn't comprehend what Bekah was doing.

Who was she talking to?

When she was done, Bekah said *goodbye*. I was familiar enough with the shape your lips make when you say that word, blooming out on *good*, then curling and budding back out with *bye,* that I didn't need to hear it to know that's what she said. She hung the yellow phone back up on its receiver, pried open the shattered glass doors, and shuffled her way home again.

The very next day, Bekah came back.

And the next.

She'd stand out there for about an hour, holding the phone to her ear.

Chatting away.

The rest of us just watched her talk, lips moving, not hearing a single word she said. We all wondered out loud if she'd lost her goddamn mind. *Poor Bekah*, we said. Once she was done, she'd simply rest the phone back in its cradle and step out of the booth. Wander home again.

It wasn't until the fifth day that I finally mustered the gumption to ask her just what in the hell she was doing. I didn't want to... to, well, *interrupt* her conversation, so I waited until she was done, struggling to pry herself out from the rusted doors and close them back up again.

Bekah? You doing alright, hon?

Just fine. She definitely didn't look *just fine.* She hadn't run a comb through her hair in days, wearing the same damn natty bathrobe. She had on a pair of fuzzy slippers, all clumped in mud. Her right ear was flushed pink from pressing the phone against her lobe for too long.

But her eyes... I swear, there was a light inside. Burning bright.

I knew that look.

Hope.

Why don't you come inside? Have a drink, on me. I placed a hand on her arm, ready to guide her back to the bar, but she resisted. Pulled free from me. She's stronger than I thought.

It took Bekah a moment to say anything, adrift in her mind, but when she did, her face brightened with this delirious giddiness that sent a chill through me. *He answered my call.*

... Who?

Hank.

Bekah came back every day. She slid into the booth. Picked up the phone. Brought it to her ear. And *talked.* We all watched her laugh, occasionally cry, as if someone was on the line.

On the other end. Talking back. Listening.

How many days do you think it took before the idea popped into my own head? How many times do you think I saw Bekah laugh and laugh before I wondered if I could laugh, too?

How long did it take me to gather the strength to try?

You'd laugh at me. I just knew you'd tease me for doing it. But I wanted to hear your voice again. I'd happily let you rag on my ass for hours on end if it meant hearing you jeer.

I knew it was silly. I knew I was being an absolute idiot. I didn't care. I simply did not give a rat's ass anymore. I needed to try. Just once. I waited until after closing time. I said goodbye to the last survivor, locking up behind them. I couldn't even call these people customers anymore. We're all just survivors, simply getting through the day so we can do it all over again tomorrow.

It was around eleven. Maybe midnight. The sun dropped long ago, the water nothing but a flat obsidian. There just wasn't anything to see out there now. No boats, no docks. Nothing.

The sodium lamp in the parking lot was the only source of light for miles. Most other streetlamps were still knocked down, leaving the waterfront in darkness, but I knew it was there. The only thing lit up around here was the booth. A spotlight shining on that payphone.

I stepped forward. Then hesitated. When was the last time I actually slipped inside?

With you. Always you.

I had to force the door shut. It oddly felt bigger without you cramming in with me. The air was muggy, trapped behind the cracked glass. Even though most panes had been knocked out, it was still difficult for me to breathe in here. Shards of glass crumbled under my feet.

I couldn't believe I was doing this. Not that it stopped me. Bekah seemed so convinced, so sure of herself. The warmth in her eyes. The belief. How couldn't I try? Just once?

I lifted the scuffed yellow phone off the receiver, the plastic mouthpiece all chipped.

I held my breath. Brought it up.

And listened.

Ever hear the ocean when you press a shell against your ear? I didn't know what I was expecting, exactly. A wave crash of static. A dial tone. Or nothing. Just silence on the other end.

What I heard was you. Your voice.

... Jenny? That you?

I dropped the phone. More like my fingers loosened, the phone slipping out from my hand. The metal-coiled cable caught it, going taut right away and bouncing back up in the air in a hangman's rebound, where the body ricochets back up after its neck snaps around the noose.

I leaped back, away from the phone, hitting my head against the window behind me. I felt trapped all of a sudden, pinned behind a pane of glass. A butterfly staked in place, all framed.

The phone dangled on its wire, swaying like the pendulum on a grandfather clock.

There's no way, no possible way I heard—

Heard—

—you.

I quickly reached for the phone and brought it back to my ear, listening.

Jenny? Can you hear me? Are you there?

I barely had the breath inside of my lungs to say it, to muster up the single word—*Yes.*

Thought I'd lost you there.

My knees softened. Legs gave out underneath me. I felt myself slide down the shattered glass wall until I slumped into this limp heap of limbs along the bottom of the booth.

I hadn't let go of the phone. I kept my grip, fingers tightening around the plastic handle. Its chipped mouthpiece so close to my lips. The receiver at my ear. *Is... is it really you?*

Your voice seeped through. *I knew you'd find me.*

Word got around quick. A town as small as Brandywine, it wouldn't take long for it to spread. Not everybody believed it at first, but most folks who'd lost someone were willing to try.

What did we have to lose that we hadn't lost already?

What was left?

I remember seeing Franklin Hull, all eighty years of himself, slip inside that booth and seal himself in. Even from here, I could see his wrist tremble as he lifted the phone off the hook.

I saw Tammy Watkins talk to her son.

Carl Jessup spoke to his brother.

You always wanted to give people their privacy. This was their call. Their time to connect. You never wanted to ask who they'd been talking to. We didn't need to. We all knew.

This hurricane had taken so much, but Aubrey left us a miracle. A beacon.

The booth.

We set up a system. Rules for using the phone. No longer than thirty minutes at a time. Not a minute longer. You'd make your call and then it was someone else's turn. If you wanted to call back, you'd have to go to the end of the line and wait for your time to come up again.

And no telling anybody. No pictures. No social media posts. Nothing. This was just for us.

The survivors.

You wouldn't believe how busy things are at the bar, I told you. *They're picking up*.

I hadn't realized I was the one doing most of the talking. You didn't seem to mind. You listened as I filled you in on everything happening at Braddock's. In Brandywine. At home.

I filled the silence. There was far too much of that nowadays.

I miss it there... Miss you.

Your voice tickled my ear. Your words felt like the faintest filament brushing over the lobe. If I closed my eyes and concentrated, focused all my thoughts on you—the undertow of your voice—it almost felt like you were there, leaning over my shoulder, whispering into my ear.

Almost.

Shelby drew a picture of you.

Oh? How do I look?

Blue.

We'd talk for so long, my ear would sweat. I'd finally hang up and realize how sore my neck was, feeling that familiar crick from childhood, where my shoulder bones held up the phone. Remember way-back-when, the landline days, when we were still kids, when you talked to your friends on the phone, spending hours on end in bed just chatting away until well after bedtime and your parents finally told you to get off, hang up, and get some sleep, and there would be this kink in your neck and your ear would be so hot, still warm from the other person's voice? Remember? That's what this felt like to me. Like being a kid again, chatting on the phone.

Don't go. Please.

I have to...

Stay with me. Just a little longer...

It's somebody else's turn, hon.

One more minute? Just one? Please? Your voice...

I... I can't.

I need to hear your voice. It's all I have to hold on to. It's so lonely here. Your voice, your voice is all I've got. It's a lighthouse without the light. Your voice guides me home... I need it.

A lighthouse without the light.

A soundhouse, maybe?

A voicehouse?

The graffiti changed. For years, it had been nothing but lewd pictures and curse words. But somewhere along the way that vandalism was scrubbed off and replaced with the names of those we'd lost. That kudzu of Sharpie marker now luxuriated in a long-sprawling patch of loved ones, as if this phone booth were a memorial set up in an honor of those lost in the storm.

People repaired the broken windows. Someone swapped out the cracked glass for fresh panes. The hinges were oiled. The rust was scraped away. The metal frame polished until it shined.

Who, though?

I pulled into the lot one morning and wouldn't you know it, but somebody had brought in a couple terracotta pots full of fresh gardenias, lining them around the outside.

The booth's become a shrine.

A sanctuary.

We could speak to our loved ones. Reach out to them. Connect. Wherever they were, they were just on the other end of the phone. We just had to hold on to them. Stay on the line.

Where are you?

Here.

But... where is here?

With you. Your voice had the faintest crackle of static to it, as if we had a bad connection. You'd cut out for a breath and I'd feel my heart skip. I was afraid I'd lost you.

It was better not to ask so many questions. This is just the way things were. Aubrey whisked you away but the booth brought you back, somehow. Brought all of our people back.

What was the old AT&T commercial? How'd it go again? *Reach out and touch someone.*

I'd talk your ear off, if there wasn't a line forming outside. It was so hard to keep our calls within their designated time limit, just to be fair to one another. It was so hard to say goodbye.

Don't go. Not again.

I'm sorry, I—

Please, Jenny, you can't leave me again... I get so lonely when you're not here.

I've got to give somebody else a turn. There's a line—

Tell me about Shelby. Please? Tell me about our girl.

She's doing OK. As OK as can be expected. There's a lot she doesn't understand. There was a hell of lot I didn't understand, either, to be completely honest. How's this possible?

I need to talk to her... Could you put her on the line?

Put her on the line. Something about the way you said it felt strange.

Do you think that's a good idea?

Why not?

It's been hard enough trying to explain what happened. This might make things harder.

She's my daughter...

I know, it's just—

I need to speak with her. I need to hear her voice.

I'll... I'll think about it.

Put her on. Please.

I've got to go—

Put her on the—

Nobody had seen Franklin Hull for a few days. I'm ashamed to admit this, but I hadn't even noticed. My mind was elsewhere. On you. In the booth.

When Franklin's body washed up on the shore, miles away from the payphone, we'd already gone through so much grief, there wasn't much left to give. His ears had been chewed off by crabs, the fish feasting on the soft parts of his flesh. It's unclear if he wandered into the water or if it'd been an accident, but all I can remember is the last time I saw him. In the booth.

He hung up the phone without saying goodbye. I watched him expel his frail frame from the folding doors and slowly wander through the lot. It didn't strike me as strange at the time, but instead of heading home, he slowly made his way toward the wharf. For the water.

I didn't give it much thought because it was finally my turn to—

reach out

—use the phone and I'd already been waiting for over an hour by then, so of course I didn't want to waste another second. Not another breath.

There you are.

I'm here.

I was worried you'd forgotten about me...

How could I forget you?

Stay. Stay with me. Please.

I'm here. I'm not going any—

Just stay on the line.

Shelby finally asked about you one night while I was tucking her in. *Is it true?*

What's that, hon?

You're talking to Daddy?

Something about her question caught me off guard. I wasn't ready to tell her. What was I supposed to say? Yes, yes, hon, your father is on the phone right now. He's always on the line...

Just waiting for us to pick up. Answer his call.

Why couldn't I tell her?

I'm steering her clear of the booth. I can't explain why, but there was a part of me that still felt uncertain about it all. Maybe I was just being selfish. Maybe I wanted you all to myself.

Is that awful of me? Depriving our daughter of hearing your voice?

Put her on the line, you said. It didn't sound like you meant the phone.

It felt more like a hook.

A fishing hook.

Tammy Watkins vanished a couple days later. Same thing. She took her call. Went over her time limit. When she finally hung up, the blank expression on her face was hard to read.

You OK, Tammy?

She never said. She hasn't been back to the bar since.

Nobody's found her body yet.

Shelby's birthday is coming up, I told you. *This one'll be hard. Her first without you.*

How old's she again?

She's turning five.

Five, right.

It was easy to forgive you if you got some facts wrong. You made mistakes. Misremembered certain things, simple things, easy to correct and move on with our talks.

Why hadn't you remembered your own mother's name?

How could you forget the name of the bar?

How could you forget your daughter's birthday?

It didn't matter. None of that mattered. Not really. I chalked it all up to the fact that you were... wherever you were. It was bound to be hard to remember every last little thing.

I knew I just needed to hold on to you however I could.

Keep you on the line.

On the line. Jesus, it even sounds like you were some kind of fish, not some voice on the phone. *Just stay on the line*, I thought to myself. Prayed every time I picked up the phone.

Just stay on the line...

The line only got longer the more word spread about the booth, which meant the wait for our turn stretched on, too. Carl Jessup kept growing more impatient, kicking gravel in the lot.

That was longer than thirty minutes, he muttered to me as I stepped out.

Sorry?

It's my turn. I notice how red his ear was. Infected, almost. A fiery coral complexion, bruised and blistered from too much chafing.

I followed Carl after he finished his phone call. Just to see where he went. I kept my distance, unsure if I should intervene when I watched him wander onto what remained of his own dock, this rickety old thing barely holding itself up by its barnacle-covered posts. He kept walking toward the end, never stopping. Not once. His focus was on the water. On his brother.

I shouted out his name the second his foot stepped off and he—

crrsh

—dropped right into the water. By the time I reached the shore, he was gone.

Our calls were changing us. Crossing our wires, somehow.

Crossed lines.

We all had people we wanted—*needed*—to speak to. People on the other side. All you had to do was slide the door closed, pick up the phone, answer the call, and there they'd be.

Their voice.

But something was wrong. This didn't feel right anymore. You didn't feel right.

I need to talk to Shelby. I need to hear her voice. Put her on the line.

People are making their pilgrimage to the payphone now.

New people.

Word got out somehow. I don't know how it spread, but news of the booth has gone beyond Brandywine. The lot is always full. I've told Shelby she can't play out there anymore on account of the cars. So many strangers. I don't recognize their faces. These people came to—

reach out

—communicate with the other side. It's no longer only our loved ones. Not just the people Hurricane Aubrey took from Brandywine. It's everybody, *anybody* who's passed on. It doesn't matter where they died or how. The phone booth is for anyone who wants to—

touch someone

—put in a collect call to the afterlife. Business has never been better, if I'm being honest. The bar is alive. Thriving. Brandywine is becoming a town again. Almost feels like home.

Isn't that what I wanted? You gave this to me. This was your gift.

Bekah Brunstetler's body had been submerged underwater for so long, it was practically impossible to identify her beyond the strips of her bathrobe draped over her bones, most of the meat pecked clean by the crabs. She'd been the first to answer the call. Look where it got her.

It's time, you said. *I want you to join me. Come to me.*

Where?

Here.

How?

It's so easy... All you have to do is follow the sound of my voice.

What about Shelby?

She can come too...

Callum, I... I'm sorry. I can't do this anymore.

Then put someone else on the line. Put Shelby on. Let me speak to her.

I couldn't help but notice the change in your voice.

No.

A wave of static crashed over my ear. *PUT HER ON THE LINE.*

There was sand in your mouth. Stones in your throat. Rocks between your teeth.

It didn't sound like you at all.

It wasn't, was it?

You?

A hand smacked the window just at my face, startling me. I dropped the phone. I let out a shout, spinning around to see the desperate face of a stranger just outside the booth. His nose was practically pressed against the glass, his breath fogging up the window. He hammered his open palm flat against the outside of the booth once more, slapping the glass, eager to get in.

My turn, he muttered. Whoever he was. His ear looked chafed. Inflamed.

I hear the ocean wherever I go now, even when I'm not on the phone. It's this slight hiss of static always at the back of my head. A white noise machine. Crashing waves in my skull.

Your voice. I don't even need to be on the line to hear you now.

You're in my head.

I had a nightmare about you. We were on the phone together, talking for what felt like hours. Maybe even days. Who can tell anymore? It must've been night because it was completely dark outside. I'd lost track of time again. Where had the day gone?

There was something strange about the darkness beyond the booth. It was murky. Green, almost. I leaned forward and squinted, trying to get a better look at what was on the other side of the glass.

Water. It was the ocean. The booth was now submerged at the bottom of the bay.

Do you see— I started to ask you, but cut myself off.

See what? You asked. *What do you see?*

There was the slightest tickle at my ear.

I yanked back the phone.

Gasped.

There. *Right there.* Roots reaching out of the receiver. Tiny red buds rose up from the colander of holes in the mouthpiece. Every last one had the thinnest living rivulet. Reminded me of a Play-Doh Fun Factory, the colored clay seeping through. All these splurging worms. Tendrils fanned out from the phone, reaching for my ear. My mouth. They wanted to come in.

See what, Jenny? The tendrils trembled with the sound of your voice, vibrating like living guitar strings, as if they were your own vocal cords. *What do you see, Jenny?*

If I opened the door, the ocean would flood the booth. I was trapped as the roots wrapped around the wrist of my hand still holding the phone, lacing their way up my arm.

They found my throat.

Choking me.

If my lips split to scream, the tendrils would slip into my mouth. I had to keep my lips sealed, *batten down the hatches*, and hold the phone as far away from me as possible.

I can't breathe...

The tendrils kept coming, pouring freely from the phone. A latticework of angry red roots wove over my chest. I could feel them working toward my ears. My nose. Any way in.

I can't breathe...

I had to snap it off at the source. Cut off your voice. I tugged on the phone, pulling so hard. The cord gave, but instead of breaking, it stretched—stretched beyond the coiled cable, beyond its wires, melding into a red stem that tugged back on itself, pulsing under the dim light.

I can't breathe...

The roots cinched tighter around my throat. The oxygen in my lungs burned. A constellation of black spots scattered across my eyes. I kept yanking on the phone, suddenly playing tug-of-war with the booth. Hand over hand, I pulled and pulled on its pulsating cable, but that stem kept coming, unspooling from within, falling into a livid, wriggling heap at my feet.

I can't...

I knew I was fading. I couldn't hold out much longer. The root in my hands had the same fleshy consistency as a tongue, wet and pink. Not a tongue. A sea anemone. Something from the bottom of the ocean. Something stirred up by the storm. *Reaching* out for me. *Touching* me.

I...

Just as I was about to black out, just as all the ink spots in my eyes nearly eclipsed my vision, those roots noosed around my neck, squeezing so tight I had no choice but to open my mouth and gasp for air, letting them in, letting them all in, a tiny hand—a child's hand—smashed against the glass.

Shelby.

Shelby, my baby girl. She was on the other side of the window. Outside the booth. In the ocean. She floated through the water, her feet off the ground, hair fanning as if it were kelp.

Her father must've finally found her, I thought.

You took her from me.

Shelby grabbed hold of the folding metal door and pulled. A spate of water spilled through the crack in the phone booth's door, the surge growing the more she tugged. I barely had the strength to push the door shut. The booth was flooding. My baby girl was coming in.

When Shelby's lips lifted into a grin I couldn't recognize, her own mother, the same sea anemones slipped over her lips, a dozen different tongues branching out from her mouth. They wormed their way over the glass until it cracked, winnowing through the fresh fractures.

I saw the sea anemones reach out from her eyes and touch me—

When I woke up with a start, letting out a shout in bed, in my own home, the dream wasn't what terrified me. What scared me the most was the sudden compulsion to call you.

Tell you what happened.

Teens gather in the lot. Not coming into the bar, simply hanging out. Waiting their turn. It's become a dare. A thing to prove. Kids come from all around, mustering the courage to pick up the phone. Answer the call. They'll simply stand there and tilt their heads back, listening to the sea. The ocean crash of static on the other end of the line, rushing right into their ears.

Whose voice is on the other end of the line for them, I wonder. Who have they lost? Maybe it doesn't matter. What if it's been the same person on the other side, calling us all?

What if you just want to keep us all on the line?

Here's what I think: It was never our loved ones. Never the ones we lost.

It was just you. Only you. Whoever—

whatever

—you are.

You've been feeding off our grief. And when we're empty, you sever ties—cut the line—and let us go, what's left of us at least, catch and release, back into the water where we drown.

It was never my Callum.

It was you.

You.

I caught Shelby in the booth today. I was behind the bar, losing myself to the water beyond the window, when I glanced at the payphone and spotted her. So small. Her head barely reached the number pad on the phone. She had the receiver up to her ear. I couldn't hear what she was saying, but I saw her lips split into that grin I'd never seen before. Only in my dreams.

I ran for the booth. Ran so fast. When I reached the folding doors, I yanked them open. Shelby gave a start, nearly dropping the phone. Her back pressed against the glass.

I told you, I shouted as I grabbed the phone right out from her hand and slammed it back on the receiver. *You can't be in here. I don't want you ever,* ever, *in here.*

Shelby shrieked at me and didn't stop, this endless peal of a scream reaching out from her throat. It didn't sound like her, barely sounded human, and oh God, for the life of me, I couldn't make her stop. No matter how hard I shook her, trying to snap her out of it, she kept on screaming and screaming, *I was talking to Daddy I was talking to Daddy I was talking to Dad—*

You can't have her. Shelby's not yours.

Please. Not her.

I waited until the crowd had thinned out for the day. Bound to be around midnight. Maybe later. The only illumination was the sodium light overhead, casting its dull beam over the booth. Once I knew no one else was around, I crept back into the booth. Sealed the glass door.

I lifted the phone off the receiver one last time. How couldn't I? I brought it to my ear. I didn't say anything. I just held my breath and waited for you to answer.

Jenny? That you?

I asked straight away: *Who are you?*

It's me... Who else would it be?

Who are you?

The line went dead for a second. Then you started to laugh. It was a husky chuckle, unfamiliar to me, but you kept on laughing, the volume only growing louder. Harsher.

Whoever you want me to be...

It wasn't your voice anymore. All that sand and sediment scraping over your throat. The awful sound of it filled the booth, so loud, flooding the suffocating space until I was drowning.

There was water at my feet. So cold. I could feel the surface rising up my legs, my hips.

I couldn't escape the booth. I kept pounding against the glass with the phone, but it wouldn't shatter. Your voice kept rising up my waist, reaching my chest, my throat... my mouth.

How long have you been feeding off our grief? Feeding off me?

reaching

out

touching

some

one

I cricked my neck back and took one last gasp of air before the water rose over my head.

I wrapped the coiled wire around my hand and made a fist.

I pulled as hard as I could.

Yanked on the cable until the phone finally snapped free.

The doors to the booth finally yawned opened on their own. I burst out and gasped for fresh air on a wave of expelled seawater, washing over the lot, taking the phone with me.

The cable was still wrapped around my fist. The wire dug into my skin.

... Jenny? You still there?

I ran to the edge of the marina, overlooking the bay. It was far too dark to see the water, but I heard it. The ocean. Its sibilant hiss, like a bad connection.

Just stay on the line, Jenny, just stay on the—

I threw the phone as hard as I could but I never heard it splash.

The following morning, the first people to stand in line for the phone are going to find what's left of the booth, now smashed and toppled on its side, its glass shattered, the folding door crushed under the front of my car. I'll be behind the wheel, staring out at the Chesapeake.

Just waiting for you to call me back.

nathan ballingrud's haunting horror recs

Holy shit, we're driving down to North Carolina to get Nathan Ballingrud's horror recs. Once the thought locked in our collective heads, there really wasn't any getting rid of it. Wasn't like Asheville was all that far away, anyhow. We're talking seven, maybe eight hours, tops. Straight shot down I-240. Who wouldn't make a pilgrimage to meet the Man? The Legend?

Nathan fucking Ballingrud.

The idea came about on our couch, about four tokes after my friend Benji mentioned Ballingrud worked in a bookstore.

Yeah, right, I said. *That's some cockamamie fanboy bullshit if I've ever heard some.*

Hand to God, man... I read it somewhere. Reddit, I think. He repeated himself, just under his breath, a record skipping: *Read-it-on-reddit-read-it-on-reddit-read-it-on-reddit...*

Dude's a horror icon, I said. *What the fuck does Ballingrud need a day job for?*

Keeps him real, Benji said.

He's got a book coming out on a top-five publisher—

Allegedly.

That's some six-figure shit right there. The hell's he doing working at a bookshop? Maybe he just likes books. Then Benji does this thing with his fingers, wriggling them in my face like they're a bunch of haunted hotdogs or something. *Scaaaary booooks.*

Knock it off.

You think he just sits behind the counter all day, Benji wonders out loud, *then when some customer comes up and asks for a recommendation, he like, recs his own stuff? I fucking would.*

Here, I imagine Ballingrud saying. *Try this book. I think you might like it...*

Dude doesn't need to recommend his own books. I felt like I needed to defend Ballingrud's honor. Not that he needed it. He's got his rep locked down tight. The man doesn't do conventions. Doesn't make public appearances. Doesn't show up for the Stokers or accept whatever award he nabs. The dude doesn't even do interviews. Not anymore. No social media presence what-so-fucking-ever. He's got one author shot—the same damn photo for over twenty years now. *People probably just come to him. Bet they bring copies of his books all the time.*

He's classier than that. Bet you he's got, like, a no autograph policy when he's working.

Damn straight.

Benji discovers something tucked between the couch cushion. A shard of a potato chip. Still crisp from the crunch of it. *Wouldn't it just blow your fucking mind to walk into that bookshop and spot Nathan fucking Ballingrud behind the register? Like he's just waiting for us?*

Waiting for me. *You made it,* he'd say. *I thought you'd never come.*

I'd lose my shit, Benji says. *Dude's a legend.*

An honest-to-God legend, I agreed. *Bet he recs so much scary stuff. Like, books you've never even heard of before... Books that would just shatter your mind into a million pieces.*

No doubt.

Nathan. Fucking. Ballingrud.

Legend, Benji says.

God, what I wouldn't give... And there it was, all teed up, the idea formulating from the fog in my mind just as the words abandoned my mouth. *How about we go find him?*

Who the hell is Nathan Ballingrud, you ask?

Dude's a fucking legend. Anybody who's dipped their toe into contemporary horror lit knows about *North American Lake Monsters*. That short story collection is a fucking classic. Canon, man. They'll be teaching that shit in college lit for centuries. Why Hulu had to change the title of the TV show was a dumb fucking move. Now nobody knows it's based off his book. They're, like, *actively* denying their own core audience demographic. But they've been fucking us fans over from like the get-go, you know? When it comes to Ballingrud, you've learned a little about heartbreak. Ever read *Wounds*? His batshit-insane novella? Trick question, asshole. If you were a *real* fucking fan you'd know that it wasn't called *Wounds* until they made the movie. Its original title is *The Visible Filth*, published back in 2015. Don't come at me like you're some Nathan Ballingrud afficionado if you don't know the difference between *Wounds* and *This Visible Filth*. Fucking amateur hour, man. You and Armie Hammer fucking deserve each other.

When word got around that Ballingrud was finally writing a novel, I nearly shat myself. Finally, at long goddamn last, fans were getting a full-blown masterpiece from our main man The Notorious N.F.B.

Not that most folks would have a chance to read it.

The book got pulled five months before its release date. Before that shit even hit shelves, the publisher got all weak-kneed and yanked it. Nobody knows why. Not really. I've heard dozens of reasons—beta-readers losing their shit, bloggers vomiting, Bookstagrammers posting suicide selfies—but I'm calling BS on all of that. His move into the mainstream was always going to cause some ripples. Like Dylan going electric. Whatever the hell it was, you'd have better luck nabbing the Holy Grail than an advanced reader copy of Ballingrud's new novel.

Like I said: *Legend*. The man's mythic.

I'd be lying if I didn't admit I've spent a few late nights traipsing through AbeBooks. eBay. Amazon. I even peeked at the pirate sites. Just to see if somebody out there's selling a copy.

Nothing. Not a single goddamn PDF. That shit simply doesn't *exist.*

*Is it Ballin*grood *or Ballin*gruud? Benji asked somewhere around Kingsport, Tennessee.

*I hear you pronounce it Ballin*gruhd.

I think it's grood.

The hell, man? I grip the steering wheel, ready to pull this piece of shit around right then and there on Interstate 40. *It's got to be* gruhd. *Who says* grood? *It's* uhd. Uuhd.

The humidity has climbed to neck-sweat proportions by the time we cross into Carolina. The A/C doesn't work so well, spitting out dribs and drabs of cool air, so I roll my window down. There's a shrill hiss in my ear, eclipsing our conversation. We've got to holler at each other now.

That's how I heard it, I shout over the windshear. *With one of those l'il umlaut-thingies.*

Dude's not Mötley Crüe. It's grood. *Ballin*grood.

Grüd with an umlaut.

Fuck off with that umlaut-bullshit...

Five bucks says it's Grüd.

You're on.

We'd been driving nonstop for about six hours by then. No pit stops, no piss breaks, fueling ourselves up on Mountain Dew and Andy Capp's Hot Fries. We didn't want to lose any momentum. At the rate we were going, we'd reach Asheville with a few hours to spare before closing time. Maybe Ballingrud would want to hang with us after he locks up. Maybe he'd shoot the shit for a bit, tell us what he's working on next. There's just no telling what he'd want to do.

And maybe, just maybe... he'd have an advance reader copy of his new novel, *The Weird,* from uncorrected proofs, just tucked under the cash register. *Not intended for resale. Please check any quotes for review against the finished book. Final cover to be revealed.*

Benji really needed to pee. *Bladder's about to burst.*

I told him to go in his bottle. No way I'm pulling over. Not when we were this close. I could nearly feel the gravitational pull of Ballingrud, reeling us deeper into the Blue Ridge like the man was some cosmic black hole in the mountains, rupturing the whole horizon. My bleary eyes could nearly see the skyline distorting into blurred bands of pink, purple, and green. An oil spill in space, blotting out the cosmos, all because Ballingrud's fans demanded his new book.

We'd already gone through his stories. Picking which one's Ballingrud's best. "The Monsters of Heaven." Obviously. The dude won a Shirley Jackson award for that shit, so you know it's top shelf. Benji said his favorite was "Skullpocket." Fine. I'm not going to quibble.

You think he gets people coming in all the time? He wonders. *Asking for autographs?*

Maybe, maybe not... Maybe we're like, the chosen ones. Like, not everyone's got what it takes to make this quest. Maybe only a few select fans even go on the journey... and maybe not everybody makes it. Reach the mountaintop or mecca or whatever the hell Asheville is.

We're totally Frodo-ing this shit, Benji shouts.

Hell yeah, we are!

One ring to rule them aaaaall, bitches!

All we wanted were his horror recs. What book is Nathan Ballingrud going to point to and say, *Hey, yo, this is some scary shit.* If he says it's terrifying, then you know it's true. Fucking Ballingrud seal of approval. Slap that sticker on the cover and see how fast it flies off the shelf.

Or, maybe, just maybe, he's got something else. Something special. Something just for me.

Why all this fuss over some author? Why Nathan Ballingrud?

Dude. If you even need to ask...

You get guys like John Langan. Or Laird Barron. Or, sure, even

Paul Tremblay. Kick-ass writers. Fucking A-list cosmic shit. But none —and I mean none—of those guys are putting themselves out there like my main man Nathan Ballingrud is. Do you see Tremblay working behind the counter of his local B&N? Nope. I mean, I heard he teaches high school math somewhere. But still. You think Barron is putting himself out there? On the consumerist front lines? Fuck no.

Only Ballingrud. You just got to find him. Make the effort. *Come to me*, he's beckoning.

Who's listening?

We are. Me and Benji over here, sitting shotgun. Damn straight we're answering the call. This all had to be more than just some job for Ballingrud. Dude's got Hulu money. He doesn't need to work at a bookstore. There's got to be a secret reason, some under-the-counter specialty, he's hiding. He's putting out this psychic evite to his fans and we're RSVPing: WILL ATTEND. Only those who are brave enough, willing to put in the pilgrimage, are going to get his horror recs. His *real* recs. Not a Goodreads list or some algorithmic suggestions from Amazon.

The real fucking deal. The truly scary shit.

Or maybe, just maybe, a little something-something. For my eyes only. Not even Benji. *I'd really love to hear your thoughts*, I imagine him saying. *You're one of the first to read it...*

Me. The first. The chosen.

The Weird.

So we didn't *actually* know what store he works at. Malaprops was the obvious call. That's the shop everybody knows. But by the time we walked in, they're all like *Ballin-who?* Fucking kid behind the counter's acting like he didn't even know who Nathan Ballingrud was.

He lives here, I told him. *He's like, your neighbor and all. You don't know who Nathan Ballingrud is?*

Does he know you're in town? Can't you call him?

So it turned out Ballingrud doesn't work at Malaprops. *Fuck.* Where else could he be? How many other bookstores can one Podunk town even have? Two? It's not like it's a big city. It's just some rinky-dink mountain town. Crusty granola hippy-dippy shit. Artsy-fartsy yoga shit.

Where the fuck was Ballingrud?

Turned out there's another bookstore. A used one. Made sense, if you thought about it. Of course Nathan fucking Ballingrud is going to work at a *used* bookstore. None of that new shit. He's surrounding himself in dusty editions. Low lighting. Yellowing pages all around. Books stacked so high, reaching the ceiling. Pull the wrong one off and they'll all come toppling down.

Now we just needed to find it.

Nobody seemed to know where this used bookstore was. Or if it really even existed. The fine citizens of Asheville sure didn't seem to take too kindly to us guests and our goddamn quest. It got to the point where it felt like everybody's just fucking with us. Acting like they don't know. *Never heard of it*, they all said. *You sure you're in the right town?* We couldn't even get a name for the place. Like the locals didn't even realize they had a used bookshop to begin with.

It's an act, Benji whispered. *Bet they're just protecting him.*

Ballingrud?

Hell yeah. He's, like, a hometown hero. They want to keep the fans away, you know? Total Salinger-style.

Made sense. They're all in on it. All of Asheville. Somebody was probably calling Ballingrud that very second, wherever he was hiding, tipping him off that we were here.

We better hurry, I said. It's not like there are many roads to pick from. The town's on a mountain. Go too far in any direction and the switchbacks spit you right out in the valley below.

We'd been driving for an hour before Benji spotted a wooded turnoff. *Stop the car.*

You see something?

Turn around, he shouted, leaning his head out the window. *Turn around, turn—*

Where? There's nowhere to—

Just turn the car around!

I perform a three-point-turn in the middle of a highway, dumb fucking call, but I circle back and turn on to a backroad I didn't even notice before and immediately we're immersed in a new neck of Asheville. Crab grass chokes the shoulders. Trees on either end. The pavement crumbles the further we go and now we're plopped into a ghost town. Not exactly a ghost town.

There's only one building. That's it. Just one.

Looks like it's been here for centuries. General store-style shop selling sarsaparilla and shit. Gold-rush shit. Old fogie in a rocker on the front porch shit. Banjoes and six-shooters shit.

No name on the storefront. But this has to be the place. Where else is there? I can nearly feel it calling to me. Feel *him*. His name's whispered through the mineshafts at our feet.

Ballingruuuud.

In we go.

The front door's got one of those brass bell thingies that rings when you open it. I'm hit with mildew as soon as I step in. Smells like a library that sprung a leak in its roof, drenching all the books below. The air is thick. Fungal. There's some NPR playing over the sound system, but the music's all muffled because the speakers are buried behind stacks of yellowed paperbacks.

There he is.

Standing right behind the front counter. Pricing out some paperback.

Holy mother of God, it's him. Actually *him*.

Nathan fucking Ballingrud.

He *almost* looks like his author pic. Almost. If I squint, he sort of resembles the dude in the photo—only the man in front of us is way older now. Thinner now. We're talking *gaunt*. He's got that same bald pate from the photo. His beard is a little longer, but the colors are sort of the same. Tawny mustache. White chin whiskers. He looks like a cigarette after someone's taken a long drag, nothing but a slender column of ash now, gray skin barely holding the rest of himself together. One simple blow would send Ballingrud just toppling right over, crumbling into dust.

Let me know if I can help you with anything, he says, totally nonchalant. No big deal. He doesn't even look at us for long, glancing back at the stack of paperbacks he's pricing.

Nathan fucking Ballingrud.

It's you. What else can I say? It's all that makes sense to me in that moment. We've come so far, crossed state lines, ascended the mountaintop. We answered Ballingrud's call.

I want to fall to my knees. I want to weep.

Now Ballingrud takes both me and Benji in. Sizes us up. Weigh our souls on the scale. Determine if we're worthy. *Is there something in particular you're looking for?*

My throat's all dry. I want to say, *yes, yes*, but it comes out like a croak. I cough a bit, clear my throat, but I can't speak. I fantasized about this moment—this exact second—going over what I'd say in my head a million times, but now that I'm here, actually here, in his presence, I've got nothing. I'm all empty. The words are just not in me anymore. Fucking fail.

Benji speaks up for the both of us. *We came for you.*

I'm sorry...? The dude doesn't get it. Doesn't understand.

It's a test. Got to be.

We're here for your horror recs, Benji says.

But it's more than that. *Let's be honest with ourselves here*, I want to say. This isn't just about getting Ballingrud's top reads. This is about getting his book. *The* book. The novel I was promised before Penguin pulled it. I didn't come all this way just for a recommendation.

I want The Weird, I blurt out. Whether Benji was ever aware of it or not, I don't know. Don't care. He can pick up as many paperbacks as he pleases, but I've come here for one book and one book only, the forbidden publishing fruit, the fucking book I was promised months ago.

I came so far. I have nowhere else to go. I can't go home without it.

Ballingrud doesn't say anything. Not a fucking word. All sound gets absorbed by the surrounding books, sponging our exhales up. I can't breathe anymore. He must get this question a million times. Does he know who we are? What we've done just to be here? Are we worthy?

Then Ballingrud asks, *Are you sure?*

Who says *yes* first is up for grabs. Maybe me and Benji answer at the same time, but Ballingrud grins. He's got this skeletal leer going on, all teeth, thin lips. He slips out from behind the counter, nodding his head toward one shoulder.

Then follow me.

I turn to Benji and attempt to telepathically broadcast: *Can you believe this shit? It's happening! Actually happening!* But something about Benji's expression throws me. My boy looks nervous. He's not saying anything. Just staring at me. Eyes wide. Like we shouldn't go.

The hell is that all about? There's no turning back now. Not when I'm this close.

Ballingrud leads me down an aisle. There's a turn I hadn't noticed before. It leads to another aisle, which then connects to another aisle. How big is this shop? Definitely didn't seem this expansive from the outside. Maybe it's carved into the mountain or something.

Benji's behind me. We don't say anything. We just follow. We want to be, uh, *deferential.* Respectful, you know? Simply being in Ballingrud's presence makes us hush. We're waiting for him to say something, but the dude picks up his pace, slipping down the aisle and turning again.

The bookshelves tighten. Constrict. The aisle tapers, closing in on itself. Books brush against both shoulders the deeper I go. I have to actually turn, side-stepping now, nearly crab-walk down the aisle, for fear my shoulders might knock these books over and cause a cave-in.

Ballingrud is way up ahead. He's moving at such a quick clip, I've really got to hoof it. I almost ask him to slow down, *wait up*, but then Ballingrud turns down yet another fucking aisle.

Where in the hell is he going?

Where's he taking us?

The lighting is dimmer now. I glance up and I see the books reach the ceiling, eclipsing the fluorescent lighting from the neighboring aisles. It's colder here. Got that subterranean climate vibe, you know? Like when you're in the basement and the temperature just drops?

Only this isn't a basement. This is a bookstore. Or supposed to be. There's a part of me that wonders what would happen if I pulled a book off the shelf. What I'd see. I'm getting the sneaking suspicion that there wouldn't be a shelving unit behind there... but rock. A cave carved into a mountain. I'm following Nathan fucking Ballingrud into the deepest cavities of Asheville.

Where the hell is Benjamin? He's not behind me anymore. I turn and look and can't find him. We must've gotten lost. Separated somehow. Did he take a turn down a different aisle?

I call out his name—*Benji*?—and it echoes back.

Ballingrud halts. He doesn't turn to face me. He's just frozen. Peering over his shoulder, I realize the aisle just... *stops*. Dead end. The bookshelves tilt a bit, the walls no longer straight. They're curving now, arcing overhead, pushing the books out at loose, awkward angles. Almost clinging to the ceiling. Stalactites. Water drips off the paperback's spines in these distant plips.

In faded marker, I see the section is marked HORROR/SCI-FI/MYSTERY.

Ballingrud glances up and down this one particular shelf. He's searching for something. Something special. Not just any book, but The Book. A book just for me. I'm ready to get weird.

Please let it be The Weird, *please let it be* The Weird, *please let it be—*

Here, he says as he tugs a book off the shelf. He has to really yank, the book giving him some resistance, refusing to release itself easily from the shelf. I hear the slightest *snap* and suddenly I don't believe it's a book, *that's not a book at all*, but a piece of subterranean fruit.

Ballingrud holds the book out to me. It doesn't have a title. Its cover is a faded red, and in my head, I remember something Benji echoed hours ago: *read-it-on-reddit-read-it-on-reddit-read-it...*

Start with this, Ballingrud says. *Let me know what you think.*

I take the book out of his hand. It's so light. It squishes a bit between my fingers, like it's more of a sagging bag than book. All the words inside are gelatinous tapioca pellets.

I think you'll really like this one, Ballingrud says.

What is it?

Something I've been working on, he says. *Maybe it's been working on me.*

I can't help myself. I have to ask. *Is it* The Weird*?*

They're all weird.

How much?

Whatever you're willing to give, he says. Then Ballingrud is off and wandering back down the aisle, leaving me behind. He calls out over his shoulder, *Stay as long as you like. Until you're finished. Don't worry about closing. We keep odd hours.*

So I do as he says. What else am I going to do? Nathan fucking Ballingrud just told me to sit and read, so I'm going to hunker down in the aisle and read.

I start flipping through. The book's got gauzy, almost hazy, pages. Practically transparent. Like onion skin. No—not onion. More like fly's wings. Whatever that stuff is called. *Membranous.* My fingers keep getting stuck every time I flip. The pages are so sticky, tacky, like a spider's web.

I hold on to the book, nestled into my lap, cradling it against my crotch. Just as I'm ready to begin reading, dive in and get this horror show on the road... the words start to wriggle, working their way off the page. Not words. Eggs. Spider eggs, hatching, crawling all over me. On my legs. I try brushing them off, but I can't let go of the book. My skin is clinging to the cover. I'm trying to pull my fingers free, but the tips start to tear and now they're bleeding all over the book, blood guttered by the crease. Whatever part of me the book touches, it sticks, like a glue trap for mice. The more I wrestle against the book, the more its pages cling to me.

If I bring my knee up to my chest and get my foot in between me and the book, maybe I can kick it off, but it just kind of folds me in more, wadding my body into a ball. Now the book is sticking to my shins. Its pages are, *shit, shit,* its pages are expanding out, spreading over my legs.

What the hell am I even reading? Or is it reading me?

I glance up and notice the novels oscillating on the shelves. Every last book looks as if it's about to burst, the yellowing paperbacks ripe and ready for plucking off the stacks. Succulent.

The pages are draped over my shoulders. I've wrapped myself in its chapters, cocooned by its cover. I don't want to believe the paper is somehow sealing up around me, but once that thought worms its way into my head, there's not much else I can think of. The open book is only inches away from my face, sliding over my shoulders, squeezing, hugging me, bringing me in.

Ballingrud's horror recs really are spot on. This book is fucking terrifying.

acknowledgments

Sincerest thanks to all the editors who gave these stories a home.

Special thanks to Daniel Carpenter, Julia Lloyd, Bahar Kutluk, Joseph Barnes, Richard Mason, Rob Clark and everyone at Titan Books for bringing the tales together.

Thanks to Nick McCabe at The Gotham Group and Michael Hartman at Ziffren Brittenham LLP.

Love to Indrani, Jasper, and Cormac.

Thank you so much for reading.

about the author

Clay McLeod Chapman writes books, comic books, YA and middlegrade books, as well as for film and television. You can find him at claymcleodchapman.com.

publication credits

the fireplace was originally published in Hello Horror, Winter 2017, Volume 5, Issue 27. It was subsequently anthologized in *"Come Join Us By The Fire"* audio anthology from Tor Nightfire.

cyan, magenta, yellow, and key was originally published in *Ink Stains: A Dark Fiction Literary Anthology*, Volume 9, edited by Stacey Longo, from Dark Alley Press, 2018.

who brings a baby? was originally published in *Ghoulish Tales* #1, edited by Max Booth III and Lori Michelle, from Ghoulish Books, 2023.

the spew of news was originally published in *FOUND: An Anthology of Found Footage Horror Stories*, edited by Andrew Cull and Gabino Iglesias, 2022.

stowaway was originally published in *Southwest Review*, Volume 106, Number 3, edited by Andy Davidson, 2021.

baby carrots was originally published as part of the Chapman Chapbooks series by Shortwave Publishing, edited by Alan Lastufka, 2023.

fairy ring was originally published in *34 Orchard* # 2, Autumn 2020, edited by Kristi Petersen Schoonover.

room with a boo was originally published in *Black Telephone Magazine* #1, edited by Leza Cantoral and Lindsay Lerman, from CLASH Books, 2021.

pump and dump was originally published in *Obsolescence: A Dark Sci-Fi, Fantasy and Horror Anthology*, edited by Alan Lastufka and Kristina Horner, from Shortwave Publishing, 2023.

keep it civil was originally published in *Dark Corners of the Old Dominion: An Anthology of Virginia Horror*, edited by Joe Maddrey and Michael Rook, from Death Knell Press, 2023.

battlefield séances was originally published in *Dark Moon Digest*, issue #34, from Perpetual Motion Machine Publishing, edited by Lori Michelle and Max Booth III, 2019.

pick of the litter was originally published in *Makeout Creek* #8, edited by Andrew Blossom, 2023.

sisterhood of the salamander was originally published in *Blood & Blasphemy*, edited by Gerri R. Gray, from Hellbound Books, 2019.

knockoffs was originally published as part of the Chapman Chapbooks series by Shortwave Publishing, edited by Alan Lastufka, 2023.

debridement was originally published in *Fangoria*, Issue 9, Volume 2, 2020.

psychic santa was originally published in *Literally Dead: Tales of Holiday Hauntings*, edited by Gaby Triana and John Palisano, 2023.

our summer in the pit was originally published in *Shadows Over Main Street* Volume 3, edited by Doug Murano and D. Alexander Ward, for Bleeding Edge Books, 2023.

sweetmeat was originally published in *October Screams*, edited by Kenneth M. Cain, from Kangas Kahn Publishing, 2023.

nail on the head was originally published as a limited-edition chapbook by Theurgical Studies, illustrated by Erik Waterkotte, in 2022. It was reprinted by Weird House Magazine #2 in 2023.

publication credits

the nocturnal gardener was originally published in *Long Division: Stories of Social Decay, Societal Collapse, and Bad Manners*, edited by Doug Murano and Michael Bailey, for Bad Hand Books, 2024.

hermit was originally published in *Fangoria*, Issue 22, Volume 2, 2024.

all ears was originally published in *American Cannibal*, edited by Rebecca Rowland, from Maenad Press, 2023.

stay on the line was originally published by Shortwave Publishing, edited by Alan Lastufka, 2024.

nathan ballingrud's haunting horror recs was originally published in *Shadows in the Stacks: A Spirited Giving Charity Anthology,* edited by Vincent V. Cava, James Sabata, and Jared Sage, from Shortwave Publishing, 2024.